BAD BAD BOY

RATS OF RICHSTONE - BOOK ONE

ANGEL DEVLIN

Cover design by Tracy Lorraine.
Photo of Tommy Dee @tdupche by Michelle Lancaster @lanefotograf
Formatting by Tammy

To **Taylor Swift**, whose songs made this story bloom to life in my mind and not let me go until I'd written it.

Also, to **Michelle Lancaster** and **Tommy Dee** who sealed the fate of it being written when a photo popped up in my feed that I couldn't let anyone else have because it said Bad **Bad** Boy all over it.

And to **Tracy Lorraine**, who kept hearing me talk about it and encouraged me to finally write it!!!

Thank you!

Angel xo

Liam

They called us The Rats.

Said we were vermin.

Sat in their million-pound houses and stereotyped us all.

We were scum apparently. Braindead, worthless scum.

Yet we weren't so different to the elite. We all left our morals at the door while we conducted business.

I did what I did to survive. They did it to buy their next ride. Why have an underground garage if you can't fill it with luxury cars you barely ever drive, hey?

They underestimated us though. Because my crew were far from braindead, and I was determined one day I'd cross the sewer and obliterate their paradise.

I would be the apple.

And there would be someone there who'd be tempted to bite.

"I need you to fuck off out of the house." My mum's boyfriend, Vin, sneered.

I snorted loudly. We had a mutual admiration thing going on as you could see. He'd been banging my mum for two months and had moved in a month ago. Saw opportunity, however small, in our tiny council house.

"What's it gonna cost me for you to vacate the premises for at least two hours?" Cold eyes tried their best to intimidate me.

"What's it worth to you for me to be gone? I'm guessing you're bringing some skank back or sorting out a deal. Either way my silence needs buying." I gave him a chin tilt and stood my ground.

He threw two twenty-pound notes at me. "One day you'll get what's coming to you, you little shit. Now fuck off, and don't come back any earlier than six."

He was so stupid. I was going out anyway.

"Next time you want to ask me a favour, make sure you knock and wait for me to say to come in. Or I might just come back early without knocking and see what the fuck you're up to." I flashed him a cold smile to show my insincerity.

His mouth pinched and he banged my door behind him as he left.

My next smile was genuine and smug. I was a far

bigger bastard than Vin Johnson and one day I'd show him just how much.

I finished conducting my evening's business, selling bud to the teens of Sharrow Manor. Jace, the kid whose house I used as a trap house, was swaggering about in the background as per usual as if he was a major fucking player. Stupid cunt. I paid him in weed for the privilege of using his house while his dad was at work. His mother was nowhere to be seen, having left them when he was young. When people left Sharrow, it was a toss up whether they'd escaped the hellhole by bus or via a shallow grave. I didn't ask about his background because I didn't care.

When I'd first friended him, knowing his house was a suitable new base for my business, he'd been a largely unwashed waste of space who got picked on for being thick, both in his head and round his waist.

He'd fallen for my patter like a cheap whore on a fifty-pound note. But he kidded himself. He thought my friends were his friends and that my holding court in his house was a party where he was the host. To keep him sweet I had to let him hang around, but his low IQ was dangerous. Like right now, as I caught him taking a selfie while he held up a spliff.

"Delete that, you stupid motherfucker." I yelled, throwing a cushion at his head. He was lucky it wasn't my fist sailing in his direction instead. "My reflection's in the television set, you thick piece of shit."

"S- sorry, Liam. Erm, you want anything? My dad got some beers in."

"I'll take a can, yeah? But remember, no photos, no evidence. Got it?"

He nodded. His head bobbing superfast like one of those fucking sad things people put on their car dashboards.

I needed to find a new place to sell my stuff. Jace was a liability.

Truth was I needed to start thinking bigger now. I was in my second year of sixth form, eighteen, and the big wide world came ever closer. I didn't want to be yet another low-grade dealer, and neither did I want to sink into the murky depths of a career in it. I had a brain, for which my mother had insisted I stayed on at school, and since my customers largely came from there, I'd agreed. That way we were both happy. I liked to make my ma happy. She was one of the few people in life I could trust.

The other three who I reckoned would always have my back were with me now: Brett, Daniel and Marlon. They'd been my friends since nursery school and though we fought at times, we all stayed together. We'd been united by our circumstances and our determination. Wanting to escape, to do better, but accepting this was the hand we'd been dealt.

For the next hour, kids visited the house, and I sold my merch. I sold weed and I sold fags. That was my lot. It kept me in enough money to buy what I needed and to shove some in an envelope and pretend to my ma that I worked a regular gig at a warehouse at evenings and some weekends, cash in hand.

She probably knew the truth, but we didn't talk about it. Just like I didn't talk about the nights she drank herself to sleep or about her taste in men. You had to find ways to endure life in Sharrow, a place where the streets never seemed clean and the sun never seemed to shine on them.

Not like over on the other side of the river.

Richstone River. A breadth of water was the dividing line between poverty and privilege. An ironic name given its location.

No one from that side of the river came anywhere near Sharrow, and as tempting as it would be to burgle the houses of the monied, we largely kept to our own side. Their security and the fact you had to walk for thirty minutes to reach a front door if you got past the electric fences, meant it was easier to go to the other neighbouring estates than over there. A few from Sharrow Manor worked for them, but mostly each despised the other.

Just looking over and seeing the swaying lush branches of the row of trees at the other side that largely hid us from their view was enough to tighten my stomach and make me hate them. Why some were born that side of the river and I'd been born this, a cruel twist of fate.

I wanted what they had. Money and options. I did not want to have to play small for much longer. Maybe it was time to take a chance, to get out of here once and for all? Time to cross the bridge. Richstone trolls be damned.

Why should they have everything at their fingertips when all that was available to mine was the alcohol and ink the pigs used to process prints at the station.

Packing my things away, I felt the same dissatisfaction that skittered up my spine whenever I was in Jace's vicinity. I was done here. This dickhead needed excising from my life. Going in my bag, I threw a twenty at him.

"Thanks for use of the yard, Jace. Won't be needing it anymore though. You take care, yeah?" I began to make my way out of his living room. The walls seemed to be closing in on me. I needed out, even if it was to the smoggy air of Sharrow. My hoodie felt like it was strangling me.

"What do you mean?" Jace jumped up like a ho I'd let suck me one time too many. Clinginess made my skin crawl. In this world you needed to be able to survive rejection.

I breathed through my nose audibly and frowned at him while crossing my arms. I slowed my speech down so he'd be in no confusion as to what my next words meant. "I mean, I'm moving on. Place gets used too much, people get fucked off. Time to leave the neighbours in peace and take my biz elsewhere."

"Oh, okay. So where are we going next?"

Seemed I was wrong about him understanding my statement. I sighed, scrubbing a hand through my hair. Thick shit needed it spelling out. "*We're* not going anywhere next. *You're* gonna ask your dad for a job helping him clean windows and learn the family business. There has never been a '*we're*', Jace. I run my business, alone. You supplied a place for me, and I supplied a payment in return. Now I'm done here. You fucking getting it now?"

He fidgeted on his feet, pacing. Sweat beaded his brow. "What did I do wrong? Was it the photo? I'm sorry, man. I promise I won't do anything that dumb again."

Looked like it needed a hammer to deal with this screw-up. "Listen, you whiny bitch. Stop acting like my girlfriend. You had a place we could use, now I don't need it. The end. It's not me, it's you. Now, I'm leaving and if you follow us, or talk shit about us, you'll find yourself with broken arms and legs and won't be any good up your dad's ladder. *Understand?*"

"Y- yeah."

As we walked away, he looked like he might cry. I might feel sorry for him, but I'd learned to not have feelings a long time ago. Buried them deep with my father's body. That way you couldn't get hurt. That way you managed to survive.

By the time I got back home, my mum and Vin were sat on the sofa together watching TV. She was tucked into his arm as if he was someone to keep her safe, not a cunt who'd ply her with more booze so as to not have to deal with her twenty-four-seven. I'd get rid of him as soon as I worked out what he was up to. I needed to make sure I benefited from his exit. I'd have told my mum, but she was as addicted to the idea of true love as she was booze.

"I'm gonna make myself pasta. Anyone want any?"

"I'm okay thanks, honey. Oh, have you by any chance seen the small purse I usually keep in the kitchen drawer with my emergency money in it? I've mislaid it." She twisted her fingers in her fringe.

My body tensed up. "No, Ma. You probably just put it in a different drawer. It'll turn up. How much you missing? Do you need an advance on my board?"

"If you don't mind. I need to pay a few bills. Can you lend me about sixty quid?" My mum's cheeks burned with shame and she couldn't quite meet my eyes.

"Sure, Ma." I went into my pocket and got out three twenties. Vin smirked at the side of me. He'd taken her fucking purse. "How much was in the purse?" I queried.

"Just over a hundred pounds, so I need to find it soon." She ragged at her bottom lip with her teeth.

That fucking cunt. He'd paid me to fuck off using my own mother's savings and still had over sixty quid left. That was it. He was on his way out of Sharrow. Not only had he double-crossed me, but he'd robbed my hardworking, but gullible mother.

I'd make him pay a lot more than one hundred fucking pounds, I could guarantee that.

2

Phoebe

"Arabella will be dropping by later this morning, darling, with some choices for the dinner at the Barratts' this evening." Mum said while trying to delicately eat a scone. I watched her. It crumbled in her fingers and I could see the frustration on her face. It was just a scone, for goodness' sake, not the end of peace on the planet.

But of course, the Ridleys were all about appearances, hence my being informed of a designer wardrobe arriving for an evening dinner. Heaven forbid, I wear what I wore there last month.

I nodded and ate my pancake with honey and lemon. Our cook's pancakes were my favourite ever food. Especially washed down with copious amounts of coffee.

Mum finished, wiped her mouth on a napkin and got up from her seat. "Right, I'd better get back to the study. The school won't run itself."

Smiling, I told her I would catch up with her later. Every Saturday was the same. She insisted we eat together and yet within fifteen minutes she was gone to her study. Mum was the principal of Richstone Academy, a small, private school. As the principal's daughter, I was expected to set the example for all pupils of the school. It was exhausting because I had to work hard for my grades and yet it was expected that I'd excel. There were just a few months left of the year before my exams were done and I was finished there. Not that I'd be any freer of responsibilities.

My father ran a publishing company, and he and my elder brother were currently over there because there was a hitch with an advertiser. I'd have rather my family felt there was a place for me at his company, but no. Eddie was the golden boy and heir to the empire, and I would make a loving wife and support to whichever rich husband I managed to land for myself. And although they said I was free to choose whichever husband I wanted, I kept being pushed in the direction of the families they thought worthy.

The fact my mother was a career woman made no difference. All she ever said to me was I could train for a career if that was what I wished, but that with a rich husband I'd never have to strive. Mum's family hadn't had much money and mum had worked her way up to the top. First training as a psychologist and then switching careers and acing her teaching studies. She'd met my father when he'd attended for therapy due to work-related stress. It would make a wonderful Hallmark Christmas movie.

Anyway, that was my Saturday all arranged for me.

Homework now.

A French lesson at one pm.

Arabella would be here for two thirty.

I'd whine onto my best friend, Renee for at least an hour after that on Facetime and then I'd get ready for the evening dinner.

The Barratts' were my parents' oldest friends, and as such we had regular dinner parties with them at either of our houses. Stefan Barratt was their only child and heir. He was in my year at school, and although I'd been told I could choose my own future husband, there had always been mumbles of 'Oh but wouldn't it be just perfect if the two of you got together'. It might be perfect for our parents, but it wasn't for us. We did actually get along, but it was like cousins would. We'd spent our lives growing up in each other's company and had become fond and protective of each other in a way you would with family. The idea of us together was laughable to both of us.

I dragged myself back up to my bedroom and sat at my desk, reaching out for my first set of homework and then I paused. This life to the outside looked privileged but I was so damn bored. I was like a pretty robot. Most days were the same: school, homework, socialise, sleep. Money certainly did not make you happy. It made you not have to worry about money, but it brought with it an agenda. Usually to attract more money.

Staring out of my window that looked over the manicured lawns and flower beds of our grand six-bedroomed, four-bathroomed house, along with a separate two-bedroomed bungalow where my grandmother, my father's mother, had lived until she passed two years ago, I yearned to see life beyond the garden's walls. I missed my grandmother fiercely. She'd refused point blank to live in the house with us and have everything done for her. Said she would go insane. The compromise had been to build her the bungalow and lure her into the house a few times a week to have dinner with her grandchildren.

She'd often spoken of travelling the world with my grandfather before he'd died prematurely in his late forties of a heart attack. We got to travel in as far as luxury holidays with butlers and other staff on hand. Villas that were next to the sea in places like the Bahamas. But I wanted to see the rest of the country I lived in. To pretend to be ordinary. To walk on a sandy beach alone, eating an ice-cream. To paddle in the sea. To eat fish and chips in a tray like my grandmother had spoken about. Not blackened salmon and dauphinoise potatoes set out on the finest bone china. Just for a small while I'd like to swap my silver spoon for a wooden fork.

Rain began to patter onto my window. The kind that came before a thunderstorm. Within minutes the sky had darkened. Turning on my desk lamp, I turned my focus away from the window and onto my schoolwork, because there was no chance of not handing in homework when your mother was the head of the school.

No chance of a lot of things.

. . .

My French lesson passed without incident. Learning French motivated me because I hoped one day to go visit there alone. Mum had taken me once when I was around fifteen, but it was to dine in fancy establishments and buy fancy clothes in the boutiques. I wanted to see the Eiffel Tower and the Moulin Rouge and eat crepes.

Before I knew it, Arabella had arrived. She knocked and flounced into my room, pushing in a rack with about eight dresses hanging from it, along with shoes, bags, and accessories.

"Hey, Phoebs. Come on, time to play dress up." She laughed.

Arabella was our family's personal stylist, but while Mum took it all ever-so-seriously and Bells would be on her best behaviour around her, with me the twenty-eight-year-old Bells would do her job while taking on more of an older sister role. A come-on-you-know-it-has-to-happen-so-let's-get-it-done manner. She'd try to make things fun, sometimes bringing along outfits she knew were a complete monstrosity, but that magazines were lauding as the 'must-buy' item of the season. She'd make me wear them and then we'd fall about laughing.

I sent for refreshments for us both and started to peruse the rack.

"Are they...?"

"Trousers? I know, shock horror. Going against regu-lations tonight, but look," Bells took them off the rack and showed me the off-the-shoulder frilled top that went with them. It was a black trouser suit with little white polka dots and it was too cute for words. "There's a hair band that ties in a bow to match. Super cute. Your mum will approve. Makes you look kinda fifties housewife but with a modern twist." She pulled some white glossy Jimmy Choos off the bottom of the rack. "Kitten heels, and a white shoulder bag and you're good to go. Go try them on and then tell me how fabulous I am at my job while we gossip for the next forty minutes."

"Sounds perfect." I grinned.

The Barratts lived around five minutes' drive from us. It was a warm day and I'd have preferred to walk the twenty minutes to their house, but heaven forbid that happened. The Bentley and our driver George had to take us from outside our own property all the way to the entrance of the Barratts'. As George opened the door to let us out of the car, their own staff greeted us.

One took coats, one directed George, one asked us to follow them. My mother would be hiring more staff when we got home. It was all about outdoing everyone else. Showing your lifestyle was the most lavish, that you were the more stylish Richstone resident. Then people would follow your example until they found a way to lead.

Sometimes I'd give my parents an idea for the sheer hell of seeing if they'd be gullible enough to go through with it and most times they would. We now had our own cocktail lounge, something Renee and I would make the most of when my parents were out of town.

Mr and Mrs Barratt greeted us after we were shown into their sitting room.

Stephanie Barratt walked over to me after she'd greeted my parents. Air-kissing my cheeks, she held me at arms-length and looked me over from head-to-toe. "Such a beauty," she said to my mother as if I were a rare antique rather than a human and as if I wasn't actually standing there right in front of her. "You and Stefan would have beautiful babies," she whispered to me. I'd never felt more like an empty vessel—like a vase she was admiring in a store—but I just smiled and walked over to greet her husband.

My brother had managed to get out of the dinner. You could do that when you were twenty-two and had your own successful circle of friends. He was at a poker night at a hotel casino that was raising money for a charity. Any excuse to try to have fun in Richstone.

After passing pleasantries with Allen Barrett, I finally made my way over to Stefan, who'd just endured the exact same moments with my own parents.

"How long before we can escape with a bottle of wine?" he whispered in my ear.

"Can't we replace our table water with vodka?" I quipped.

"You just wait. My mother had a new idea and she's *dying* to talk of it."

I groaned. "Is this going to set my own off?"

"You fucking bet. This is going to set all the women of Richstone off."

"Give me a clue."

15

He grinned. "She's saving the world. One poor child at a time. That's all you're getting."

The announcement came with the cheese and biscuits. "Oh, did I tell you? I've been thinking for a while now about how else I could use the advantages I have in life to help someone else and it came to me." Stephanie dabbed her mouth with a napkin. "I'm going to pay for my staff to do open learning. Then, even though I will be loathe to lose them, they may go on to a better life." She put a hand over her heart. "I'm starting with Theodora. She's going to take a course in hotel management." She took a sip of her wine. "Her skills should benefit us while she handles the house and then she can go forth and hopefully make something of her life."

Stefan kicked me under the table, but I wouldn't look at him. I was ready to vomit onto my plate. We all knew that Stephanie hated Theodora with a passion because she felt she was a little too pretty for the household. This was nothing but a way to get her to leave and replace her with an older, less attractive employee. She'd been out of town when Allen had employed the new maid, and Mrs Barratt was clearly not convinced that tucking in bedsheets was all she was employed for.

My mother gave a compassionate gaze to Stephanie and held up her glass. "Oh that is simply wonderful. It's such a selfless act to actively encourage someone to better themselves so they can move on. Especially when they've been such an important part of your life."

Another kick from Stefan because we were waiting for it. The comeback.

"It's so funny that you've had that idea because I have also been thinking of bequeathing a new future to those less fortunate."

"Really?" The smile returned by Stephanie Barratt was through gritted teeth.

"Yes. I'm making four scholarship places at the school," Mum announced. It was the first any of her own family had heard about it. "Four sixth form places to four kids from Sharrow Manor."

Audible gasps came from Mr and Mrs Barratt and my father.

"Who better to try to improve and change than those most unfortunate?" Mum beamed and then she tucked into her cheese as if she hadn't just dropped the equivalent of a nuclear bomb at the dinner table.

3

Liam

Sharrow Manor had no endearing qualities. There was little green space and what was there wasn't anywhere kids should be playing. Discarded needles and tab ends laid discarded near the swings because as soon as dusk came it was where the teens met. Rather than a row of restaurants and boutiques, Sharrow had fast-food kebab joints, pound stores, and boarded up windows. There were a couple of hair salons and a barbers, a beauty salon that to my mind had women come out looking worse than they went in, and mini-marts and corner shops that were occasionally robbed because the people here couldn't help themselves but to shit where they ate.

If I wasn't in a trap house, I'd be sitting in a fast-food restaurant, buying a drink and waiting until they got fed up and kicked me and my mates out. Mostly they didn't. Not unless there were a lot of youngsters in and then

19

we'd be told to behave and mind our language or find somewhere else to go. Those kids were going to turn into us anyway; it was only delaying the inevitable. Sometimes we'd meet in a pub, but they tended to be frequented by the older residents of Sharrow.

Saturday mornings always found us rats in the mess room at my uncle's garage. I might not have a dad, but my mum's brother let me tinker with cars on a weekend or hang around the mess. No pressure, just whatever I felt like doing. He'd taught me to drive, and while I couldn't afford a car or the insurance, I had my license. It was an investment for my future. When maybe there'd be a job with a car, or I'd actually earn enough to get me a set of wheels.

The four of us had hung around here on a weekend since we could roam the streets. We now brought our own refreshments and sat plotting life and some people's destruction. This room had heard a lot of secrets.

And that's what we were discussing right now.

I sat with a foot up on the edge of Daniel's seat because I knew it pissed him off.

"We need to get rid of Vin. He's robbing my mother and he's also using the house for something dodgy. He needs to go."

"What d'ya wanna do to him?" Daniel knocked my foot off his chair, and I sniggered. It was like an unspoken test as to how long he'd put up with it before he got annoyed. He'd lasted about a minute. Good job he had more staying power with women apparently.

"Something painful." I sat with my fingers steepled.

"Next time he's home alone, you need to come to the house. Let's show him what fucking with rats and their families does."

Brett exhaled. "We need to know what he's up to first. Could be something we can work with. Make some profit."

"I fucking doubt it, seeing as he's stealing from my mother. More likely he's paying for a whore."

"You got our numbers. Just ring when he's alone and we'll take it from there." Daniel said. He was the one who had your back without even asking why. Jumped in with both feet, whether it was a good idea or not.

"Thanks, man." I looked at the other two. "You in?"

They nodded.

"I can't live like this much longer." I told them. "In this shit hole. I feel like I want to blow Sharrow up. Just take my baseball bat and smash up the cars, the shops. Set fires. This can't be my life."

"No one would notice if you did do any of those things," Marlon pointed out. "You said it yourself. It's a shit hole." Anyway, you made us all stay on at fucking school. We have a few months of that left and then we can look at moving on."

"Move on to where though, Marl, huh? Where's the money coming from? Who's gonna want to take on a rat anywhere but here in the sewers?"

"We'll make our own business then." He huffed.

I rolled my eyes. "We'd need start-up money." I looked around the garage. "I know my uncle wants me to work here, to take on the family business, but he barely breaks even. His customers have no money. Most of the time he just shrugs his shoulders and tells them to take care. Charges 'em just for parts. I can't do this. Fuck can I work for peanuts and end up with a nagging wife and screaming kids. We need to think big, guys. Out of the box."

I knew I was rambling like a crazy person, but I was so fucking done. I needed away from the likes of Vin Johnson and that idiot Jace before I ended up in prison for a crime that just wasn't worth the time.

"Like what? Robbing a bank? A hold-up out of town? Can't see another way you're making money fast without upping the biz into harder stuff and that's just gonna get you dead." Brett's brow creased.

Drumming my fingers on the table, I met each of their gazes in turn. "We need to be able to get to the other side. To the riches. They're our meal ticket. Somehow we have to cross the bridge and show that rich pussy what a real man fucks like."

"What exactly are you suggesting?" Marlon asked.

I kicked Daniel's chair in frustration and got a look that said if I did it again, I was going to be on the floor with fists raining down on me. "I don't know yet. I'm just thinking out loud. Just always had a feeling that our future lies that side of the river."

"So we get jobs there. A few other people have done that," Brett suggested.

I shook my head vehemently. "That's not going to make us rich. I don't want a job and a normal wage. I want to be so fucking minted that I never have to worry about money again." I tapped my fingers on my knee. "Or maybe we need to get a job to start with, but then we need to get... a girl." My mind started to warm up to the crazy ideas floating around my brain. "I've fucking got it. We need to get into the rich bitches' lives, the ones our age, and trap them. Like, proper entrapment. Drugs, sex, blackmail. You name it. Fuck it, we could even get them pregnant."

"What the fuck?" Brett shouted. "Have you gone out of your actual mind?"

"Think about it." I tapped the side of my head. "You get one of those mogul's daughter's pregnant. Think the Bridge Bosses are gonna want half-rat bastards? They're gonna buy our silence and their daughters' abortions. It's perfect." I sat back with my hands behind my head, my mind spinning with enthusiasm for this completely psycho suggestion.

"Say we went with your crazy arse idea. How the fuck you think we're going to get over there?" Marlon scrubbed a hand through his hair. "This is madness."

"What's madness is staying in this fucking dive a second longer than we have to. Why should they have all the money and the capacity to make even more? Don't you want to try? Don't you want to at least get over there and see how the other half live? We find a way to get into Richstone and then we take it from there."

"I think you need to lay off the wacky-backy. You're supposed to sell it, not smoke it." Marlon eye-rolled me.

"If I find a way over there will you come?" I asked them.

They looked amongst themselves.

I put my right hand down in the middle of the table. "Those who want to cross the river, tell me you're in."

"You're a mad fucker," Daniel said, but he put his hand over mine. I thought he would jump first.

The other two followed, Brett last.

"From rats to riches", I quipped, and the others groaned at my lame-arsed joke.

Now I just had to find a way to cross the bridge.

But first I needed to give Vin the sending off he deserved so that I could hope my ma was okay while I was gone.

The following Thursday, Vin asked me to leave the house again, this time throwing a hundred quid at me. "Your mother's purse is back. It was only a loan, so you can calm your tits. Now fuck off."

I gathered the money up, slipped it into my jeans pocket, and kept my eyes narrowed on him the whole way out of the room. Then I shrugged on my jacket, slipped my feet into my Nike's, and went out wearing a shit-eating smirk.

I texted the others.

We're on.

Heading to Best Burger, one of the fast-food joints we preferred, I could feel laughter wanting to rumble in my throat. Did Vin really think I'd just roll over and let him fuck with me and my mum? Underestimating me. Many had done that before and lived to regret it.

Within thirty minutes the others were sitting with me.

"So, what's the plan?" Daniel asked, flexing his fingers, already psyched for a potential fight.

I picked up my phone from the table. The fizzy drink I'd bought to be able to sit here was largely untouched because I'd been watching my phone since I'd got here.

"He's got someone coming around he wants to impress," I told them. "I've set up one of those dog cams in my ma's bedroom and another in the living room. I figured his business would take place in one or the other."

"A dog cam?" Brett chuckled.

"Yep, twenty quid each off Amazon. Used the money he fucking bribed me with. Seemed fitting, like it's coming full circle." I clicked between one camera and the other.

"Well, fuck me," I exclaimed.

"What?" Daniel tried to look over my shoulder.

"I've got a blow job waiting, so any time today." Marlon tapped his fingers on the table.

"His date just turned up." I grinned. "It's Mrs Handley." Mrs Handley was a teacher at Sharrow Manor.

"Fucking what?" Brett was about to piss himself with excitement. "He's giving Mrs Handley one?"

"Well, she's already got her tongue halfway down his throat so looks like it." I watched as Vin opened the living room door. "And they're on their way upstairs."

My lips pursed as I thought about what was happening, because his sudden windfall didn't make sense unless he was taking money from Mrs Handley's purse too.

"Don't we need to go bust up the lovebirds?" Brett said.

"Not yet. I'm recording them." I winked. "Might as well make the most of everything."

I'd give Vin his dues, he made the most of what he'd got. But then he presented his fuck buddy with a bracelet before she departed. Now I knew what she saw in Vin Johnson, but I still didn't know where the money was coming from.

Until she'd left and he went in my mum's jewellery box, where, coming up with nothing, he banged his fist into the dressing table. My mum didn't have much in the way of valuables and it looked like anything she did have was now gone.

Oh fuck. Not her wedding and engagement rings. Don't let them be gone.

I'd kill him.

"It's time. I have what I need." I told the others, my voice as cold as the ice remaining in my drink.

"Hey, Vin." I called out into the house. The others followed me into the kitchen, taking a seat each at the kitchen table, leaving one spare. It wasn't for me.

Vin came downstairs and walked to where he could hear our noise.

"Thought you were going to be out all night?" There was no mistaking the scorn in his tone.

"Well, you were done, so I figured it was safe to come back." I winked at him before sharing a smile with the others.

"What the fuck did you just say?"

"I said," I raised my voice. "That you seemed to be done fucking Mrs Handley and so I figured me and my mates could come hang in my own fucking house, shit-for-brains."

He leaped forward, but the others were too fast for him. Before he knew it, he was on the other chair facing me, with his hands tied behind him and his feet tied together.

"You'll regret this," he spat out.

"I don't think so." I lifted my fist and punched him hard in the nuts watching his face contort. "I think I'm going to enjoy myself so immensely I might even need to wank."

"Your mother will kick you out when I tell her you've been stealing from her. I've already planted enough doubts in her mind. She thinks it's you, you know?"

"Yeah, well, my video says otherwise," I told him. That shut the fucker up. I showed him a little clip on my phone, so he knew I wasn't bluffing.

"You're done here," I informed him. "But I'm going to give you a little goodbye present and how big that gift is depends on your answers to a few questions."

Vin no longer looked so smug.

"Did you sell my mother's wedding and engagement rings?"

He was silent, so my next punch went in his stomach. He almost puked.

"I'm done being nice here now, Vin." Marlon handed me my knife. "Next time you give me the silent treatment you're not going to look so pretty and then how you gonna score pussy, huh?"

"I pawned em down the high street. Browns."

First thing in the morning, I'd be there, school be damned, trying to get my mother's rings back.

I held my knife to Vin's throat. "You get your stuff and you get out of here and you don't come back. Right now."

"I've nowhere to go," he said carefully, knowing every word moved his throat against my blade.

"Not my fucking problem. Go see if Mrs Handley's husband fancies a polyamorous relationship. Maybe he'll fuck you in the arse like you have my mother."

I let my blade bite into his neck, enough to bring a couple of beads of blood to the surface and to sting. "You going or am I finishing the job? One way or another you're out of here. I have three witnesses who say you attacked me after I confronted you about stealing from, and cheating on, my mother. Self-defence, innit, boys?"

"He pulled a knife first. Far too unpredictable. You just tried to defend yourself. You didn't know you'd kill him." Marlon said with cold-blooded menace.

"Okay, I'm gone. Gimme five minutes to pack the few things I have." His eyes remained wide as my blade remained against his throat.

"Five minutes where I watch you." I moved my knife

away. "And that's only because I can't be fucking arsed to burn your crap."

Ten minutes later, Vin was gone, and I was pouring us all a scotch. I held up my glass tumbler in a toast. "To the rats."

"To the rats." They clinked their glasses against mine and we drank.

Mum came home from work, looking weary. "Hey, boys. Would you mind going into the living room so I can fix myself some supper, only I feel ready to drop." Mum worked shifts in a care home and it could be draining.

"No probs, Mrs Lawson." Daniel said, and the others got up. "We need to head off now anyway. School in the morning."

"You sit, Ma. I'll fix you some supper once I've said goodbye to this lot."

They left and when I came back, she turned to me and said, "Whiskies on a school night? You want to tell me what you were celebrating, and why Vin hasn't come to kiss me hello tonight?" She pulled the rest of the bottle towards her, lifted it up and put it to her mouth.

4

Phoebe

To say my dad was apoplectic was an understatement. My parents rarely raised a voice at each other in front of me, but dad had clearly decided my mother had gone too far this time. He'd waited until we'd walked through into the hallway and the staff had departed before showing his true feelings.

"Could you not have donated a huge amount to charity? I mean we could have had a school built in India or something in our name. But Sharrow Manor. Kids from Sharrow at our school? You do realise that Stephanie Barratt is already on the group chat setting up a committee to get this crazy idea stopped, don't you?"

"Oh, let her. It just makes it more fun." Mum actually looked smug. "I've had this idea for a while. You know how much I love psychology. I want to know what happens when you put children from a life of struggle into a life of privilege. It's only for a few months, for heaven's sake. The school year is almost over. But if we can get Sharrow kids having prospects, well, I'll look like Mother Theresa."

"It's going to cause uproar," Dad snapped.

"Don't be ridiculous, darling. I'm the principal of one of the top five London academies. They might all hate me and bitch behind my back, but not one of them will say anything to my face, or protest. I mean they employ people from Sharrow Manor to do their manual labour. How would it look if they publicly denounced giving them a chance at improving their prospects? Stephanie is putting one of her staff through education. Hers is just online. It would look extremely hypocritical if she then said my idea didn't have merit."

You had to hand it to my mother. Dad might run the huge multinational publishing company, but mum was the biggest badass I knew.

"Looks like you have it all in hand," he said with a raised brow.

Mum ran a hand down her immaculately straightened chestnut brown locks. "Oh, I do, Maxwell. I so do. Do I take it I have your full support in this endeavour?"

Dad paused for a moment and then sighed. "Of course, darling. I trust you implicitly."

"Fabulous. I'll get the guest residence aired." Mum began to walk off towards the staff entrance, my dad in hot pursuit.

"What are you talking about, Daphne?"

She turned around to him, folding her arms over her

chest. "Oh, did I not mention that part? My error. I'm going to let one of them stay here. The other three can commute, but I want to see what happens when one is fully immersed in the lives of... what is it they call us? Ah yes, the riches."

"Daph, they aren't guinea pigs," Dad protested.

"No, they aren't guinea pigs, they're rats." Mum mentioned the nickname given to them. "And I'm their new Pied Piper."

I'd have excused myself had they even noticed I was still there. With my mind spinning with what the evening had brought, I instead went up to my room. Firstly, I removed the 'costume' of make-up and clothing I'd worn for the evening's 'performance', and then I poured a huge amount of Jo Malone Pomegranate Noir bath oil into my copper, double-ended roll top bathtub. Lowering myself into the blissfully hot water, I called Renee. My bath-room was fitted with music, television, and the ability to conduct a conversation with my friend by saying a pass-word to unlock the system.

"You survived then?" Renee's voice came out through the speakers.

"Well, for once Stefan and I weren't the main topic of conversation."

"Oooh, do I smell gossip?" she said, and I heard her clapping.

"I'm surprised you haven't heard it already." The sarcasm in my voice was highly evident.

"That juicy? Spill."

"My mother is going to offer four scholarship places at the academy. Just until the end of the sixth form year..."

"And?"

"To four rats from Sharrow Manor."

There was a silence.

"Can you repeat that? Because I'm sure you just said there'll be four rats from Sharrow Manor in our school."

"That's exactly what I said. She got competitive with Stephanie and the next thing I know she's announcing this, and that's not all..."

"There can't be anything else surely?"

"She's having one of them stay here in the guest residence."

"Nooooo."

"Uh-huh. I'm just thankful they won't be in the house. I know what my mum will do though. Get some poor sap of a girl here and then expect me to entertain them. We'll have to have her with us, and how will that work? We'll be having to deal with all the shit that comes from the other students and put up with having a cuckoo in the nest. I mean she could be lovely, or she could be a brat rat. Who knows?"

"Who says it's going to be a girl?" my friend announced.

"Yeah, my mum's going to put a rat boy on our estate. Then she'll see what happens when her only daughter, who she wants to marry off to Stefan Barratt, makes friends with him."

"Hey, make sure at least one of them is a hot boy. I'm

fancying a bit of rough. All these polished princes are *so* last year."

I giggled. "Renee, you are so bad."

"I bet they know what they're doing in bed. All fucking hard and dirty."

"Stop it," I screeched, sitting up in the bathtub and splashing water over the edge.

"Got you laughing, didn't it? It'll all be fine. It'll be a novelty for a day or so and then the rats will go home, I'm sure. They'll hate it here. Think about it. The focus of everyone's attention and most people's hate. No way are they going to stop here among the snobbery of Richstone."

"Maybe."

"So I'd better bed one as soon as possible. When are they coming?"

I laughed. "No idea, but Mum is already arranging to have the guest residence aired, so I'm sure it won't be long."

"Okay, tomorrow night we need to go eat at The Aegean and talk this over in depth with the other girls. It's too good an opportunity to miss."

"What opportunity? Please tell me you're not serious about sleeping with any of them?"

"If there's a hot one, I so am. I want to see if there's a difference between a rat boy and a rich boy. If your mother can run an experiment, then so can I."

"What on earth has my mother set in motion?" I said my thought out loud.

"Probably not much. Like I said, I don't think they'll

stay, and the parentals will be onto the next thing, like having a large seascape built and adopting endangered sharks or something."

"We have plenty of sharks here already." I said thinking of Ivy Sackville, the poisonous, self-appointed Queen Bee of Richstone Academy.

God, how was she going to react to a rat? She barely tolerated anyone else outside of her esteemed circle of minions.

Just what had my mother started?

The Aegean was a luxury fish restaurant and the favourite place to dine in Richstone. It tended to attract the parents rather than the children and so made it the perfect spot for us to meet and eat without wondering if we'd bump into Ivy.

"People are looking over at you and whispering," Flora stated.

"I've noticed. Seems news is travelling fast. Well, if any of them come over to ask me about it, I'll be directing them to my mother. It's her baby, not mine."

"God, I bet they all hate the idea. No recollection of the fact that most of them are self-made." Renee looked around the place with a narrow-eyed gaze making several diners look away uncomfortably, having been caught staring at us.

"That's the thing though isn't it?" Our other friend Lucie said. "They don't want a reminder of where they came from, or for anyone who's not nouveaux riche to suddenly put them in the same bracket as a rat."

"I wonder just how ratty they are? Like if they were to dine here, I guess they wouldn't know which silverware to use. I mean goodness, half the time I don't remember," Lucie admitted. "But would they like slurp their food, or ask for a burger and fries with ketchup?"

"We'll find out soon enough," Flora replied.

"Mum's going to spend this week getting the paperwork sorted so that she can approach Sharrow Manor's headteacher."

"They aren't going to do an exchange, are they?" Flora went wide-eyed and as pale as her ash-blonde hair. "I wouldn't survive. Without my personal dietician I'd get very, very fat."

I laughed. "There's no exchange, just four of them coming here. That's if any of them agree, because any kid with a brain knows they wouldn't be invited here without a pay-off for Richstone."

"Maybe they don't have brains."

"Or they're all in their dicks," Renee winked.

"They're in the second year of sixth form so they must have some intelligence," I stated. "I hope my mum isn't underestimating the students she invites. If it was me, I'd want to take every advantage of the opportunity and I don't just mean the education side of things."

"What do you mean?" Lucie bit on her bottom lip.

"If it were me, I'd be trying to impress people to get a job, show my worth; but these people barely have the money to feed themselves. If I were them, well I'd be looking to try and embezzle the rich morons and blackmail them, so I left with some of the money I'd been surrounded by."

"You watch too many episodes of Dallas," Renee laughed.

"Maybe so, but it's human beings we have coming, not ready to be re-programmed robots." I huffed.

"I disagree. If they're desperate for money, then I reckon I can get one of them to do my exact bidding," Lucie said, twiddling a tight red curl around her finger.

"Well, I want to get one into bed," Renee added.

"Don't leave me out. What can I do?" Flora pouted.

"Make one over. Like in the movies. Turn an ugly duckling into a swan?" Renee suggested.

"Oooh, yes. I love it." Lucie clapped. "What about you, Phoebe. What are you going to do?"

"Try to survive the whole experience," I said dramatically.

"No. That won't do. We need you to commit to a plan of action with a rat. Makeover's gone, fucking one is gone, and controlling one is gone." Renee taunted me. "So what'll it be?"

I thought for a moment. "I'll try to get one to ruin Ivy. Knock her right off her pedestal." As I said it, and as my friends' faces lit up at the very idea, I actually looked forward to the possibility of it happening.

Flora picked up her Bellini and we all followed suit.

"To the upcoming experiment," she said. "All we need now is a prize to whichever one of us does the best work."

"How will we choose?" Lucie asked.

"We can ask Stefan. He'll keep our secret and he'll absolutely love being involved," I said. "Once we know when they're coming, we can make more of a plan. Get a timeline in place. Be thinking of a potential prize."

"Everyone needs to buy the winner something huge, like a holiday," Lucie beamed, getting ever more excited.

"Well, that's worked up quite the appetite, and if I can't have my bit of rough yet, I'll have to settle for dessert." Renee beckoned for the waiter. I didn't miss Flora's sigh because she couldn't have one, her dietician would not approve.

"I'm not having one either," I put my hand over hers to show my support.

"It's fine. Don't do it on my account."

"No. I'm full. You can talk to me about makeover ideas while they eat something they'll regret later," I said, louder than I'd anticipated.

"Oh I'm definitely hoping to eat something I regret later." Renee winked at me, then she sighed. "What if your mother just brings all girls?"

"I'll make sure she doesn't," I assured her. It was time I showed a keen interest in my mother's plans given she would have me at the centre of them anyway.

5

_____

Liam

Sharrow Manor secondary was as dull as every other part of Sharrow, but at least they'd tried to make a bit of an effort with the sixth form annexe. The education department had thrown grants at us in an effort to get us to not turn out like almost every other disadvantaged individual: with a lower mortality rate, poorer diet and health. Like giving everyone an iPad was going to perform miracles.

It was only the fact they'd marked them all over with security pens that meant they were all still there. An iPad could pay for your next fix.

Not everyone in Sharrow Manor was a deadbeat though. Some people had never known anything else and were perfectly happy living life the way they always had. Some of the sixth formers were intent on leaving once they'd passed their exams and were hoping for scholarships to other, better areas.

Skye Drummond was one of them.

She might have bright-pink bobbed hair with a buzz cut above her right ear, but she had a brain, and when she was in school, she was quiet, studious, and eager to learn.

She was quite eager to learn out of school too, and I'd taught her how to give me a blow job well. She was a fuckbuddy, though she called herself a friend-with-benefits. She was no friend. My friends were my homies and that's as far as my circle went. Kept small.

"You got any plans for the weekend?" she whispered, leaning over. She'd sat right next to me in class today, making the lads smirk. Someone seemed to be getting too attached.

"Not sure yet," I said honestly. I wasn't about to bin her off when her mouth was so capable, so I'd keep her on a leash like an eager puppy for now.

My plans to get us to Richstone had been fizzing in my brain all night. Saying it had been one thing, making it happen quite another. Who did I think I was? As if I could just snap my fingers and get us into Richstone. My mouth had run away with me and my cockiness didn't have a condom large enough to contain it. Now the guys were expecting me to perform some kind of miracle, even though none of us believed in a higher power other than that given by recreational substances.

I had options. Let's face it, I had a teacher at my disposal now should I want it. One caught on camera with her naked body riding my mum's ex's dick. After my ma had seen the footage last night and heard the full extent of her lover's thieving and dishonesty, she'd been ready to go find him armed with a rolling pin, but I assured her he'd bother her no longer.

I'd also reassured her I'd get her rings back. My mother had sobbed at their loss, not at Vin's. First thing this morning I'd used some of my savings to get them back from the pawn shop. As far as I was concerned, Vin still owed me a debt and one day I'd make him pay, but right now, I was happy Ma's rings were in my backpack safe, ready to go back to their true owner. This time I was putting them in the safe in my bedroom for which only I would know the combination. They could keep my cash and supplies company. If she wanted them, she'd have to ask, because I couldn't trust that when drunk she wouldn't spill the numbers out like her cider missing the glass after a fifth top-up.

"If you'd like to answer the question, Mr Lawson." Clive Billings drawled sarcastically as I realised I'd been daydreaming. Fuck, that wasn't like me. For all that most kids hated the education establishment, I actually wanted to learn.

"Sorry, Sir. Could you repeat it?"

He rolled his eyes but did repeat the question and I provided the answer succinctly. His eyes met mine and he gave me an imperceptible nod, communicating that he'd also keep me on track because he realised I was one of the few kids where his investment might not be a complete fucking waste of time.

We were almost at the end of his lesson when the

head of the school walked in. Mrs Whitstable was a formidable looking woman. One of those who as she'd grown older had become more masculine. Her drab grey suit didn't help and neither did the grey hair and ageing face, no doubt caused by being in charge of two thousand kids. She chatted to Mr Billings for a moment and then walked to the front of the class.

"If I could have your attention."

Oh God, what now? No doubt she wanted us to do a sponsored swim for school funds.

"Something rather extraordinary has happened. Last week the principal of Richstone Academy contacted me to say she wished to offer four students the chance to finish their sixth form education at her school."

There was a gasp from several students.

"I know." Mrs Whitstable acknowledged the noise. "This is unprecedented. Such an opportunity has never been touted before."

Skye raised her hand and Mrs Whitstable looked at her. "I'll take questions after I've finished."

I turned around and looked at Marlon who was in this class with me. He mouthed, "What the fuck?" at me and I grinned back.

No fucking way was anyone but us four getting those places. So I needed to listen to everything the old bat said.

"If you wish to be considered for the scholarship, then please fill out one of the forms I've just left on the desk. Also..."

God, she was making the most of this.

"There is the opportunity for one student to live in a guest residence on Principal Ridley's estate. All expenses paid. If you wish to be considered for that, there's a tick box on the form."

I'd never wanted to swear so much in my life. One of us could fucking live there? In Richstone? Don't get me wrong, you'd be the bloody fool of the place for everyone to treat with disgust and poke fun at, but only if you allowed them to. And I wouldn't. I needed that place, or at least one of the four of us did, so that we had a base with the riches.

"Okay, Skye. What was your question?"

"I just wondered how you would choose the winning candidates."

"We'll see who applies first and if there are more than four then Principal Ridley will choose based on your application."

"And when do applications need to be in?"

"By close of school Monday. Principal Ridley wants things moving quickly."

"Thank you." Skye smiled and it made me clench my fists. There was no place for her at Richstone.

I waited for the head to leave and then getting my phone out of my pocket, I sent her a text.

We should do our applications together tomorrow? Wanna come over?

Her message back came in less than a minute.

Yes! Can you imagine us both there at Richstone?

No, I couldn't and that was why she needed to come over tomorrow.

After school, I delayed going home and giving my mum the news her jewellery was back, so that the four of us could meet. This time we met at the park, sitting on two graffitied benches put there in memory of someone's lost loved ones.

I'd filled the other two in about the scholarships on the way there.

"So is everyone up for it still? Speak now if not because I'm going to make sure we get the places."

Everyone said they were still in.

"Does anyone here want the guest residence placement?" I asked them.

"Not me. They're going to watch whoever it is like a laboratory rat. In fact, I reckon that's what we are. A fucking test of some kind. Either that or it's a favour for the Prime Minister or she wants a mention in the Queen's honours list," Marlon stated.

"Well, I want it," I told them. "They can try what they fucking like with me. I intend to stay one step ahead of them all the way." I looked at my friends. "Of course, she's doing it for a reason. No one invites rats into school without one."

"I'm happy for you to have the accommodation," Brett said.

"Me too," Daniel added. "We can just hang whenever we like, anyway, right?"

I shrugged. "Who the fuck knows? But we have to get in there first."

"How are we going to make sure it's us four?" Daniel asked. "Whatever help you need, man, I'm there."

I laughed. "You don't even know what I have planned yet."

"I don't need to. I will always have your back. Remember that." He told me seriously. One of the rare times he was.

He held out his fist for a bump and I bumped it back.

"Right, this is what I'm thinking," I said, and I told them of my ideas.

My plan had three parts to it and the first part had me at a door I'd not been to before.

Lisette Handley opened the door to me and sighed. "I knew you'd be here to extract payment for your silence before the week was out." She tilted her head behind her. "You'd better come in before someone sees you here. The last thing I need is gossip I'm fucking a pupil."

As if. Lisette Handley might be in her late twenties, but she wasn't anything I'd ever fucking go near, especially after she'd laid herself spread-eagled for the disease otherwise known as Vin.

"Do you want something to drink?" She walked over to a wooden cabinet at the back of her living room and pulled out a bottle of gin. "I'm having one seeing as I don't suppose you're here to tell me anything good." She didn't even get a glass. She just took a swig straight from the

ANGEL DEVLIN

bottle. Classy. Even my drunk mother used a glass most of the time, though half her alcohol ended up on the table or the carpet after a few.

"I'm good thanks, and you don't need to worry too much. What I'm here for isn't anything you can't handle."

She flopped down onto the sofa. I took a chair at the side of it even though she'd not asked me to sit.

"Come on then, out with it. Then you can fuck off and leave me alone. I've got plans and you're not part of them."

"There's a scholarship being offered at Richstone. You heard about it?"

Lisette sniggered. "Yeah. God knows what's got into that prissy bitch to offer such an experience. Didn't offer a teacher a place though, did she?"

It was clear to see that the bitterness that was insidious in Sharrow was invading Lisette Handley.

I paused to examine the way she held herself. She showed an air of bravado, but it hid the truth. That she felt shame. "Why d'you fuck Vin? You knew he was seeing my ma."

She emitted a long, low sigh. "Because it made life just a little bit more adventurous, Liam. You're too young to understand yet, but the daily grind, the boredom. I'm twenty-seven. There has to be more to life than this. Vin's fit, and screwing him in your mother's bed, well, that made it all the more exciting that we might be caught. It was more about that than it was about him." She huffed. "I didn't really think we would be caught though." She

48

took another swig from the bottle. "So here we are. What do you want?"

Another bitch who underestimated me. This time because of my age. She'd live to regret that. I was doing all of this because of the boredom and lack of prospects of being in Sharrow Manor.

"There are going to be applications submitted to Mrs Whitstable for the scholarship places. Your job is to make sure that none except that of mine, Brett's, Daniel's, and Marlon's are seen by her."

She shot forward. "How the fuck am I supposed to do that?"

"Not my problem." I smirked. "But you say you like danger and lucky for you, her second-in-command is male. I can think of a way."

"I'm not going to sleep with Mr Berringer to fix the applications."

"Sleep with. Suck off. I don't give a shit. You just make sure there are only four applications there, or your performance with Vin is going on Pornhub."

Her eyes narrowed at me with such derision that if she'd had a leg to stand on, she'd have kicked me in the balls with it. But she didn't.

"Get out of my house."

"Nice doing business with you." I rose to my feet. If I had my way, I wasn't quite done with Mrs Handley yet. She'd given me an idea that if I managed to get to happen would screw her over one final time, just as she'd screwed over my mother.

. . .

Saturday afternoon saw part two put in motion. I had Skye in my bedroom and the dog cam was back in place. I could take stills off it. Hopefully, I wouldn't need to use it if Lisette did what she was supposed to, but I wanted contingencies in place. I never rested on my laurels. Never assumed what I was doing would work. You had to cover all bases, or in Skye's case, uncover them.

I laid on my bed and watched as she performed a sultry striptease that would be my insurance against her getting anywhere near those scholarships. And I enjoyed every minute of it. Enjoyed watching those perky tits with the rosebud nipples jiggling around. Enjoyed the way she twerked her arse at me. Enjoyed the fact I was rock hard from both her performance and the power I wielded. By the time she sat on my dick I was about to explode, but I made sure I took my time, made sure she was begging for me, until we were both satisfied.

The only part of the whole thing I hated was the way she wanted to cuddle up and talk afterwards. I knew she'd decided she wanted more, even though I'd made it clear we were just sex. I was laid back against my head-board waiting to get my breath back and trying to enjoy the afterglow of a fuck, but no, Skye was like a downpour on a bonfire.

"Did you do your application yet?" She wrapped herself around my body.

"No. I'll get it done tomorrow, ready to hand in on Monday morning."

Those big, brown eyes looked up at me, full of misdirected hope. "Wouldn't it be great if we both got out of here? Got a place there? Just think, if one of us gets the house we'd have the place all to ourselves." She began to stroke my cock which liked her movements more than my brain liked hearing her suggestions.

"Dreaming gets you nowhere in life, babe." I moved my hand between her legs, running a finger up her slick wet snatch and pushing it inside her. "You have to make life happen."

Her eyes shuttered closed as my fingers stroked and I distracted her from the conversation. Then when I'd fucked her again, I told her I had to meet the boys and that I'd call her.

A call I never intended to make.

6

Phoebe

I made sure I was at the dinner table on Monday evening with my mother. My father and brother were still at work again. Having the whole family together at a mealtime only happened once or twice a week.

"Was school okay, darling?" My mother asked me. It was usually a throwaway question where I'd just nod or say yes, but this time her shrewd gaze on me meant she wanted to know what they were saying about her plans.

"Well, my friends think it's an amazing idea, and so do many other pupils, as a lot came to ask me about it today. It's very much seen as a charitable opportunity. I think when these pupils turn up and they have a brain, it'll be the Richstone pupils who'll look the dumbest."

My mother smiled at that.

"But there are an equal amount who think you've lost your mind. They don't want rats amongst them, and, I don't know, it's like they think they're going to catch lice or poverty from them."

"And that's one of the main reasons I want to do it. To challenge those stereotypes."

I took a mouthful of soup while I considered whether or not to ask my next question, but in the end, I just had to ask it.

"Did you do this to get one over on Stephanie, Mum? Because it's not too late to call it off. You could just say that your idea wasn't approved, or Sharrow Manor didn't want to take part."

Mum smiled. "I've wanted to do something like this since my psychology days, darling. It's going to be so interesting seeing what happens when you drop a rat in with the elitist snobs. I started making calls today and the feedback was good. I fully intend to get this happening as quickly as possible. With exams being in May and June, for this to have its best chance of a positive impact I want to try to have the four in school straight after half term."

"*In three weeks?*" My spoon clattered as I dropped it in my soup bowl.

"Yes. I figure I try to get it officially announced at Sharrow Manor this week. I mean it's only a matter of time before one of the Sharrow people working at Richstone lets the cat out of the bag by gossiping anyway. It's only fear of losing their jobs that can usually vouch for their silence. I want to get there first if I can. Then a few days for applications. I'll review and interview and then they can start on the twenty-fourth of February after the half-term break. The one who wins the accommodation can spend half-term moving in and getting acclimatised."

I arched a brow. "You seem to have it all figured out."

"I have the logistics figured out. I don't have the actual experiment figured out. It could go without a hitch and the rats just make the most of the opportunity offered to them, or..." Mischief hinted in my mother's eyes. "It could be like dropping a bomb on Richstone."

"Don't you care that you might cause chaos and have the residents of Richstone want to drive our family away?"

Mum wiped her mouth on her napkin. "I couldn't care less, Phoebe. I've made that school what it is, and I'm asked... no... begged persistently to go head up other schools in London, New York, Paris and beyond. I may just ruin the place for my own amusement and then leave. Don't you think watching the Stephanie's and the Ivy's of the world have nervous breakdowns over their perceived superiorities being challenged would be fun?"

This was my chance. "Well, you need to make sure, Mum, that we have some boys in the mix. Preferably good-looking ones."

My mum looked so proud of me at that moment you'd have thought I'd just told her I'd won a Nobel prize.

"Oh, Phoebe. Do you think that Ivy might be a little more accommodating of a rat if it was a good-looking one?"

"It's something I'd be very happy to study."

It seemed that my mother and I were bonding more

over upsetting the residents of Richstone, than we ever had over any of her other ideas for me and my future.

"And what about you though, Phoebe? If I put a good-looking rat here, what's to say you won't fall for one yourself?"

"Never," I told her. "There's no room in my life for romance, Mum. I keep telling you this with all the silly ideas that me and Stefan would ever get together. I want to concentrate on my exams and get ready for university."

"Well, I don't like to say this out loud, but I will anyway. One of them will be living here, and as the principal's daughter you'll be expected to befriend all four and be a point of contact for them. A connection between them and me and someone their own age to help them. But you must not let yourself get over-involved with any of them, and certainly not romance one of them."

"Your words aren't necessary, Mother."

She nodded her head.

"I don't want you involved with Stefan Barratt now anyway. It would tie us to that insufferable bitch. It's time to hit the brakes on that friendship. Send her a clear message on what happens when you try to get one over on me. Are there any other boys you might want to date after your exams? We can invite their parents for dinner instead."

I rolled my eyes. "No. And you must keep your friendship with the Barratts. Dad likes Allen and Stefan is my friend. I'm sure Stephanie will have learned her lesson."

Mum smiled at me. "My wise daughter. You will make an amazing wife one day."

"I want an amazing career. Like you."

She wrinkled her nose like something smelled off. "Me and your father have worked this hard so that you don't have to. Land yourself one of these rich heirs and spend your time doing things that don't cause wrinkles that no amount of Botox can fix, darling. Travel and see the world on their riches."

Here we go again, I thought. Why could my mother not understand that I wanted more out of my life than being bankrolled by some rich husband? Okay, maybe I would meet one and fall madly in love and be happy travelling the world with them, but I wanted options, and right now those options were studying hard and going to university.

The rest of our evening meal was spent on general chatter where Mum told me the rest of what her and Dad had planned for the week.

As soon as the meal was over, I excused myself to my room to do homework. The evening had started so well, with Mum and I colluding over the rats coming, but in the end, she'd showed me that despite bitching and complaining about the people who lived here, my mum plainly couldn't see that she was actually one of them. Maybe even the Queen of them all.

By Friday she had it all signed and sealed, and the announcement was being made at Sharrow Manor. Friday evening, she texted me to meet her at the guest residence where Granny had lived.

I walked down to the house, which was only five minutes' walk away from us, but that Granny had insisted on being built so that trees shielded the view of it from the main house. It was a bungalow as Granny didn't do stairs well, but it wasn't small. It was formal from the front with a large, central front door with wide windows either side of it. Our main driveway had a turn off point to a double garage and large gravelled driveway where Granny had insisted on keeping two of my Grandad's cars, an old classic Porsche that hadn't been touched in years and the modern Bentley he'd driven her around in. Any guests she'd received could park on the driveway and then follow the designer-done path to the front door. In front of her house was a large lawned area, with the trees to the right and partway around the back garden.

Mum waved me in from the front window and I realised she had her interior designer, Movadi with her.

Pushing open the front door, I stepped inside. I swore it still smelled of my granny's perfume, a choking scent of rose she'd insisted upon. I was always surprised my brother hadn't wanted to move in here after Granny's death, but he always said when he moved it would be to his own large home with a wife.

I'd missed my gran too much to consider it, and plus, I was only recently eighteen. I didn't want my parents having heart failure that I might want my independence.

"Hey." I said to my mum and to the six-foot-two skinny male who had an iPad in his hand. Movadi was of course not his real name, but he'd told me designers got much less work when they didn't have an artistic name and Andrew hadn't been cutting it. He'd also told me that the flamboyant silk shirts he left half open, and the tight trousers he strutted around in were swapped for loungewear the moment he was through his front door and his wife basically had them laundered and waiting along with his slippers in a designer looking storage box in the hall. I'd overheard him talking to his wife once and I'd agreed to keep his secret, so Mum thought this was his usual day-to-day attire and his genuine personality.

"Well, you get more beautiful every time I see you." Movadi said heading over and air kissing me on both cheeks. "Did you get a new colour because that chestnut is divine."

"Yes." I put a hand under my long hair and swished it. "I fancied a change from it being lighter."

He tipped up my chin with his finger. "It suits your eye colour more. You look ravishing." He turned to my mum. "Is she fitted with a chastity belt because she won't be safe around any hot-blooded teenagers."

"Thankfully, she has no time or interest in any," Mum acknowledged him and then she moved her gaze to me. "We're going to make some changes to the place based on what a younger person would want. I thought you could help. The whole thing needs modernising so that afterwards it can be a modern looking guest residence." She whisper-shouted to Movadi, cupping her hand. "I've been desperate to get my hands on this place, but Maxwell wouldn't hear of it being altered. Yet another advantage to my plans."

"You're up to speed with my mother's new project, I take it?" I asked him.

"Fully up to speed and ready to cause as much change to this pensioner property as your mum is to the school and neighbourhood."

And with that we went from room to room while Mum reminded me that there couldn't be anything too drastic because time wasn't on our side.

"Rip out all the carpets and replace with hardwearing and easily cleaned floors, whether that is real wood or laminate." I got into my stride quickly and became determined that once this student had moved out, I would insist on moving in. Maybe Mum would let Renee share with me? "Take all the formal curtains down and all the fancy pelmets and replace with venetian blinds that let in light but offer privacy at all the front windows."

So far, Mum was nodding along, so that was good.

"Paint out all of these dark colours and swap it all for creams, whites, and maybe sand or beige colours. I don't know what's in style but any of those."

"Calico, my darling. Calico, Ice-Cream Vanilla, Snow White, and a touch of Glastonbury Field brown."

I smiled at him. "Perfect."

"I'm thinking large modern square dining table in complementary tones. Chairs that look modern but are comfortable, because a bunch of you might hang here and do your homework."

"Do we have time to knock through from the kitchen and make it a dining kitchen, Mum? It's a lot more user friendly. You know, make snacks and pass them over?

"Should be doable. The hatch is there anyway and the kitchen is modern, thank goodness, as your granny didn't care what that room looked like because she was never entering it." She rolled her eyes.

"The sitting room will need two sofas, a coffee table in front of each, bookcases, and of course a large television on the wall with cinema style surround sound for when it's time to stop studying and relax."

"You're really thinking about everything this *new person* will need, darling." Mum raised a brow and I realised she'd fathomed out what I was up to. "I suppose I could talk your father around were you to agree to attend a local university."

As if I'd be able to attend one anywhere else. But if my mother thought it could be used as a bargaining chip then I was all for the idea.

I beamed. I couldn't help it. Not with the thought this could all be mine in a few months' time.

We toured around the rest of the property. At the side of the dining room and facing the patio was a bedroom. Adjacent to that was the second living room. "Mum. This is a large ask, but given that the better weather is approaching, could a pool be installed?"

"I don't want student parties being held here, Phoebe, and I fear that would encourage them."

"I'd make sure it didn't and you want to provide fitness for them don't you, without them having to come to the main house? You could have a summerhouse built next to the trees and put a few items of fitness equipment in there." She looked like she was about to say no, so I took a gamble. "Yeah, probably best not to. Granny would turn in her grave at all the mod cons."

"Oh, go on then," she relented and inside I smirked hard. "Can you take note of all this, Movadi, darling, and contact Anthony about the outdoor space and work together on the project?" Movadi nodded and then winked at me when she wasn't looking.

"So given there'll be a pool, can the back sitting room hold waterproof but comfy furniture, waterproof floors and the main bathroom have a large shower stall?"

I gave some last instructions but on the whole, my mum looked bored and ready to be out of here. Movadi looked like he was going to jump up and down on the spot with the size of the job, and me? I couldn't wait for this student crap to be over so I could live here.

The future looked bright.

Bright Calico, Snow White, and Ice-Cream Vanilla to be exact.

7

Liam

It took me all the rest of Saturday and a whole heap of Sunday, but I wrote my application form and then read it over. After that I got hold of and revised parts of the others' forms. They were all ready to be handed in first thing Monday morning.

And then I waited.

Tuesday morning Mrs Whitstable sent for me.

I walked into her office, directed by the school receptionist. The head sat behind her desk as if she was Don Corleone. Her jaded green gaze assessed me as she gestured for me to take a seat opposite her.

Then while I sat there, she picked up her mug and took a slow sip of her drink. If this was all some power play, it was lost on me. I was a call a spade a spade, let's-sort-this-shit-out-and-be-done guy. Next, she picked up the application forms and thumbed through them.

"I really thought given the rare opportunities these scholarships offered, that more than just four people would apply." Her next stare was like an X-ray.

I shrugged. "Maybe most people are happy as they are?"

She tilted her head to one side. "Should I ask them, Liam? Should I go into the sixth form classrooms and see how many of my pupils did actually apply for those places?

She'd got me there, but ultimately it didn't matter what she did. Somehow, I would get over to Richstone because I sure as fuck wasn't staying here.

"Well, that's your call, Mrs Whitstable, but personally, I think you have four amazing candidates for the scholarships and don't need to look any further. Each one is a credit to the school in terms of their academic achievements and the forecast for their future results, and they can shine a massive light on just how amazing a school you manage to run despite the disadvantages and obstacles in your way."

"Four male students is going to be a tough sell, Liam. They'll expect at least one female."

"It's non-negotiable for me. Either all four of us go or none goes."

She took a deep exhale and sat back in her chair, resting her head against the headrest.

"When they recognise how good you are at your job, you're going to be offered work out of here. Will you take it, or are you the saviour of Sharrow Manor?" It was my turn to stare at her.

She let out a deep exhale. "I'm getting older, Liam. I would take it and go. There are younger people than me who have fresh ideas and enthusiasm for improving the prospects of our students. You yourself would make a great teacher. You're resourceful, hungry, forward-thinking."

"Ha. I want to get out of here, not cement myself in as one of the bricks of the school hierarchy."

"That's a shame, but I've mentioned it. Planted a seed as they say."

She sighed again.

"I'm going to talk to Principal Ridley and see if she can take five students instead of four. I'll say it's impossible to choose between you. And I'm sending a female. If she says no, who are you leaving behind, Liam? Because we both know that despite the strong bonds of your friendships, the chance to get out of Sharrow Manor would win."

"I'm not going to choose one of my friends to be dumped. It's not *Love Island*."

"No, it's your first real test of your resolve, Liam. I'll go into class, get newly submitted application forms and pick none of you, unless you can give me a name of who you'd leave behind."

"Is this a game to you?" I spat out, "because this is my life."

Her eyebrows pulled down in concentration. "Yes, my dear. It's the game where you realise life at Richstone is going to be damn hard. Do you think they're all going to treat you with respect? They aren't interested in the fact you deal a few drugs, or that over here you're revered because you're a tough guy. Over there you'll be small fry and a joke. To survive, you're going to have to make a lot of tough choices, so here's your first. If you had to leave one friend behind, who would it be?"

I took a deep inhale, my nostrils flaring and jaw taut as I considered which of my friends I would cut loose if I had to. Brett, I felt, would fit into Richstone well, with his level-head; and in a completely opposite way, Daniel, who would have a go at anything, should fit in too. So that left Marlon. Marlon had been the most reluctant to get on board with the plan anyway. He'd been the one to say I was out of my mind. Yes, the decision wasn't so difficult after all.

"If she says no, then I'll leave Marlon behind," I told her.

"See, that wasn't so hard, was it? Now tell me which girl I should send to Richstone?"

Goddamn it. There was only one girl I knew who had actually applied and I didn't want her there. I had my insurance though, to use if she didn't get the message when I dumped her. Something I'd have to do now she was coming with us.

"Skye Drummond."

Mrs Whitstable nodded.

"Okay. I'd better make my calls then. You realise Skye is likely to get the accommodation?"

"That's sexist shit. Just because she's the only girl doesn't mean she should get the place."

Getting up, I walked out of the room and slammed

the door behind me because this hadn't gone according to plan and I had no time for diversions.

There was only one thing left I could think of for the third part of my plan. Vin was an electrician by trade and so I disabled the wiring in Ma's bedroom ceiling and got her to call him to repair it. I'd not wanted him back at the house, but hopefully he'd not be sticking around if my plan came off.

When I came home later, Mum told me he'd fixed it. She'd been drinking and I had no doubt she'd also paid him in a way where no money had exchanged hands.

"You want another while I pour myself one?" I said, holding up a bottle of whisky.

A normal person would wonder why I was offering alcohol when I usually took it away from her, but my mother was too much of an addict to the feeling of numbness it provided. All she did was raise her glass for a refill. Eventually, her eyes closed, and I made sure she was safe on the sofa, and then I went up to the attic.

And started a fire.

I knew what I was doing. It would seem like an electrical fault and the blame would lie at the hands of Vin. Earlier I'd moved the contents of the safe and given them to Brett, telling him not to ask. Returning downstairs, I sat in the chair next to my mum's sleeping form and waited for two minutes. I couldn't leave here until that fire engulfed a lot more of the house, but fire was an unforgiving beast, and it wouldn't take long.

It was late, and most people would be in bed. My alibi was I'd fallen asleep on the sofa to keep an eye on my alcoholic mother, and all I had to do was choose the right moment to call 999 in a blind panic and drag my mother out of there.

Adrenaline burned within me at the thought that the fire was growing above us, that smoke was invading the air, and that we ran the risk of the ceiling caving in.

Two minutes. That moment was *now*. I dragged my mother outside onto the street. It was clear to see that the fire was burning through the roof of our property and Mum's bedroom. Leaving her sat in the middle of the pavement in a state of confusion, I phoned 999 while banging on the neighbours' door to get them out of their home as the smoke was a danger to them too.

By the time the fire brigade got here, our home was no longer fit to be lived in. The firefighters battled to put out the fire that was so intense I could feel it from my spot well back on the pavement near mum. I gave them my report. That the ceiling light and fan in Mum's bedroom had not been working and that we'd had an electrician out to repair it. I gave them Vin's name and number from Mum's phone while she just sat there.

They said we had to be checked over at the hospital regarding smoke inhalation. I knew they'd be checking my mother over for far more. Whether almost burning to death in your home gave her the motivation to quit booze would be for her to choose.

Mum sobered up enough to ring Uncle Karl, who

said we could stay in his spare room until we sorted out a new place.

"You go there, Ma. It's just one room. I'll ring Brett and see if I can crash at his."

"You sure, baby?"

I nodded.

"I can't believe my fucking house burned down. That dickhead, Vin. You think he did it on purpose cos I ditched him? Only he tried to get back with me tonight and I held out and said no."

That made me smile. "Good for you, Ma."

Her eyes were half-closed with tiredness and the remaining alcohol in her system. "I'm sorry I'm not a better mum, Kiddo. You deserve more."

"So give me more. Stop drinking. If I hadn't been in the house tonight, Ma, what would have happened?"

"I'll try, okay? I'll try."

We both knew she might try for a day, even maybe a week, but ultimately there was nothing to avoid alcohol for. Once I'd left to go to Richstone, she'd be back with a bottle as a roommate.

My uncle collected us and dropped me off at Brett's.

"Fuck, mate." Brett met me at the bottom of his path, and then as we approached his front door, he put his index finger to his mouth and pointed upstairs. I nodded and made sure I walked lightly through the rooms.

"There's a quilt and a pillow on the sofa. You know where everything else is. I'll let you tell me all about it in the morning. Just glad you're okay, mate."

"Thanks, bro." We fist-bumped.

I stripped down to my boxers as my clothes stank of smoke and climbed onto the sofa, pulling the quilt over me. I'd done everything I could to get us to Richstone.

I just had to hope it was enough.

Our house fire was the topic of conversation that next day. Everyone coming up to me at school, people who'd never bothered with me before, clambering around to see if there was any gossip more exciting than the second floor of the house having been damaged. Did they want half my face to have burned off for their entertainment? We'd lost all our clothes and shit, wasn't that enough?

I checked in with Mum who said she was okay. Uncle Karl had said she could stay for however long it took for the council to rehouse us. In the meantime, I was homeless. Luckily, I had the money to buy a few new cheap items of clothing when I got the chance and had been wearing my favourite trainers. Brett had leant me something to wear to school.

Mrs Whitstable called me to her office once more. When I walked in, she was sat fiddling with a pendant around her neck, moving it left to right on the chain.

"Please tell me, Liam, that the house fire was acciden-tal, and you didn't deliberately cause a fire to get the guest residence in Richstone."

"It wasn't accidental."

Her jaw dropped.

"I think my mum's ex did it on purpose. Or through

70

carelessness. We had a fault, and he came to repair it yesterday. The fire brigade's report will let us know."

She seemed satisfied by that. "Well, I'm sorry that happened to you." Her hand dropped from her necklace. "You understand my concern if you'd been so reckless as to do that? Fire can kill."

"It's fine. I get it. But I'd never put my mum or my own life at risk like that," I lied.

"So where are you staying?"

Now she was concerned? A minute ago, she'd thought I was an arsonist.

"Brett's. He has a sofa I can surf on. Hopefully, the council will sort us a new place sooner rather than later, but meanwhile my mum's staying at my uncles. That's all I'm really bothered about. I'm young. I can sleep anywhere really."

She nodded her head and I saw the hint of sympathy in her eyes. I'd won her over.

Making sure my body posture stayed a little slumped, I made my way out of her office.

The next day she came into the class to announce that Principal Ridley had agreed to take five students pending interviews and announced our names.

"Principal Ridley will make the final decision about the house," she added. "That's out of my hands." Her gaze swept quickly to mine and away.

Skye grinned at me like she'd booked us a date at a wedding chapel. "Wanna get lunch?"

"Sure," I told her.

After grabbing a sandwich and a bottle of coke, I let her lead me to a bench at the rear of the yard. As soon as I approached, the two kids sitting there got up and left.

"I can't believe we're in," Skye said for the millionth time.

"I know, it's amazing," I replied. "We need to make sure we make the most of it."

"Fingers crossed about the accommodation."

I tilted my head towards her.

"Skye. We have the interviews to do yet, but you have to realise I'll most likely be there with my three best friends. I'm fond of you, and we've had fun, but it's bros before hos."

Her face paled.

"The opportunity at Richstone isn't for us to have some love nest; it's for us to try to gain a foothold in a place that thinks we're the shit on their shoes."

"But..."

"But what? You think I'm going there and gonna act like your bodyguard? Anyone talks to you funny and I'll knock their head off? My aim is to impress someone so much they give me a job. There'll be no romance there, Skye. Not with a rat anyway."

Tears swam in her eyes. "We can still be together."

"No, Skye, we can't. Because we never were together. We just had a few fucks; some good times in the sack." I raised my voice slightly. "If you go to Richstone, you need to go for the right reasons—the opportunities it grants you. Have the interview and make your decision, but don't hold out your hopes for me."

Her lips were trembling now, and she wouldn't look at me.

"Who's to say there's not a much better man for you there anyway?"

That got her attention. Her eyes swept up to meet mine.

"That's what this is about, isn't it? You don't want me there, because you want to see how you get on with the riches. The pretty riches."

"I'm the one who recommended you to Mrs Whitstable for a place."

"You did?" Hope burned in her irises and I wondered why I'd said it. Maybe because her heart was in the right place? She'd just tried to hook mine and it was behind a fortress. It wasn't her fault.

"Yeah. When all the applications went in, I hoped you got one. You deserve it. But you need to make friends there, try to fit in. I'll be doing my own thing and you need to know that. I'm sorry, but that's just the way it is."

"I guess we have to sacrifice shit to survive, right?" She sniffed. "Sharrow's not the place for happy ever afters, is it?"

"No, but Richstone might be." I held a hand out to her. "Friends?"

She arched a brow. "With no benefits?"

I shook my head. "Nope, we're done."

She sighed but held out her hand. "Friends. I guess I'll

need them if I'm the only girl from Sharrow Manor at Richstone."

We shook.

"I'll have your back, Skye, where I can."

It felt like the truth to me as I said it, but I knew that if it came to it, I'd throw her under a bus if it meant I triumphed. What can I say? I had a stone-cold heart.

8

Phoebe

It was the day of the interviews with the potential Sharrow Manor students and Richstone Academy was at fever pitch. Students were hanging around their lockers, being late to class, all because they wanted a glimpse of a rat. They were wasting their time, my mother had them coming in class time. She wasn't stupid.

It was a grey, rainy day and the ends of my hair were damp from just walking from the car into school. Opening my locker, I tried to sort out what I needed without transferring the moisture off me onto any of my books. But in the process I dropped my bag on the floor, my pens and keys spilling out. Thankfully my phone was still clutched in my hand.

"Would you look at the state of that?" The voice I could hear belonged to Queen Ivy herself. I rolled my eyes at her before bending down to pick up my belongings. Of course, she looked perfect: long, straightened blonde hair, just the right amount of make-up, sleek designer wardrobe which today consisted of a straight grey mini-skirt and a red sweater, stereotypical rich-girl pearls around her neck, and Louboutins on her feet. She was a walking cliché, but her little sheep, who I'd nicknamed the Poisons, flocked around her like she was Serena van der Woodsen. Come to think of it, looking at her, Ivy probably had her stylist watching *Gossip Girl* on repeat. The daughter of a media mogul, no one liked to say anything to her, because there was always a chance she could introduce them to a Kardashian. I found her more car crash than Kardash, but the fact was that even at a school for the elite, the pecking order went from the most powerful down, and Ivy Sackville was at the top.

She hated me because I was the nearest thing to a threat to her, my father owning his publishing company and my mother the school principal.

As I stood up, Ivy strolled towards me, standing to the left of my locker. She picked up the ends of my hair before letting them go, her response looking like she'd touched a dog turd. "Have you ever actually met a set of GHDs? Your hair looks like rat's tails. Are you sure you're the right side of the river?" she cooed, the three girls with her tittering. "Speaking of rats," her voice lowered, so her minions could hear, but no one else, "What your mother has happening here is heinous. The moment things start to go wrong, my daddy is going to request for Principal Ridley to be kicked out of this school and for someone more appropriate to be put in

place." She fake-smiled me, "and then you'll be gone too."
I slammed my locker door shut trapping the ends of her
hair in it.

She squealed and as the tears hit her eyes from the
short burst of pain, I smiled back, only mine was genuine.
"Oops, sorry. I didn't realise you were so close. You heard
of personal space?" Leaning in, I sniffed near her under-
arms. "Is that body odour or are you just so rotten inside
the smell of it is seeping out?"

She clutched her hair and stomped off, the Poisons
following. After a few steps she turned around. "You'll
pay for this. You'll be gone soon and then you'll not look
quite so smug, bitch."

Renee came to stand next to me. As she opened her
own locker, she let out a leisurely whistle. "That was a
thing of beauty. I hope you managed to pull some of that
hair out right from the roots."

"She drives me insane," I said sharply. "I don't want
her crown, so why she feels the need to come threaten me
I don't know."

"Yes, you do. It's because she's threatened, babe. By
you. You're everything she wants to be. She's full of fake
assery while you own who you are. I'm glad you decided
to use a rat to help bring her down. Can you imagine if
she's caught *in flagrante* with a rat? Just think of Hector
Sackville's face. It has to be something sensational."
Renee started to spread the fingers of her right hand wide
and swept the hand across the front of us both, as if
showing us. "Like her sucking one off, her little shiny
haired head bobbing up and down. Get him to ruin what

she looks like completely. Like throw her in dirt or something."

My mouth slackened, "You've thought about this way too hard already. We haven't even seen them yet. Anyway, you're going to fuck one, aren't you? And don't you want it dirrrttyy?"

"Hell yeah, but I'll make sure mine is without an audience. Whereas you need to make sure hers is viewed by everyone. Just food for thought. How very satisfying it would be to see the Queen fall right off her throne."

She was right. It would.

"So is there no chance we can sneak out of class to go peek at the rats? I could fake a migraine and ask to see the school nurse. Say I've got an aura and need you to guide me there."

I had to admit my own curiosity was frustrated at my mother's appointment timing.

"We could give it a try." I shrugged. "If she only lets you out, you'll have to do the spy mission alone, that's all. But," I reminded my best friend, "we won't see them all. They have staggered appointments. Tomorrow, she's going to hold a special assembly for the school, announcing the details. Then one of them will be here in the guest residence by the weekend." It was surreal to think about. A student from Sharrow Manor would be living in our guest residence in less than a week's time. They'd be in school two weeks from today.

"Personally, I can't fucking wait. This place has needed some excitement for way too long. The spoiled little rich boys will have some competition. Shit. Is.

Going. To. Go. Down." Renee's green eyes flashed with excitement like light catching a disco ball.

"I don't know what on earth possessed my mother to do this."

"Maybe God himself spoke to her through a dream or something. I know I'm thinking of visiting the Chapel in school."

I shook my head at my best friend. "You are an atheist."

"Yeah, but I might have to go apologise, get on my knees and pray for one of those boys to be heaven sent."

"That's not the get on your knees you'll be doing, and you know it." The bell had gone and most of the crowds had dispersed. "Come on, lets head to class, and you need to look a lot less happy, Mrs Migraine."

Renee winked at me and then clutched at her head groaning.

"Yes, Renee?" Mr Sadler, the maths teacher looked at my friend with concern, because he usually had to ask her to stop chattering and all she'd done in his class was be extremely quiet and keep rubbing at her head and squinting occasionally.

She put her hand down. "Sir, is it okay if I go see Ms Jenkins? The lights are hurting my eyes and I'm getting spots in my vision." She blew out a breath. "Oh God, I feel sick."

I put my hand on her back and rubbed it. "Are you okay? Can I help you?"

She shook her head. "I'm fine. It's not far to first aid."

"Get yourself straight there," Mr Sadler said. "You do look a tad peaky."

Renee stood and swayed slightly, "Oh my god, I'm so dizzy."

Mr Sadler's face paled and he fidgeted with a pen on his desk. "Phoebe, could you please accompany Renee to first aid, and you might be as well taking my wastepaper basket with you, just in case." He grabbed the bin with speed, holding it out towards me as I approached.

I 'helped' Renee out of the classroom. She popped to first aid and said she felt like she had a migraine, scored two Ibuprofen to cover her tracks, and then as we left the nurse's office she smirked.

"We don't have long, so let's go."

"Okay, so what's our official story for walking past the main reception in the middle of classes?" I asked my bestie.

"Why do I have to think of everything? Maybe you need to ask your mother something seeing as the principal who is seeing these people is *your mother*."

"Which wouldn't have helped you if I'd not been allowed to accompany you."

She gave a heavy sigh. "You are really going to have to raise your game with this competition we have going on if you're going to get a rat to bite Ivy." She lifted her chin, thrust her chest out and walked in the direction of the reception.

I hurried to follow behind her. Once Renee was determined, nothing stood in her way. She pushed through the double doors and into the entrance hall. There were seats here outside of the glass fronted reception area. Attached to the wall at the side of reception was a computer where you signed in and out of school.

There was a guy sitting in the reception. He wore smart, black trousers and a plain grey shirt with a light grey tie. His matching black jacket was across his knee. He did actually look like he'd come for an interview. But not to be a student. Like he'd come to join the staff. His hair was dark brown, a little grown out on top and his eyes dark brown orbs. Renee was chatting to the receptionist and I'd hung back nervously, wondering if I was going to bump into my mother. I caught the guy's eye and gave him a half-smile. He gave me a chin lift in return and then let out a nervous exhale.

Renee turned back to me, looking over my shoulder and taking a good look at the visitor. I noticed the receptionist had disappeared into the back room. She walked over to me. "I told her I'd misplaced my house keys and wondered if anyone had handed them in."

"Renee. She'll know it doesn't take two of us to ask for house keys."

"Oh, I know. You're on your own. When she comes back out, you'll need an excuse ready."

"Why am I friends with you?"

"Because I love you and I'm not boring as fuck. I'll wait for you through the door."

The receptionist beckoned me forward. I needed to think of something fast. "I just wondered if my mum was free. I need to ask her something real quick?"

Speaking of the devil, my mother came out into the reception at that point, but my eyes only flicked over her and past her to the man at her side. Because he was no boy.

Short dark brown hair was shaved short but to perfection. His face looked personally carved out by God as an example of how man should look: chiselled cheekbones and a perfectly sculptured nose, made more interesting by the slight bump near the top. His chin hinted at a dimple, though was largely covered by a light scruff. His eyes were grey, and intense, like a stormy night. His lips soft, pink and plump, a moustache shadowed above his top lip.

But what knocked me sideways was how he held himself. This man hadn't dressed to impress. He'd turned up intent on presenting himself. He wore dark black jeans, a tight white t-shirt and a black leather jacket. A group of friendship bracelets adorned his left wrist, the colours standing out against the black cuff of his jacket. He had Nike's on his feet and a thick silver chain around his neck. I realised I'd looked him completely up and down.

Those grey eyes landed on mine, his facial expressions fixed and giving away nothing. Locked down. Then he dropped the frozen features, turning to shake my mother's hand.

"Thank you for the opportunity, Principal Ridley," he said.

My mother shook his hand. "It was good to meet you. As I said, I'll be in touch, Liam."

Liam.

He stepped forward and nodded to the guy sitting. "Good luck, my friend."

Then he was gone. I watched as he went to stroll confidently out of the building.

"Excuse me? Erm. Liam." I shouted out.

He spun back around and tilted his head without saying a word to me.

I pointed at the computer screen. "You need to sign out. School policy."

"Oh, of course. Thank you." He half-smiled. It was an Ivy smile, fake as her nails.

"Brett?" My mother queried, "If you could just give me a moment."

I heard him mutter his agreement.

She stepped towards me. "Are you waiting for me, only I'm very busy right now." Her brow furrowed in annoyance as she watched me watching Liam.

"Oh no. It's okay now actually, Principal Ridley. I can see you're very busy."

"Indeed." Was the one word answer I received, before she took Brett with her.

Liam had finished signing out.

"Thanks," he said, his voice a mix of having talked a lot and needing a drink, mixed with the lilt of Sharrow Manor. He sounded rough and ready. He sounded unapologetic. I knew if my mother let him into school all hell would break loose.

And I hoped she did and it did.

. . .

Pushing through the door, Renee looked like she had ants in her pants. "I know I've not seen them all yet, but I'm claiming Brett. His eyes were like the blackest coffee and we know how much I love coffee."

"Fine with me," I said. "I'm claiming Liam, the one who just left."

"The one who hadn't even bothered to make an effort? You think you'll get Ivy to sleep with him?"

I smiled. "I never said she had to sleep with him, I said he had to ruin her."

And if anyone could ruin someone, I reckoned it was him.

9

Liam

The G.P. and my uncle were trying to manage my mum's alcohol intake. I listened to my uncle telling me how it was going. How she'd seemed to do brilliantly for a couple of days before he'd found himself missing twenty quid from his wallet and Ma spark out on the spare room bed.

The truth was that our National Health Service couldn't provide what my mum needed—a stint in a rehab. They'd do what they could, but waiting lists were long and my mum's memory of committing to giving up alcohol, short. If I had money, I could pay for a place in a proper facility. If one of those bastards from the other side of the river had a problem with alcohol they wouldn't be fobbed off and left waiting for treatment. They'd just ring a private health care provider and it would be dealt with immediately. Wealth was the answer to my escape from Sharrow and from my ending up with a noose called Ma around my neck. I loved her dearly, but I did not want her strangling my future prospects while I dealt with the fact she'd been found in a pool of her own vomit outside a pub. Her alcohol issues were rooted deep into the bottom of my father's grave, and she had the ghosts of the past to deal with before she started on trying to live in the present.

"So are you okay at Brett's still?" Uncle Karl pulled me from my thoughts.

"Yeah, fine, don't worry about me. You've enough on with Ma."

"I'll still worry about you. You're my nephew."

"I might have somewhere else to live soon, I hope," I announced.

"Oh?"

"Richstone."

There was a silence on the other end of the phone that I presumed was a stunned one, before my uncle gathered himself enough to utter, "Run that one by me again."

After visiting my mum at Uncle Karl's on Sunday, he'd given me a couple of hundred quid to go towards the replacement clothes and shoes I needed. I knew it would have been hard earned, but he wouldn't hear of me refusing him. He'd also given me the keys to the garage so that I could meet my mates in the mess room, warning me that if there was any damage to the place, he'd damage my head. It was idle threat banter. I knew he'd never touch me, and he knew I'd never do anything to his pride and joy

It meant that on Sunday evening, I was able to meet Brett, Marlon, and Daniel on private land, out of earshot of anyone else. Marlon dropped four cans of beer down on the table. I dropped a bottle of scotch at the side of it.

There was a bitter chill in the air. I put the small electric heater on to keep us warm, and we stayed in our coats. All three of my friends were looking at me, waiting. I'd put this whole thing in motion and as such I was responsible for them. The leader. "So, lads, interviews are tomorrow. Anyone want to ask anything else before it's too late?"

"I'm good," Brett answered. "My inherent good looks and charm will win the principal over."

That earned him three groans.

Daniel reached over for a can popping the top. Marlon must have shaken it on his way over as it fizzed up and out, dropping down his mouth and top. "Fuck's sake," he grunted.

"She offers you a glass of water or a cup of coffee tomorrow, you say no. You'll probably throw it down her suit," I warned him.

"I'll be fine. I've got my own suit out ready. Look very dapper if I say so myself."

"Suit? It's not a fucking wedding." I looked at the others shaking my head.

"I'm wearing a suit, it's an interview," Brett looked at me as if I'd said I was planning on turning up naked.

"Yeah, I've got a pair of trousers and a shirt and tie," Marlon added.

"Fucking swots," I laughed, grabbing my own beer. "I suppose it's the right thing to do. Make a good impression. Show them how you'll fit in."

"Exactly," Brett replied.

Yeah, it was exactly why I wouldn't be wearing one.

My interview was the first of all five of us, at eleven am. I'd woken up bright and early, my mind working out every possible angle I anticipated Principal Ridley would come at me from. I wanted that guest residence and she'd know I had no home, but it didn't mean she still wouldn't give it to Skye.

If she offered it her, I'd just have to show Skye my footage of her naked to ensure she didn't accept.

Walking over to the other side of that bridge was the weirdest fucking feeling ever. Like I was a male Cinderella and on my way up the street someone would step out, wave a wand and I'd suddenly end up dressed in D&G and a Cartier watch. The people I passed looked twice at me, but then turned their heads to ignore me. One even crossed the street to the other side. Whatever. This wasn't about them, it was about me and my friends and how we could free ourselves from scrimping and scraping or having to deal.

I followed the directions Ridley had given me until I eventually reached the gates of the academy. I had to stand and stare for a few minutes before I walked in.

Where Sharrow Manor was grey brick built—resembling a block of flats that needed knocking down—and tarmac floored and potholed outside, Richstone Academy was its antithesis. You still had to speak to reception to get buzzed through the main gates, but metal detectors didn't search you for concealed weapons here as you walked through. The building was a bright cream colour and set out in an L-shape. The main reception was in the centre section. To the front was a landscaped driveway, where arrows pointed to parking for both staff, students, and visitors around the side and back of the building. In the middle of the front grounds was a statue with the school's coat of arms and the Latin phrase *Audentes fortuna iuvat*. Helpfully underneath the English translation told me their motto was Fortune Favours the Bold.

I could get behind that.

As I walked up to the reception counter I was greeted with a friendly smile by the receptionist, a woman who looked around the same age as my mum, but who wore make-up, rather than a look of having given up on life. "Good morning. Can I help you?"

I nodded. "I'm Liam Lawson. I have an appointment with Principal Ridley at eleven."

"If you'd like to just tap the screen, Liam, and sign yourself in as a guest. It will direct you to having your photograph taken and then I can print off your visitor pass."

"Okay." I did as asked and the receptionist placed my photo in a lanyard and handed it through the small gap on her reception counter.

"Just take a seat, Liam, and Principal Ridley will be with you shortly."

Sitting down on the brown leather sectional sofa, I looked around the reception. There were pieces of abstract art on the walls besides the school rules. Everything was polished and perfect.

"Liam?"

I'd not even heard Principal Ridley come in, I'd been so lost in my surroundings. I got straight to my feet and held out my hand. She smiled and shook it.

Tall and slim, her hair was sleek, bobbed and dark brown. She wore a charcoal-coloured skirt suit with a pale-green blouse. "Come through," she gestured for me to follow her.

Going through a door at the back of the reception, I found a carpeted area with a reception desk and a secretary sat typing. Principal Ridley pushed open a door marked with her nameplate and we entered her office.

Dark mahogany furniture: a desk, bookshelves, even her filing cabinets matched. Not the battered grey shit we had at Sharrow Manor.

"Take a seat, Liam. Would you like a drink?"

"A water would be good."

I expected to be passed a bottle. I was being ridiculously naive. She pressed a button and asked for water and a coffee. Of course things would be brought to her door.

While we waited for the drinks, she introduced herself formally. About how she'd been the principal for over a decade. That there were approximately five hundred pupils there from Richstone. The exam pass rates. It was superficial stuff and I just nodded my head. Once I had my drink and we were left uninterrupted, the real interview started as I'd known it would. My water had come in a jug with sliced lemon before being poured by the woman who'd brought it into a glass and handed to me. The rest of the jug had been placed at my side, on napkins not made of paper.

"So, Liam. I'm going to be upfront with you about why I've offered this opportunity to students from Sharrow Manor. I used to be a psychologist before I was a teacher. After spending all these years at Richstone, where I've made it into an elite academy with incredible results, I want to see if I can make a difference in the lives of those less fortunate. I know you'd only be here for part of a year, but having seen your progression, I can see you are on course to do well. I think I could help you get higher marks. Improve your future prospects."

She took a sip of her coffee.

"If this is successful, I'd offer the scholarship every year, but for now I'm doing this as a trial. For five of you, it would be a case of come to school here, get your head down with your studies and let's see what happens. If you made friends then by all means you could hang with them, and if they wanted to visit Sharrow in return then that would be up to them, but no one else from Sharrow could come here other than those invited to school. Not your mother, and not any of your friends who also applied if I choose not to accept them."

Fuck. I'd at least hoped that if any of the lads didn't

get in, they'd be able to come here if I got the residence. I was starting to feel out of my depth and needed to get myself back in the game.

"Sounds fair." I deliberately yawned in an attempt to show my supposed indifference.

"So I've read your application but can you tell me yourself why I should consider you for a place?" She sat back in her seat.

I sat up straighter in mine. My legs spread, I leaned forward resting my forearms on my knees. "As you've said, I'm doing well in my studies, and I have no doubt I could pass my exams. Mrs Whitstable said I'd make a good teacher at Sharrow. She gave me something to think about." It was 'over my dead body' but I didn't need to elaborate on that. "But the fact remains that in Sharrow I have responsibilities." I decided to be brutally honest. "I deal drugs, Principal Ridley. Weed and fags to teenagers."

Her eyes widened just a little, more I assumed at my admitting it, because the woman wasn't stupid. She knew what activities happened in Sharrow Manor.

"It's not what I want to do. But when your mother could be an alcoholic and you need a roof over both of your heads, you do what you have to."

She nodded, "I understand that. There are drugs here too, Liam. Just because people have money doesn't mean they don't get high. It's just here I guess it's more for recreational purposes than survival."

I went for my Oscar winning performance. "I want a life where I don't have to be struggling for things that come easily to others. I'm not scared of hard work. I just want a chance to prove myself. I know you're only offering a school place, but to be able to say I studied at Richstone Academy in itself gives me an advantage when applying for jobs."

We chatted some more, and she asked me further questions about my home and school life.

"I'm glad you've decided to be frank with me, Liam. Mrs Whitstable told me about the fact your house had been destroyed in a fire recently. That must have been quite a shock?"

"It was, but then I just chalked it up to life giving me one up the arse again."

Principal Ridley smiled. "Are your friends like you, Liam?"

I smirked. "They're all coming in suits and will be doing their best to impress you. I wanted to come as myself. I will work hard. I will try not to cause any problems. But I'm not going to stop being myself. I'm not from Richstone and to pretend I was would be laughable."

"Is that what you feel your friends are doing? Aren't they just trying to make a good impression?"

"Has the psychological experiment started already?" I arched a brow.

She just laughed.

"Liam, I'm going to cut to the chase here. I've spoken to your headteacher and to your teachers, and I'm aware you've fixed it so that I'm here interviewing your friends and the one girl you asked to be included under duress." She steepled her fingers.

Fucking Whitstable.

"I like the lengths you went to. I'm not convinced about the electrical fault and if there are any suspicious fires in Richstone you'll be in need of a lawyer."

"You mean....?"

"I'm offering you a place here, Liam. You're perfect. I know you'll work hard because you know it's your way out of the situation you find yourself living in. I want to see how you make use of the opportunities offered to you when you're no longer forced into a life of crime through circumstance. I'll offer you the guest residence too, but you mustn't say anything of this to the others at this stage. As you have nowhere to live and they do, I would have to be cruel to not offer it to you."

Was this really happening?

"You'll move in at the weekend, and spend half term getting familiar with your accommodation. Saturday evening you'll come up to the main house and meet my son and daughter. My son is twenty-two and my daughter is the same age as you and attends here."

"Okay. Well, you don't need to warn me to stay away from your daughter. I've no intention of messing up the amazing opportunity you're offering me."

"Oh, Liam. I don't want you to stay away from my daughter," Principal Ridley said, and my eyes snapped up to meet hers. *What the fuck?*

"Phoebe needs some lessons in life too. She has dreams of a career and a life outside of Richstone. I've been there, done that, and it's not the right thing for her. She needs to see just how very privileged she is here. If she spends time with you and you show her the other side of life, then maybe you can convince her she needs to marry well and stay here."

"So what exactly do you want me to do?" I asked, my tone now a lot lighter.

"Befriend her. She's your link between us, and she'll help you at school. Just make sure you don't hurt her, or your life at Sharrow Manor will have seemed like a dream at the nightmares I can throw at you."

I didn't doubt it. She was clever and monied.

"Is there really a social experiment?" I asked.

Her smile was like something the Joker would give you.

"Yes, my experiment is to see if showing my daughter the worst, will make her strive for the best. Let her visit where you live, see it for herself. I can't guarantee your exam results, Liam, but I can guarantee that if my daughter changes her attitude and agrees to marrying a Richstone man, I'll make sure you never have to face a return to Sharrow or a lack of money ever again."

So there it was. The true reason for all of this.

"I can do that," I told her.

Her next smile was genuine. "Excellent. Hopefully we can make this a rich experience for us all. Richstone is a great place, Liam. Make the most of it all. Though having met you, I'm sure you will."

"There's one more thing I'd like to ask," I told her, and her tongue poked her cheek as if her patience with me was running out.

"Yes?"

"Would you consider also letting a teacher from Sharrow Manor come here? Clive Billings is a fantastic English teacher and it would be good if we had someone we could go to at school if we had a problem, someone who understands us and who we are. It would also be an incredible experience for him."

"Hmmm, that's not a bad idea actually. I'll give it some thought."

She looked at her watch. "Right, your friend is probably waiting so I'll bring this to a close. Someone will be in touch with you about the coming weekend and any other arrangements."

We walked outside, where sure enough Brett was sitting there, his foot tapping with anxiety, but before I could engage with him, I became aware of a girl standing in front of me looking me up and down. One of the riches. I would have liked to have thought she was checking me out, but no, she'd be assessing me ready to go and tell the other riches that she'd seen a rat. I turned away and addressed the principal once more. I thanked her for the opportunity and once more she said she'd be in touch. Then I walked over to Brett and wished him luck.

That was me done. I wanted to punch the air in excitement but needed to wait until I was somewhere out of sight of other people.

"Excuse me? Erm. Liam," a loud but yet gentle voice said from behind me.

I span around to come face to face with the rich girl, all shiny red-brown hair. I noticed her amber eyes though. They were stunning and if she wasn't one of the riches I would probably have been interested. But right now, all I needed to do was think of my plans and concentrate on this daughter of the principal's.

I tilted my head at the girl, waiting.

She pointed at the computer screen. "You need to sign out. School policy."

"Oh, of course. Thank you." I fake smiled and signed out, hearing her approach the principal. With a "thanks," I walked out of the building. Making my way past the motto, I cracked my knuckles, along with a huge grin.

Yes, fortune did favour the bold.

And there would be no one bolder than me, now I knew I was in.

Phoebe

My mother wouldn't tell me anything that evening, saying that just because I was her daughter didn't mean I got the advantage of finding out before the others. I don't think she trusted me to keep my mouth shut with my friends. She might have been right. All I knew is I actually felt excitement fizzing in my stomach because something different was happening here. Not a fundraiser or one of the residents being knighted. Something fundamentally different.

Renee called me. "Please tell me that brown-eyed boy is in."

"I've told you already, she won't tell me a thing. Not one clue."

"Hmm. I wish we were on FaceTime so I could check you for tells of lying."

"You know I tell you everything. She says I get to know when everyone gets to know."

"Your mother is always so utterly fair that it's sickening. I want to know whether to make an effort to book in for a Brazilian."

"You still have to sleep with one, even if they're fugly. It's what you agreed to. There was no 'as long as they're good-looking' in your bet."

"Oh God. What have I done? Can I swap with you if there are only ugly ones? Yours looked worth banging. Then mine could just be revenge on Ivy."

"Not a chance. I won't be sleeping with a rat. Can you imagine what that would do to my mother's reputation as principal?"

"He could be your dirty little secret."

"No bad boys of Sharrow Manor for me. And he most definitely was one."

"He sounds hotter every time you describe him."

"No one says he's getting a place either. In fact, I doubt he will. He didn't even make an effort to look smart." I thought of his friendship bracelets, wondering if his girlfriend had made them for him. "Right, is there anything else, because I've some homework to finish?"

"No. I'll see you in the morning to hear our fates. Love you, Fifi." She called me my pet name. When we'd first met at nursery, she couldn't say my name properly.

"Love you too, Ren."

· · ·

We sat in the assembly hall. As the oldest we were given seats near the rear, the youngest at the front. My mother took to the stage, standing behind her lectern. She took a sip of water and then waited for a hush to descend before she began to address the staff and pupils of Richstone Academy. Ivy Sackville had deliberately taken the seat behind me with the Poisons.

"Principal Ridley always looks so well put together, and yet her daughter can't get a grip on style. I guess she's too busy thinking of other pupils to bother with her own daughter."

I ignored her. My pleasure would come when she was knocked off that pedestal she'd put herself on.

"Good morning, Richstone Academy."

My mother waited for the returned murmurs of good morning.

"As you are all by now well aware, we will shortly be welcoming some new arrivals to Richstone Academy. I had the pleasure of speaking with five new students yesterday who will be taking a position with us in our sixth form after the half term break."

"Five? Wonder why there's an extra?" Lucie whispered from my right. I shrugged my shoulders.

"I shall expect the usual welcome from Richstone both in and out of school. The students who are coming, have as you know come from a disadvantaged area. We will get to know them as individuals and not make judgements as to who they are before we've had the opportunity to get to know them. If there are any problems, you will report them the same way as you would if it were another pupil."

"Except another pupil wouldn't give me lice," April, one of the Poisons said, making the others behind snigger.

"So from Monday the twenty-fourth of February we shall be welcoming Liam Lawson, Skye Drummond, Brett Mayer, Marlon Rowe, and Daniel Preston."

"Four boys and one girl. My hot boy must be in that mix," Renee's eyes were lit with excitement.

"Look at her best friends pretending to be excited that she's bringing trash into school," Ivy kicked the back of my chair. I was desperate to get up and escape her being behind me, but my mother wasn't finished.

"I have a further announcement. After making a very quick phone call to my seniors, they agreed that it would also be an opportunity to extend an invitation to a teacher too. So also on Monday we will be welcoming Mr Clive Billings to our English department."

"Oh, this has gone too far. Now a rat will be telling us what to do. As soon as we're out of here I'm phoning Daddy."

"Can anyone else hear an annoying whining noise?" Lucie leant round behind her. "If I hear it again, I'm going to hit it with a rolled-up textbook."

I sniggered, feeling a little better with Lucie having our backs, because if Ivy wasn't careful, Lucie would carry out her threats.

Mum carried on giving information about the scholarship opportunity and then we were free. "I wouldn't be surprised if my mother gets some huge accolade for this,"

I said loudly so Ivy could hear. She narrowed her eyes at me and stormed off ahead.

"I'm guessing this Skye will be staying in the guest residence. I hope she's nice. We'll have to arrange a welcome party," Flora suggested.

"Good idea. I'll check with Mum tonight that we're okay to go ahead and plan one."

God, I hoped she was nice too seeing as I was going to have to spend a lot of time with her. I also hoped she respected the guest residence. Mum had thrown money at the place getting it fixed up in super quick time and it was almost ready to move into. Huh, I'd be in my bedroom while a girl the same age as me got a whole house to herself. Maybe I could persuade her to let me move in?

I was surprised to find both my parents and my brother sat at our large dining table that evening. Either they'd been summoned by Mum or my dad wanted to know what the hell was going on.

Taking my seat, I said hello to Eddie and my dad.

Our cook brought in a starter. Today it was chicken liver pate which I adored. Marjorie gave me a little wink as she walked out. I loved our cook. Marjorie would sneak me extra dishes of her sticky toffee pudding, which was to die for, when mum wasn't looking.

"How did today go?" Dad asked once Marjorie had gone.

"Better than I could have hoped," Mum replied. "I

thought there'd be much more opposition, but I feel having not got it stopped, people are waiting for it to go wrong instead.

"That's what Ivy Sackville said. That once something went wrong her father would step forward," I added.

"Well, we'll just have to ensure that nothing major does go wrong, won't we? Because if I can make Hector Sackville's face look any sourer than its usual delight, that would just be the icing on the cake."

Dad shook his head, but I smiled, because if I got my way, Hector's face would be more than sour; he'd be unable to show it around Richstone.

"Mum, the girls and I were thinking of getting the house ready for Skye. A welcome party."

"Oh? What sort of thing were you thinking?"

"A kind of picnic? We could lay it out in the kitchen. You know: huge welcome basket, decorate with welcome bunting. That kind of thing."

"That would be lovely."

I smiled.

"If it were Skye taking the guest residence, but I've offered it to Liam."

Both myself and my father choked on our food at the same time.

"There's a boy moving into the guest residence? I'll need to be having a word then, Daphne, to make sure he knows not to come within two feet of our daughter."

Eddie laughed. "Mum, did you wish to give Dad a heart attack for dinner?"

Mum pursed her lips. "Liam knows there will be no

romance. He's unlikely to wish to scupper his placement dallying with Phoebe. There are plenty of other Richstone girls he can choose from. I'm sure not everyone will be so immune to a rat. He has very hypnotic eyes."

"Mother," Eddie was disgusted.

"Anyway, I've told Liam that Phoebe will be available for helping him navigate his way around Richstone. He'll be moving in on Saturday, and then Saturday evening I've invited him for dinner so that the two of you can also meet him, so make sure you're home from work please."

"I wouldn't miss it for the world, seeing Dad's reaction to the new man living on his land, a rat, in a guest residence, with access to his daughter."

"There is no access to me, you idiot." I scowled.

"I'm just winding Dad up, Phoeb. Take a chill pill. I bet Liam will be bringing some."

I swear Dad's face went paler still.

"Enough now, Edward. I shall be expecting you to be a good role model for the younger man. You can tell him how you progressed from your education. He might yet show aptitude towards publishing."

"I can't help feeling you're heading towards a severe disappointment or headache, Daph," Dad said, making Mum's chin tauten. "These children are from one of the roughest places in England. A few lessons at a posh school is not going to suddenly turn around their fortunes. Prepare yourself. Because if they don't cause the trouble themselves, their being here will certainly bring it. The people of Richstone will not want this to be a success, because if it is, what comes next? We encourage more mixing? You need to tread very carefully. This is going to make you new enemies."

"And it might just change some people's judgemental attitudes, so we'll see how it goes." She turned to me. "I think you should still do a welcome basket and then go down and introduce yourself. Just you, not the others as well. Renee will have him running screaming from the house if she starts with her relentless, enthusiastic questioning. At least warn him before he meets her. See if he wants to do a mixer on the Sunday evening. Maybe he brings the others from Sharrow and you invite a few people from here. I've no doubt Stefan would be happy to come along."

"Okay," I said.

"Maybe lose the welcome bunting and the picnic blanket. Add an Xbox, Playstation, and some beer."

"Perhaps Eddie should be the one to meet him?" I suggested.

Mum shook her head. "He'll be wanting to know about his new peers, school, what you do for recreation. He might appreciate a drive around Richstone to get used to his new surroundings. I've already told him you'll be his contact between him and me when I'm unavailable."

"Bet he was thrilled." Eddie raised a brow.

"Liam Lawson is not to be underestimated. He showed an intelligent mind and maturity beyond his years. He's not going to do anything to jeopardise the opportunities offered to him, I can assure you."

The rest of dinner proceeded in a similar vein, with mum telling us how it would be, Eddie trying to get a rise out of our father, and me becoming increasingly nervous about the fact that the steely-eyed boy would be moving into our guest residence on Saturday, and I was expected to befriend him.

I felt like I was walking on ice and hoping it wasn't going to crack.

11

Liam

The day had arrived. I was moving into a guest residence in Richstone. As I picked up my suitcase and headed out of Brett's house towards the car idling at the kerb, I once more found myself scratching my chin, while my stomach clenched.

I didn't think I did nervous, but there was definite tingling in my chest. The drabness of Sharrow Manor gave way to the green of Richstone as we passed over the bridge. Thankfully, the driver stayed silent, so I was able to continue to stare out of the window, taking in my first real glance of the large houses that were Richstone real estate. Houses with driveways so long a car was a necessity for reaching your own front door. Sat on land so huge, Sharrow would have had twenty terraced residences on the same spot. What struck me most was the faces of the people we passed. Most didn't wear a frown.

They looked relaxed, happy, as they pushed prams, jogged, or generally went about their day.

The driver turned up another leafy street and reached a metal gate where he flashed a card at a machine. The gates drew back and he carried on through, travelling up the long, winding driveway before taking a turn and giving me my first view of the guest residence. Principal Ridley—or Daphne, as she'd instructed me to call her outside of school—had given nothing away about where I would be living other than saying it was a bungalow. I'd pictured the bungalows of Sharrow. Small rectangles consisting of two small bedrooms, a kitchen/diner, a small living room, small bathroom and if you were lucky, a small square of lawn or concrete to the rear. There was rarely a garage. Mostly if you had a car it was parked outside the front of your home on the street.

I swallowed, not wanting to give the driver any sign of my shock and awe as he pulled up outside the front door, having just driven me past a double garage. His eyes were on me and he turned, holding out a set of keys taken from the centre console.

"Mrs Ridley felt that rather than meet you, she'd let you get settled in on your own. She says to make yourself at home and that Miss Ridley will come around later to introduce herself."

I reached over for the keys. "Thank you."

He nodded. "Welcome to Richstone. I'm Christian, one of the drivers. I'm sure Miss Ridley will furnish you with the details of how to contact us if you need to go anywhere, but if not, be sure to ask her. We are at your disposal, Mr Lawson. Welcome to Richstone."

"Liam. Please call me Liam," I said, "and thanks again."

I got out of the car and Christian walked around to the boot, taking out my one suitcase. He left me standing there on the pavement outside my new home, my suitcase at my feet. I watched as he got back in, and drove to the end of my driveway, turning up the road to the main house. I could just see it through the trees.

Well, here went nothing. It was time to see what my new lodgings looked like, while I was on my own and could be honest about my feelings.

As I pushed open the door, a brightly lit hallway with a span larger than the whole downstairs of my previous house greeted me. My old home's front door had opened straight into the living room, and a back door out into our small garden. Here, cream cupboards hid a place to put multiple coats and pairs of shoes. There was a small bench for you to sit on while you put on or removed your footwear. I did so, feeling like I needed to tiptoe around this strange building.

Pushing the first door open, I entered a living room so large I couldn't begin to comprehend the size of it, given it was just for me. It held two massive dark brown leather sofas, one L-shaped, one a three-seater. A large TV on the wall looked like I was in my own cinema. Though I wanted to take it all in, firstly, I decided to just move quickly around the space. Then I could sit down and wonder if I'd accidentally smoked some of my weed on the way here.

Everything was large. A second doorway on the left led to an enormous kitchen/dining room with a funky looking square table and a modern kitchen.

The third door on the left-hand side of the hallway revealed a large bedroom decorated in neutral tones. It looked out over a vast garden area and had an en suite bathroom.

Fucking hell. This was the residents of Richstone's normal. My skin crawled with the unjustness of it all. Part of me wanted to smash the lot of it up, but I took deep breaths and moved onto the next room at the back of the hall. A further living room was next. This one however had a less formal feel to it, and I guessed it was there for people to hang around in, given patio doors opened onto the rear of the property where I looked out over the vast garden, patio, and was that a pool?

On the right-hand side there was also a large bathroom with a wet room as well as a large jacuzzi bath and finally a second bedroom that faced the front of the property with another en suite. This room had a second window that looked out over the trees and gave a small glimpse at the larger house ahead.

I flopped down onto the bed. I'd look outside later. Right now, I needed to just take a moment to get my head around my new accommodation. What the fuck would the other guys think when they saw this? Would jealousy get in the way? Nah, they could come here whenever they liked.

You're doing the right thing, Liam. I told myself. *All of this is for the greater good. It's just stuff, don't let it consume you and your soul.*

But as I felt the comfort of the mattress beneath my body, I knew that even by being here for these few minutes, I'd already crossed a line that meant I could never happily return to Sharrow.

I'd not slept well the last few nights. Sleeping on a sofa wasn't the best place to start with and then with a mind whirling with the changes ahead, it'd got worse. So when I woke suddenly, wondering where the hell I was before realising the answer was on the comfiest bed I'd ever had the fortune to meet, I'd closed my eyes again, in no rush to wake up.

But then I heard the source of what had woken me. A knock on the front door. Reluctantly pushing myself off the bed, I left the room and headed to the front door. As a third knock sounded, I yelled out, "Hold on a moment, I'm coming." This would be the daughter. No doubt a fucking do-gooder. I expected her to be standing there with a basket of cookies and some homemade lemonade.

So when I pulled open the door to find the amber-eyed girl from the reception standing there with her arms crossed firmly around her chest, I had to admit, I was wrong-footed.

This was Principal Ridley's daughter?

I wasn't sure whether to be pleased the pretty girl standing in front of me was her, or annoyed because I wasn't allowed to play, and I really would have liked an opportunity to dirty her up.

My eyes flickered up and down her body like I know hers had mine when we'd first met. I once more took in that long, red-brown hair, and those amber-coloured eyes making me hope she hid a wild side as they reminded me of a wolf. She had a slim but athletic body, dressed in black skinny jeans, a big fluffy red jumper and black ankle boots. And of course there were also perfectly manicured brows, one of which arched up at me right now.

"My mum sent me to introduce myself and to see how you're doing. Can I come in?" She looked back towards her house. "I don't have to if you're still getting settled." Her refined posh accent was like smoothed plaster compared to my rough edges.

I stood back from the door. "No, it's fine. Come in."

She took a deep exhale as if walking past the threshold of the house was crossing into some kind of lion's den, but then she'd no doubt think I was a criminal who might attack her. Her judgement fucked me off and had my hackles rising.

"Sorry it took me so long to get to the door. I've not been sleeping well, and so I just sat on the bed and that was it. Out like a light. It means I've not unpacked or anything, so excuse my case." I nodded my head towards my single piece of luggage.

"Ah, for a minute there I'd thought you weren't stopping. When you didn't answer, I wondered if you'd taken one look and left already."

My hands clenched briefly and I gave her a forced smile. "Why? Did you expect me to think I couldn't possibly live here? That I was overwhelmed by the luxury and had to bolt back to the shithole I came from?"

She flinched at the hate in my words.

"No. I thought you might have preferred the place where you live. The one that's ugly on the outside, but you manage to live in all the same. Don't be fooled by pretty packaging here is all I have to say to you right now."

I'd give the girl her dues. She'd rescued herself pretty quickly from her shock at my attitude and come back fighting.

"Oh I'm not fooled by many things, certainly not pretty packaging." Once again, I let my eyes slowly look her up and down.

She ignored my actions completely.

"So I'm Phoebe. I'm going to make myself a coffee in the kitchen if that's okay? We can sit in there while I do what my mother has asked me. Then I'll leave you to it."

She clearly didn't want to be here. Maybe I was making her feel uncomfortable after all.

"Lead the way."

"This place is amazing," she said as she stepped into the hallway, and I could hear the envy in her tone. "I've asked if I can move in once you've left. The place was really old-fashioned as my granny lived here until she died and then it just stood empty for a while."

"Huh. It seems a sin to leave a house like this empty when people like me don't even have somewhere to live."

"You don't have a home?" she exclaimed as we entered the kitchen/diner and she started gathering coffee pods and filling a jug with water.

"My house burned down recently."

"Jesus," she answered. "I hope no one got hurt."

"No. Not physically anyway. So, your granny didn't die here, did she? Because if she died in one of the bedrooms, I'll sleep in the other one."

"Ooops." Phoebe grimaced. "She died right in that very bed you've been sleeping in."

My face must have worn a look of complete horror because she then cracked out laughing.

"Oh my goodness, Liam. I don't even know which room you slept in. Granny died in hospital, enjoying the best private healthcare my daddy could buy. Also, she'd had an antique four-poster which I had put into storage, because I didn't think it would quite be your scene." She quickly added, "making no judgements except basing it on the fact it wasn't my scene and we're the same age. You want an antique four-poster, I'll have it brought back."

She set the machine to make herself a coffee. "Want one?"

"Actually, can you show me how to work it, so I'll know for future?" I hated asking for help, but I had to accept here I had things to learn.

"Sure."

I went to stand next to her. Our hands touched briefly as she passed me a pod to put in the machine. The whole system was easy enough, but I'd only ever shoved a spoonful of the cheapest shit coffee into a mug before and then drowned it in so much milk I couldn't taste the bitterness. This time I just added a splash. Phoebe had left hers black and I watched as she walked over to the sink and added cold water to the top.

She shuffled onto a stool placed against the island and I climbed onto one opposite her.

"I- well..." Phoebe puffed out her cheeks and blew out a breath. "I'm going to be perfectly honest with you, Liam. I have no idea what to say to you. My mum has set up her scholarship and told me I need to make sure you're okay. I'm here to answer any questions and to show you anything else in the house you might need help with. I can tell you about school. Oh, and Mum said that you were invited to dinner up at our house tonight. Eight pm." She raised both brows. "So prepare for a grilling from my father and maybe my brother too. Is there anything you need other than the tour?"

"Hmmm," I mumbled suggestively. Phoebe looked away, suddenly fascinated with the inside of her cup. "Okay. I do have a question."

"Yes?"

"What do the other kids in the Sixth Form at Richstone Academy think about their new fellow students?"

"Well, my friends are so excited that you're all coming because they're looking for a bit of excitement before the exams come up and all we do is revise. There have been general rumblings from some guys as to whether you'll be okay or if you're going to create trouble and bring the school down in disgrace. Mainly that's them parroting out their parents' crap. Then there are other girls who say they want you out as soon as possible, and my mother along with you."

"Harsh."

Phoebe shrugged her shoulders. "I don't think Ivy Sackville truly likes herself, never mind anyone else. If it's okay I thought I could arrange a bit of a welcome party for you and the others for tomorrow night. I know it's a bit 'throw you in at the deep end', but my friend Stefan and his friends are really nice, and I think it would be good for you to meet a few people who are pleasant before you meet the ones who are less so."

"A welcome party sounds good. Where would we have that?"

"I can book a function room, or you could have it here. I mean, it's too cold for the pool, but the patio has heaters."

"Fine. I've not actually been outside yet. Want to come with me?"

She nodded and jumped down off her stool. Walking back out to the hall, she walked towards the second living room at the back.

There were keys in the patio doors. She turned one to open it and we stepped outside.

"Perfect for parties."

"Yeah, it seems so. We can hold the party here," I told her.

I followed Phoebe across the decking. "So the pool is under this cover. It does have heating but in February it's still going to be too cold. However," she pointed to another covered up item in the corner. "That's your hot tub and that you can use." She sighed. "Are you sure I can't convince you to leave so that I can move in here?"

"Afraid not, but you can come use the hot tub. We'll trade numbers and you can just let me know when you fancy a soak. I promise not to peek at your swimwear," I teased.

A hint of a blush crept into her cheeks. She busied herself finding a key on the bunch, walked over to a large shed and opened the lock. "After you," she pointed inside.

"Is this where I find out it's all a ruse and I'm actually being locked in here and kept as some kind of lab *rat*," I asked, but as her fingers touched her parting-on-a-gasp lips, my own mouth dropped in surprise as I came face-to-face with state-of-the-art gym equipment.

"Did I actually die and go to heaven?" I asked, and in that moment I forgot to be anything but overwhelmed.

1 2

Phoebe

My mouth had been so dry by the time I'd made the small walk down from our house to the guest one that I'd wondered with that and nerves if I'd even be able to speak. My coffee had been most welcome and needed. I'd watched a myriad of emotions pass across Liam's face during the short time I'd been here with him, from his closed-off dismissiveness to what I saw now. Complete disbelief at his surroundings. I guessed it was one thing to covet wealth and dream of nice things, but quite another to be faced with it and told it was temporarily all yours.

He was wearing faded blue denim jeans with rips at the knees and a navy-blue Adidas t-shirt. I didn't know why but I'd thought he'd smell of cigarettes. He didn't. He smelled of faded aftershave, just enough to tantalise my senses.

"If you need new gym gear, we can arrange that," I told him.

"Are you like a genie? I rub you and you grant my every wish?" he retorted.

I felt my cheeks heat and he smirked. "Are you always so easy to embarrass?"

I shrugged. "No one ever spoke to me like that before."

Shrewd grey eyes fixed on mine.

"The guys around here tend to talk to women respectfully, rather than like objects."

He smirked. "You'd better remember then that I'm not a guy from around here, Phoebe Ridley." He walked away from me to better explore the gym equipment and I let out the breath I'd held in a few seconds longer than necessary.

Liam dropped down to sit on a bench press and he sighed, as if he didn't know what to do with himself.

"Is it true that you call us the riches?" I asked him.

"Riches. Rich bitches. Assholes. And you call us the rats, right?"

"Yup. But now if you take weed, I'll call you a Rich-stoner."

He burst out laughing at that. I think he was as shocked by his hearty guffaw as I was.

"Phoebe Ridley, you might not be the boring babysitter I was expecting after all," he announced.

For reasons I didn't dwell on, his words lit a fire deep down in my belly.

"After tomorrow's welcome party I'm sure you'll

make friends with Stefan and the others and not need babysitting by a girl anymore."

He got up from the bench and closed the space between us. I found myself walking backwards until my back hit the wall and I could go no further.

"What if I still want babysitting?" His voice was low, and he was too close, invading my personal space. "You intrigue me, Miss Ridley. I presumed you'd be head-to-toe Chanel, walking around with a dog in a bag, and telling me all about your ponies and how Daddy just bought you some earrings from Tiffany's."

I tilted my chin up at him. He was trying to intimidate me. Toy with me. I wouldn't give him the satisfaction. "Oh, you'll meet plenty of those, but still, be careful of presumptions."

"Because of course no one will be expecting me to say fuck every other word, spit on the ground, and talk with my fists." He flicked his tongue over his top teeth. I watched its every movement.

"Do you mean you don't? I'm disappointed. I hope you're not going to be boring."

Silence hung between us but there was something else in the air. Just hanging there as if waiting to pounce. Something that needed to not be there.

Liam lifted up my hair, tucking it behind my left ear, and he leaned in and whispered, "I would ruin you." Then he backed away, putting space between us. It happened so quickly, I wondered if it had really happened at all.

Swallowing, my eyes darted to the door. To my

escape. "I'd better get back." I pointed in the direction of the main house. I'll leave you to do whatever, and then we'll see you up at the main house just before eight?"

He nodded; that damn slow smirk back on his face. "I'll see you out."

"Don't forget that the keys to the patio doors are in this shed door. There are also keys to remove the swimming pool cover because we don't want anyone falling in there after deciding to swim after too much beer." I knew I was babbling, but I needed to give him the info quickly and get out of there.

"You mean you don't fill it with champagne?" he mocked. His tone stopped me from running scared. I felt my nostrils flare.

"I don't like champagne for your information," I replied haughtily.

"For yours, I prefer scotch to beer," was his simple comeback.

We'd walked into the house and across the hall. I opened the front door and gave a half wave. "On behalf of my family, welcome. The house numbers are next to the phone. Oh, you said we should swap numbers." I hesitated in the doorway, not knowing if he was going to give me his number or his middle finger.

"Pass me your phone," he beckoned with his hand.

"Bossy much?" I took it from my pocket anyway and passed it to him. My fingers met his palm as I did so, and I felt like I'd trespassed onto his territory by accidentally touching him. I inspected his hands as he typed into my phone. They looked like they'd seen work—rough and calloused—and I imagined them against my skin, my cheeks, my thighs.

Phoebe. What the hell?

I remained in this trance for as long as it took him to input his details.

"There. I've sent myself a message back. Lesson number one, you need to be less trusting with strangers from Sharrow Manor."

I swiped my phone off him and looked at the message he'd sent himself from my phone.

Liam: that got you thinking didn't it?

I narrowed my eyes at him. "Ha bloody ha."

"Just think. I could have sent, 'oh, Liam, I can still feel your hard cock inside me', and then I could have passed it around the dinner table tonight."

I stomped back up to the house without looking back. Annoyed that in a few hours I'd have to put up with him all over again.

"Mum. I'm going round to Flora's, but I'll be back in plenty of time for tonight."

"Okay, honey."

I'd called a get-together, but I didn't want to hold it at my house. Everyone was gathering at Flora's as her parents were away skiing.

"So what's got all up in your panties?" Renee asked as we all sat in Flora's living room drinking a glass of white wine Flora had opened as soon as she'd seen my face.

"I've only met him for like half an hour max and I

already feel out of my depth." I scrubbed a hand through my hair. "What on earth was my mother thinking? He's scowling one minute, cheeky the next, pleasant a second later, and then intense and intimidating."

"You want in his pants," Renee announced.

"No, I do not," I protested, flustered. "What I do want is advice on how the hell I make sure he knows not to mess with me."

"I think your father will handle that one for you at this evening's dinner," Lucie yawned and stretched.

"Sorry, are we keeping you up?" Renee's lips pressed flat as she looked closely at our friend. "Oh, it's not us keeping you up. Someone else did. Spill."

Lucie smirked. "Let's just say I had quite the workout with Jake from Fitopia."

"You fucked your personal trainer?" Flora gasped.

"I hope you used a condom because if the rumours about him are true, you are not the first," I added.

Lucie winked. "Oh, I'm definitely not the first. That's why I wanted him. I needed a man who could show me a good time. Show me how sex should be. Not like the crap I've had so far. Now when I order my new pet rat around, I might just command him to do a certain thing with his tongue I've discovered I really like."

We all fell about laughing.

"Gosh, this is exactly what I needed. Just an hour with my friends to decompress. It's too much back at mine, with the new boy moved in and Mum organising this dinner. Oh, also, I suggested a welcome party for tomorrow, and he said yes. Can we quickly organise that, just a select few, so I can let him know what time we'll be there, and he can ask the others?"

"A party on Valentine's Day? And you didn't lead with this? The fact we're going to meet the rats and be able to start putting our competition in motion?" Lucie rolled her eyes at me.

"We ignore the fact it's Valentine's. That's an order." I told her.

"Spoilsport. Right, who are we inviting and more importantly, what are we wearing?"

When I got back home, I headed straight upstairs to my room. My body was chilled out from the two glasses of wine I'd drunk, and I decided I'd redo my hair and make-up before dinner. I wanted to look tidy and presentable enough to satisfy my parents' expectations, but to also show Liam I'd not made a huge effort. He was good looking and I needed him to see that I wasn't Lady Chatterley looking to fuck him against a tree in the garden. I had to remember that he would have some kind of game plan about being here. The man was clearly not stupid, but I wasn't about to be the aim of his game. Thirty minutes later, my hair was up in a sleek, high ponytail, with not a stray, wispy hair in sight. I wore a Gucci black and white silk crossover dress with a scarf neck. My make-up was simple: beige tones to my eyes and cheeks and a soft pink gloss lip. I made my way downstairs, slipping my feet into kitten heels.

"Ah, Phoebe," my father turned to me as I walked

into the sitting room from his position on the leather Chesterfield.

"Dad."

"So what are your first impressions of this chap? Do I need to lock up the valuables?"

"He's fine. He was polite enough. Seemed completely overwhelmed by the house."

"I should imagine he'll feel like a fish out of water coming here for dinner then. I don't know why we have to entertain him here, especially on his first evening."

My brother entered the room. "Is the rat not here yet?"

My mother walked in. "Eddie, you will watch your mouth. Liam is our guest and will be treated like any other guest we invite to dinner."

"Oh, so polite to their face and then we have a huge bitch behind their backs. I can get on board with that." He gave my mother a wink and she huffed.

And then the doorbell rang.

"I told the staff you would answer the door, Phoebe. I thought it would put Liam more at ease to be greeted by a familiar face."

"Fine." I left the room and started the walk down the hallway to the front door where I could make out a shape behind the small rectangle of glass.

Our front door was old and stiff, and I had to really drag it open.

"Thought you'd have staff do this for you," Liam stood on the doorstep holding a very small bunch of flowers. There were like six of them and they were wrapped in cellophane.

"We do, but I was sent to put you at ease. Come in. Are those for Mum?" I asked him.

"Yeah. My mum said I needed to bring them with me." Pain flashed across his eyes for a moment, and I wanted to ask him what was wrong and if I could help. But his gaze changed, and the hard, flinty stare was back. "Are you keeping me on the doorstep, or am I actually allowed in?"

"We're in the sitting room. Come meet everyone. Dinner will be served shortly."

We began our walk down the hall. It was quiet and awkward, and I needed to fill the emptiness. "Did you unpack?"

He looked down at the different clothes he was wearing. A pair of black jeans and a pale blue shirt open at the neck, then back up at me with an expression that said, 'duh'.

"There's no need to be such an idiot. I'll not bother talking to you anymore," I huffed. His snigger echoed through the remaining silence.

Pushing open the door, we found my mother standing by the coffee table. My father and brother rose to their feet from their seats on the sofa.

"Liam, come in," Mum beckoned him inside, smiling kindly.

Liam offered her the flowers. "I appreciate this isn't much, but I wanted to show you my appreciation for this opportunity."

"Oh, Liam, that's so very thoughtful. Thank you. I shall get them put in water immediately." She placed them on the sideboard, gesturing to my dad and brother. "This is my husband, Maxwell; and this is Edward, Phoebe's older brother."

Eddie held his hand out first. "Eddie. Please don't call me that old-fashioned name they insisted on giving me."

I saw Liam's shoulders fall two inches lower as he realised Eddie had a sense of humour.

"I hear you. My mum would have introduced me as William."

Next Liam approached my father and shook his hand. "Good to meet you, Sir. Thank you for inviting me to stay."

"Well, I have no say in the matter. Happy wife, happy life is the motto I live by, Liam." Dad then winked at him.

"Maxwell!" Mum scolded. "Could I get you a drink, Liam?"

"Do you have a scotch?"

"Do we have a scotch? Come," Dad beckoned him. "Let me show you my drinks cabinet and make a recommendation for you."

Sitting around the dinner table playing happy families was so false. I couldn't wait for this to be over and for me to be out of here. Everyone together was rare. Everyone together and acting like they enjoyed it was like finding a white peacock. We'd so far enjoyed polite chit chat about the house's history and Dad was just finishing up talking about the publishing company.

"So if you want a tour at any time just let us know. I'd say Eddie would show you around, but he'd likely get you both lost in a bar on the way there."

"Which I'm sure Liam would prefer to being shown around a boring old publishers."

"Take no notice, Liam. Edward will be taking over the 'boring old publishers' and really loves working there," my mum said.

My eyes met my brother's, silent messages passing between us. My brother didn't hate it, but it was expected of him, just like I was expected to marry a rich man and have his heirs.

"So, do you have any thoughts on your future career, Liam?" Dad asked him.

"I'd like to run a successful business, but what, I'm not sure yet, maybe accountancy."

"Oh." My dad's surprise was unexpected, and I could see Liam's shoulders tense up in response.

"Phoebe's worst subject is maths, maybe while you're here you could tutor her a little?"

Liam exhaled and turned to look at me. "Happy to help if you need it. Just let me know."

"Thanks," I fidgeted with my cutlery.

"So how are you finding the guest residence, Liam? It's a lot of house for one person, isn't it?" Eddie queried.

"It is, but I'm enjoying the space. The thing I'm finding strangest is the quiet. At Sharrow Manor there's rarely any quiet. We all live so close together and there's noise from the pavement outside your home as people walk past, or cars drive by. Here, I opened the back door and heard silence, except for birds. It was quite unnerving because it was so unusual."

I imagined Liam looking out at the rear garden, thinking of how different it was to where he lived. I tried to imagine being in a small house, with people living either side, and traffic and strangers being able to walk right in front of your window.

But that was Sharrow. There were other towns and cities out there. Where you could have your space and yet still be able to see people. To be able to breathe without expectation. Liam didn't know it, but we weren't so very different. We both wanted what we weren't getting. Opportunity. Maybe being around Liam would teach me about the real world, the one I was protected from?

"I would appreciate the maths tutoring," I said. But I wouldn't be limiting it to maths. I'd want to learn all I could from him. So I could work out how I got myself away from being Mrs Rich and Boring.

Liam had been explaining about the house fire that had made him homeless prior to his coming here while I was wrapped up in my own thoughts. It struck me how confident he was. I'd expected him to feel awkward up here sitting with the family, but it certainly hadn't proved the case.

"I hope that man is sent to jail. He could have killed you both." Mum was disgusted, even though she already knew about the fire from Liam's interview.

"And so you have an uncle?" Dad questioned.

"Yes. He's a mechanic and owns a garage in Sharrow. I think he's expecting me to take it over, but he barely breaks even. It's not what I want for myself, to step into my uncle's shoes. He's a great guy, kind, loving, but even if he'd ever had ambitions about his garage being a profitable venture, it's not possible where we live. He ends up working for free more often than not."

"Such a shame. Maybe one day Sharrow will receive one of those transformation funds the government give out now and again and the tide will turn?"

Liam shrugged. "I'll not hold my breath. I do love cars though. Uncle Karl has had me tinkering with them since I could toddle, but I don't want dirty hands in my career."

"Most people's hands are dirty in their careers here," my father joked. "Just in a different way."

Liam smiled at that.

"So you love cars, hey? Then tomorrow I have some things to show you. Might be right up your street." Dad patted his stomach. "That was another amazing meal from Marjorie. You enjoy it, Liam?"

"The food and the company have been fantastic. Thank you again for inviting me into your home this evening. I can assure you I'll take this incredible opportunity given and make the best of it."

"You're welcome." Whiskey had loosened my father's tongue. "I have to admit, I thought Daph had lost her marbles when she first touted the idea, but having met you, I think you're going to be a welcome breath of fresh air."

"If we could have some coffee please," Mum said to Amy, the woman currently taking away our plates. Amy asked what we all wanted. I shook my head, "I'm okay, thank you."

"None for me either, thank you," Liam answered. "If it's okay, I'm going to make my way back and get settled in for the evening. Get used to the creaks and groans of the new place. I also need to ring my friends about tomorrow's welcome party."

"Of course. It's been our pleasure having you," Mum replied. "Phoebe, please see Liam out."

I wanted to shout, 'Yes, Miss', but I did as requested, my father's eyes watching me as I left the room.

"Your family is nice. Everyone sitting around a formal dinner table is unusual for me," Liam said.

"For me too. Except like tonight when we're putting on a show." I could feel his eyes burning into the side of my neck.

"But they're good people. I mean mine are, but Mum can barely sit upright, and I don't have my dad. It was nice seeing a proper family."

I smiled, but I knew it didn't reach my eyes. "My advice to you, Liam, while you're here in Richstone. Rarely is anyone what they appear. The place is as fake as the riches tits and teeth." His eyes were wide with surprise at the bitterness in my tone. "You seem like a person who can stand up for themselves. Strong. A survivor. I hope for your sake it runs deep and isn't just on the surface or this place will destroy you," I said and then I closed the door on him.

I turned around. I could hear he was there, and my stomach sank.

"Oh, Phoebe," my father said. "How many times do I have to tell you about that outspoken mouth of yours?"

I prepared myself for the pain I knew I was about to receive. The sort that left little or no evidence behind.

When I came out of his office and returned to my room, I opened my wardrobe, rummaged in the bottom and took out the bottle of Dad's scotch I stole previously, drinking it until the pain dulled.

As I fell into some kind of an unconscious sleep, I wondered if that was why it was Liam's tipple of choice too.

13

Liam

The meal had gone better than I had expected. They had talked to me like I was an equal where, to be honest, I'd expected them to talk down to me in some way. I was under no illusions about the residents of Richstone and that some would be fake as fuck, while others would treat us like the vermin they called us. But the Ridleys had been welcoming and as I unlocked the door to my new temporary home, I felt a warmth in my body that hadn't been there in a very long time. Part scotch, part hope. While I would take nothing for granted, right now, this evening, I was going to text my friends to let them know to come tomorrow and then I was going to find a film, drinks and snacks, and settle down in my living room in front of that enormous flat screen TV and make the most of the fact that for this, perhaps one evening only, no one in Richstone was giving me shit yet and I had luxury at my fingertips.

Even though I'd fallen asleep in the front bedroom, I decided to make the back bedroom that faced the rear garden my own. As I walked into the room and padded over to the window to close the blinds, my eyes looked into the garden. It was subtlety lit with solar lighting around the periphery. I knew there was patio lighting for if I decided to sit outside on an evening when the weather got a little warmer, but for now I just gazed at the expanse of lawn and exclaimed at the fact that right now, this was mine.

"One day, Liam, you will own a place and land like this yourself, and no one will look down on you. They'll admire you and fear you in equal measure," I said to myself with a smile.

One day.

I would exploit my time at Richstone to ensure it came my way. Right now, Daphne Ridley was promising me money if I got her daughter to marry a fellow riches and settle to life as a trophy wife. I'd keep that in mind, but there were other ways of obtaining an even larger pay off. Phoebe was the key though.

But for now, I climbed into bed. Yet another bed so comfortable it could have been made of marshmallow. It was only a few minutes before sleep claimed me, despite the nap I'd taken earlier.

· · ·

I woke feeling weirded out. Because not only had I enjoyed an amazing night's sleep, courtesy of not sofa-surfing, but I didn't have anything to worry about. Usually, I'd be thinking of what drops I had to make, worrying what my mum was doing, and other elements of trying to survive Sharrow life. But not today. Today was Maxwell going to show me cars, and then the welcome party. With school not starting until a week tomorrow this was like some dream vacation and I intended to make the most of it.

Jumping out of bed with a fizzing energy inside me, I realised this new feeling was enthusiasm. I actually had things to look forward to.

I showered, dressed and headed to my kitchen to fix a coffee and some toast. The coffee machine was a piece of piss to use now I'd been shown how to fill it and where to place the pod, and the taste was worlds apart from the trash I'd drunk before. I was taking a bite of my third slice of toast when the doorbell went.

I opened the door to Maxwell. He stood there looking suave in a maroon sweater, grey slacks and black shiny shoes. His grey-blonde hair was combed back and he was clean shaven.

"Not too early, am I?"

"Not at all. Do you want to come in?" It was half past ten.

"If you want to grab your shoes and a coat, we're not going far."

"Okay." I did as asked, then followed Maxwell as he walked down towards the double garage.

"Did you sleep okay? First night in a new place and all that?"

"I really did. My back thanks you. After days spent on my friend's sofa, it was a dream."

"The things we take for granted, hey? Like beds." He began to unlock the garage by pressing a key on a remote he carried. "So, my son disappointingly has very little interest in what's in here. These were my father's." The front of the garages rose to reveal two cars that made my jaw drop. The main object of my desire, a vintage Porsche.

"Is that a Targa?" I asked him.

Maxwell looked at me with such pride for identifying the car you'd have thought I was his firstborn and had just graduated from Oxford University. "Indeed, it is. It's a 911 dating back to 1970."

He gestured for me to get closer to it, and I approached the stunning red classic, taking it all in.

"It's been fully restored, but not driven for a while. I give it a brief burst around the estate now and again just to tick it over, but I'm getting too old for such things."

"Don't be crazy. What are you? Forties? You're not too old for a classic car."

"I think I'm considerably more suited to the Bentley." Maxwell nodded to the other car in the garage.

A true classic, this old-fashioned looking car was the kind of thing I'd expect royalty to step out of.

"The Bentley is a four-door saloon, and one of only twenty-eight produced. It's had some overhauling and resprays but has a remarkable history. It was in New York for a time belonging to a chap on Park Lane itself. My father purchased it in 1990 and my mother insisted on being driven around in it."

"I'm speechless. I had no idea what was hiding away in the garages. I never even thought to wonder. With it being the guest residence, I just assumed they would be empty."

Maxwell waved around a key. "My wife said you had a license. How would you like to take the Porsche out with me to air her off?"

There was really no other answer than the one that spilled out of my mouth. "Hell, yeah!"

I thought Maxwell had meant for me to sit in the passenger seat, but then he walked around to that side himself.

"Mr Ridley..."

"Please call me Maxwell. I'm actually forty-nine years old, which though I'm sure seems old to you, still seems relatively young to me. Not so young as to sit behind the wheel of a Porsche though. Now get in and let's fire her up."

I took a deep breath, caught the keys Maxwell threw over the top of the car and lowered myself in. Maxwell sat in the other side and then before I knew it, I was on my way down the drive. Maxwell directed me out of the main gates, and we took to the streets. I felt exhilarated even though I could only drive at the correct speed limits for the road. While I drove, he asked me more questions about my background. Nothing too intrusive, just what car I'd learned to drive in. If I'd ever had a car of my own. I told him I'd driven my uncle's car many times but never had my own.

Eventually he brought us back to the main gates and I made my way back up towards the guest residence. "No, keep going straight on," Maxwell pointed towards the main house, having me drive past it and then around the back until we reached a large brick outbuilding that I would have said was a garage were it not the size of an industrial unit.

He instructed that I left the car outside and then gestured for me to follow him into the building.

It *was* a garage. Holding fifteen different cars of varying values, from expensive to 'how fucking much?' Maxwell showed me them all. I was speechless. And while I was trying to appreciate the beauty of the vehicles, inside bitter jealousy burned through me like acid that one man could have so much. He reached the last car in the row. Another Porsche. This one was a black 911 Carrera.

"I'm bringing the older classic inside which means this one will be homed in the double garage back at the guest residence. I've had you added to the insurance."

"Whaaaaattt?" I looked at the guy as if he'd grown another head and neither of them held a brain. "No." I planted my hands in my pockets, my stance wide. I wasn't a fucking Action Man these people could change and accessorise.

"Liam, though we have drivers, don't tell me you

wouldn't prefer your own car to get to school and back, and for any other arrangements you make while you're here at Richstone, like if you go out for dinner or to a party. All I ask is you never drink and drive. You'll be doing me a favour getting the engine ticking over."

"But it doesn't have to be a Porsche," I protested.

"Liam, this is the cheapest car I have and the cheapest I intend to own, so yes, it does. Now, I'm not accepting no for an answer. You need a vehicle. All I ask is you take good care of it and given how you just drove me around like the other car was a newborn son, I know you will."

He stared at me with a curl to his upper lip. "Just think of the look on the riches kids faces when you turn up at school in this beauty. Those less keen on your arrival will be wrongfooted. How fantastic would that be?"

"Okay. Thank you. I'll take really good care of it, I promise."

He clapped me on the shoulder. It was such a 'Dad' thing to do and it took me back to another time. Another shoulder pat. *I love you, son.*

Something happened to me then, that I vowed would never happen again. Caught completely off guard, I felt moisture pooling in my eyes. Emotion. I didn't fucking do emotion. I gritted my teeth and focused my mind.

He's not adopting you; he's just lending you a car. They're lending you a house. It's a social experiment remember? It's just money. Don't be fooled by nice things.

He seems like good people. Fantastic. Treat him with respect and then remember why you're here.

To get this for *yourself.*

I blinked the water back. Held it down.

"Obviously, if you go back to Sharrow don't take it with you."

I huffed. "As if. It'd be feasted on like lions at a deer carcass within seconds of arrival. I'd have a gun held to my temple at the first red traffic light."

"It's that bad?" he asked.

"Yes. When you have nothing, there isn't anything to lose."

He nodded and then he handed me the keys. "I'll leave you to drive it back down to the double garage."

I reached out a hand and he shook it, but then he pulled me into a hug. I felt myself tense up. My family didn't do this. Even with the guys, bro fist bumps were as far as it went. Maxwell let me go and patted my shoulder a couple of times again.

"Sorry. It's just been so nice to be able to share my enthusiasm with someone. I understand you'll be busy with kids your own age, but if you want to take any of these others out anytime with me, just let me know."

"I will, and genuinely, thank you for today and for these opportunities. One day, I hope I'll be able to repay your kindness."

"You never know, do you?" he replied. "Maybe one day, hey, son?"

. . .

I climbed behind the wheel, put my key in the ignition and turned it to start the engine and I began the short journey back towards the house. I stopped for a moment just outside the main house while I did a few seat adjustments. A knock on the passenger side window made me startle. I turned to face Phoebe, who tried the door and finding it open, pulled it ajar and leaned in. "I was just coming down with a few things. Can you hold on as otherwise I'd need to make a couple of trips?"

Turning the engine off, I opened my car door. "I'll help you. Lead the way."

14

Phoebe

I'd woken this morning to a dull, throbbing pain at the back of my head caused by my father, along with a headache and furred tongue from the alcohol. For a moment I'd just laid there, staring up at the ceiling, wondering why my father turned from a mild-mannered man one minute to a monster the next. I never knew what would set him off, but it was usually connected to his drinking and my lack of subservience.

Tears had run down my face until I'd had to sit up before I choked on them.

"What have I told you about complaining about your life, Phoebe? You really think Liam is interested in hearing your complaints?"

I trembled as he picked up the pliers. Tears squeezed

from my eyes even though I hadn't wanted to give him the satisfaction of seeing them. What the hell was he going to do to me?

"The next time I hear you dishonour the life of luxury you have here, I will use these pliers to take out the teeth my money paid for. Do you understand?" He placed the pliers back down carefully. He had more respect for those than he had for me.

I nodded.

"You may go. And make sure that you never say a word to that boy that isn't based around how wonderful your life is here and how fortunate you are. Remember, he has nothing. He doesn't want to hear your poor little rich girl whining."

"Yes, Father."

I headed to the door, feeling relief that it was just a warning. That he wasn't going to do anything this time.

Then he grabbed me around the throat and smacked the back of my head into the door hard.

I saw stars and felt sick. His hand had immediately left my throat and he'd already walked away.

With it being winter, it was a time for thick jumpers, so I'd dressed in some black corduroy trousers, a thick cream jumper and boots, before I'd gone downstairs where Marjorie had made me fresh black coffee and much needed pancakes with syrup. Then we'd talked party food before I'd gone back to my room to talk to the girls about later.

Mum was in her study, Eddie had gone out to meet friends, and thankfully, my father was nowhere to be seen.

At just after one, I'd decided to walk down to the guest residence to take the food and tablecloths etc down there so it would all be ready for when people arrived later. In truth, I was bored and Liam being a stone's throw away was too tempting a possibility to ignore. I'd take his multiple personalities over being stuck here any longer.

When I left the house and my dad's Porsche came towards me, I felt my stomach clench and my head throb, but as the car stopped nearby, I realised it was Liam sat there wriggling in the seat, moving things around.

So now, here we were. Liam grabbing hold of cool boxes while he told me all about how fabulous my father was and how he'd insisted on him having use of the car. I felt like I was with someone else to the man I'd met yesterday. He was more like Stefan today. Polite, enthusiastic. All this fervour about cars was lost on me, but I'd rather he spoke about that than about my father's generosity.

"The guys at school have races sometimes. I don't know if he'd let you take the Porsche out for that though," I mentioned.

"Yeah, that might not be the best idea, after being trusted with an expensive, luxury car," Liam scoffed.

"I've never really seen the appeal of luxury cars."

"*What?*"

"It's just something on wheels that gets you from A to B."

He finished putting some boxes in the space under the bonnet and put a hand on each hip. "Phoebe Ridley. I'm not sure we can be friends now if you don't understand the beauty of these cars."

"Maybe we could go for a drive sometime and you could try to explain the appeal?" I shrugged.

"Sure. You could direct me around Richstone, so I can get more familiar with the place and I can get you to see sense. I mean it's probably like how you feel about shoes."

"That they get you from A to B?"

He shook his head. "You're an enigma, Miss Ridley. You're supposed to be a rich bitch."

I rolled my eyes and walked towards the passenger seat.

Standing by the side of his car, his body relaxed, Liam spoke. "You don't actually need to come to the house, do you? I'm perfectly capable of putting things away in a fridge."

My face must have given away my disappointment as I turned to walk away and head back to the house. Liam quickly came up behind me and tugged my arm. "I'm kidding. Come with me. I can make you a coffee. I know how to use the machine now. You can help me set up the speakers and anything else to make it a cool place to hang out later."

I worried the left side of my bottom lip. The guy was just being polite.

"Phoebe?"

"Yeah?"

"Get in the fucking car."

"You have such eloquence," I said with mock derision. But I got in the car anyway.

Liam started the engine. "So, what car do you drive?"

"I have an Audi R8 coupe."

He spluttered and turned around to me so fast the car lurched to the left. "*Liam!*" I squealed, as he righted us.

"Well, I'm sorry, but you're telling me you're not into cars and I'm saying I'll take you out in my Porsche and you have an Audi R8. I mean, you must appreciate the style, the bodywork, the drive…"

"It takes me to school… and back… and sometimes to my friends' houses, but a lot of time I just ring for a driver and they take me out in one of the business cars."

Liam took one hand off the steering wheel and curling it into a fist he pushed his knuckles into his mouth.

"What are you doing?"

He removed his hand. "I'm trying not to scream."

He pulled up outside the garage, leaving the car on the front. "We'll unpack here, and I'll put the car away later."

God, I loved his voice. His accent was like mine, only if it had been rubbed with sandpaper. Rough around the edges and dry.

I followed him into the house. He was already much more familiar with it, evidenced by his gait as he moved around the kitchen, placing a box on the countertop, then unpacking it. I went to fetch more as he started getting mugs out to put the coffee in.

Ten minutes later we were sitting with our drinks on the back patio. I'd turned on the heaters and pulled the seat cushions out of the storage bins, throwing the fluffy winter fake-fur fleeces and cushion covers on it. I pulled one over me as I sat and relaxed.

"I really think you should make yourself at home." Liam laughed, looking at me all tucked up.

"You've no idea how I covet this place."

His mouth pinched, his expression turning sour. "Phoebe, your own house is incredible. I saw only the smallest bit of it, but I can see you want for nothing. I bet you have all this in your own garden, or if you asked your parents, they'd get it for you."

I took a drink of my coffee and kept quiet. What was the point in telling him that what I coveted here wasn't the furnishings, but the peace and tranquillity? The freedom. I was talking to the wrong person. Stefan was the one who'd understand this. Liam might as well have been from another planet.

"Tell me about your friends," I said to change the subject.

He smiled off into the distance. Clearly these friendships were strong. "Brett is my best friend. You might have seen him the day of the interviews. He was the one waiting in reception for his interview."

I nodded. "Yeah, I saw him."

"He's the sensible one. He keeps me grounded. He's probably the only reason I'm not in prison."

"Why? What would you have done without him?" My brow creased.

"Who knows? Beaten someone up until their own mother couldn't recognise them? Tortured others?"

I laughed and Liam's hand shot out to my chin. I startled but his grip was strong. He tilted my head up. "I'm not joking, Phoebe." His voice was like stone, his eyes cold as ice.

My next breath came out slow and laboured.

"I know we're hanging out because of the strange situation we've ended up in, but don't forget who I really am. A drug dealer. A fighter. Someone who, if he or his family are crossed, will do whatever is necessary to survive. And I mean survive. I've lost friends to supposed drug overdoses. Or they've been found kicked to death in an alley. The things I've seen you'd never understand. The things I've *done*, you'd never understand."

"You're still a person, Liam, and I'm a person too."

His hand fell from my chin.

"Just don't expect me to be an angel while I'm here. You'll be disappointed."

"Okay. You'll be a bad boy sometimes. Who says I'm a good girl?"

He scoffed at that. "Your goodness almost seeps out of your pores, Miss Ridley."

I gave him a chin lift. "Maybe I'm a bad girl, but I just haven't yet shown my hand?"

"Yes, you look terribly scary wrapped in fake fur sipping a coffee." Liam's eyes held an amused twinkle, more a grey day than a storm right now. "Come on, show me where we're putting the tablecloths and the other girly crap you brought with you."

I shook my head. "Not yet. We're still talking about your friends." I handed him my cup. "Make me another coffee and this time bring out one of those packets of cookies."

He told me more about Brett. How his influence brought Brett out of his shell. About his kooky friend Daniel who loved a giggle and tended to act first and think later, and about Marlon who liked to observe stuff from a distance, but wasn't afraid to jump in and get his hands dirty. I wondered how my friends would receive these people.

"And Skye. What's she like?"

"Eager."

"What do you mean? That she's enthusiastic? Gets stuck in?"

"Yup," he smirked.

"Oh? *Oh!* Is she your girlfriend?" I was aware that I felt a strange feeling in the back of my throat, like my coffee had turned two more strengths bitterer.

"God, no."

"Friends-with-benefits?" I hedged.

"Acquaintances-with-benefits," he answered. "Fuck-buddies."

"Wow, she must have felt really special."

Liam shrugged. "I was never anything but honest with her. I don't do relationships."

"Because you're a bad boy?" I scoffed.

"Because I don't let anyone in. Ever."

"You let your friends in, don't you? I can tell by how you talk about them that you care. It sounds to me like you're giving yourself an excuse to be an arsehole."

He snorted coffee out of his nose.

"It doesn't sound right, a posh girl like you saying 'arsehole'."

"What do you expect me to say? That you're a reprehensible imbecile? A nincompoop? A simpleton, a dork, a cretin? None of those serve you so well as the word 'arsehole'."

He was now holding his stomach.

"I'm glad this is so amusing. This poor girl was probably in love with you and you fucked her and left her hanging. Probably onto your every word."

He stopped laughing. "Skye knows the score. And yes, I'm fond of my friends, but my heart? That's locked away. Because it makes you vulnerable, and vulnerability makes you weak." He cocked his head to one side. "I suppose you're going to tell me I'm missing out?"

I shook my head, "No. I'm telling myself maybe I need to be more like you."

A period of silence passed between us, only the outside making noises: of nature, of the background whirr of the heater.

"Your turn. Tell me about your friends," he said.

So I did.

15

Liam

After Phoebe had drunk her second coffee, she stood up.

"I'm going to go back to the house for a while. You should be able to meet your friends here alone first. I'm sure they'll have plenty to say about your new situation."

"You don't have to leave on my account."

"No, it's the right thing to do. I'll get my friends to come up to mine and we'll all walk down together around half-four. Gives you a chance to show off the place to the others."

"Okay, thanks."

"I'll see myself out. Catch you later," she said, and she walked through the patio doors. I watched her walk through the living room until she was gone, and I heard the door closing behind her. The thick baggy jumper she was wearing masked the figure underneath, but the trousers had hugged the curves of her thighs and calves. I'd be lying if I said Phoebe didn't make my cock hard. She also seemed like a genuinely okay person. We got along despite the differences between us. But I had to remember, I wasn't here to make friends. I was here to make opportunities, and Phoebe Ridley was an opportunity just waiting to be exploited.

The fact I'd probably enjoy myself immensely while doing so was just a bonus.

The sound of a car horn blared from outside. I opened the front door to see Marlon stepping out of his ancient Volkswagon Polo. He'd pulled up just in front of the Porsche. With a quick wave in my direction, he moved to look closer at the other car and I came out of the house to greet him and the other two who had now exited from the back of the Polo.

"Fuckadoodledo. So is this Phoebe's ride?" He asked. I looked at his Polo, with its road rash and stone chips, and rusted undercarriage.

"It's her father's," I said.

"Oh."

"And for the duration of my stay, it's mine."

"Fuck off, it's not," Daniel shouted. "No way. You got the house. You're not having a car as well. Enough already. What do I get?"

"You know what you get. You know what the plans are." I tapped the side of my head. "Now get inside so I can make you all feel even more jealous."

I showed them around and there was a lot of body

slamming, head rubbing, and general jubilation about my new digs and the fact we were here. That the four of us had made it to Richstone.

"So, who's coming tonight again? Just Phoebe's friends, right? No one who's gonna be a cunt?" Marlon checked.

"Even the nicer ones might be a challenge," Brett pointed out. "They're so fucking minted they probably won't even realise they're insulting us. I'm taking bets they'll look us up and down and wonder if we bathe. They call us the rats and I bet they think we carry disease."

"Phoebe's not like that, so hopefully her friends are like her," I attempted to reassure them, although I had to admit I was beginning to wonder how the evening would go myself. And then the murmur of voices and a girl's giggle sounded out from the front of the house.

"Well, here's where we find out exactly what they're like," I announced.

"Hey," Phoebe smiled at me. I saw the tremble in her lip that showed she was nervous.

"Come on, Liam, let us in, it is fucking freezing out here," yelled a girl standing just behind her shoulder. She said it like 'facking'. Looked like this friend was a party girl. She wiggled a bottle at me confirming it.

"Come in," I gestured and they all swept in. There were eight of them. Four boys, four girls. Phoebe instructed them as to where to hang their coats and then looked to me. "Rear living room and patio, right?"

I nodded.

"We'll do the introductions out there once we've all got a drink. Come through, guys."

I noted all the looks I'd garnered as they walked past. From fleeting glimpses and chin lifts to downright staring.

Phoebe and I worked together to fulfil everyone's drinks order. I felt eyes on me and turned to see the party girl watching. She raised an eyebrow at me and smirked. I didn't know what she was getting at and turned away from her attention. Was she trying to say she was amused by my playing at houses? When I turned again, she was standing between the two of us.

"Well, you two look all kinds of cute like you've known each other forever. Now, Liam, I'm going to need you to introduce me to Brett."

Phoebe sighed. "Liam, this is my best friend, Renee. She has no filter, but I love her anyway."

I looked at the sassy girl with the dark-brown hair. I wasn't sure if Brett could handle her personality. My poor quiet friend wouldn't know what had hit him with this thunderbolt of a girl. It'd be fun to watch though.

"We just have a couple more drinks to fix and then it'll be my pleasure."

"Ooh, Phoebe, watch this one, he is chock full of charm," she winked and waltzed off.

Phoebe held a hand up. "I apologise in advance for anything Renee does or says."

"Likewise with Daniel. I think they may be long lost twins."

Phoebe had brought her other girlfriends Flora and Lucie, and then Stefan, who'd brought another three guys: Sam, Nelson, and Wayne. There was a bit of an awkward silence while everyone sat in the living room taking a drink.

"So, Stefan, you're friends with this crazy girl then?" I asked him, nodding my head towards Phoebe, figuring this was as good a conversation starter as any.

"I am. Our parents want to marry us off. We developed a mutual appreciation of eye-rolling at dinner, and that was it, friends forever."

I grinned. I liked Stefan already. He was okay.

"So, you must feel like you won the lottery?" The guy called Wayne looked at me. Underneath the friendly persona he was wearing for Stefan's benefit, was a snob who didn't like what I'd been handed on a plate, even though the chances were the same thing had happened to him, only from birth. I'd usually answer such a fucktard question with my fists, but I had to play nice here.

"I feel... strange." I replied. "Like there's this fabulous house, potential new friends, but I'm on my guard. You know? Like it's a trick because things like this don't happen to people like us. I'm waiting for someone to pull the rug from under me. For the first person to treat me like trash." My eyes met his until he looked away.

The girl called Flora gasped. "Oh, Liam. It's only early days, but no one's going to do that to you. I know Phoebe's mum wants you to stay until after the exams."

She looked at me imploringly, "you just need to get used to us, that's all. It's just like when you go on holiday and it's all different."

"That's just the thing," Marlon said. "None of us have ever been on a holiday. Apart from the odd day trip to the beach."

"You've never been on holiday? Not stayed somewhere a week or two. Or been abroad?" Lucie gasped.

"No," Brett confirmed, "and if you each sold your watches, I'd bet you'd be able to buy all four of us houses in Sharrow Manor and furnish them. That's the difference the divide of the river makes."

Renee went to sit beside him. "Wow, I never even thought of that. We have all this stuff and we're just used to it. It's not like we're flaunting it on purpose or anything."

"And we don't have much and we're used to that. So, this is going to be one strange headfuck," he said.

"But we're here and going to enjoy the riiiddde," Daniel sang. "So, who's for another beer? Because this party needs to be a hell of a lot less lame. What's all this serious talking? Get the tunes on and let's paaarrttyyyy."

Flora smiled at him. "I'll help you pick some good tunes."

I watched as he smiled back.

Stefan was sitting next to Phoebe and they were chatting away. She kept glancing at me, but every time my eyes met hers, she looked away. Lucie was talking to Nelson, so I went and sat with Marlon, Wayne, and Sam.

"Sorry if I sounded like a dick before," Wayne said.

"S'okay. I'm sure I'm going to get worse."

"Yeah, I'm afraid you are. There's a whole bunch of guys and girls at Richstone who don't want you there and who are intending to try to drive you out."

I shrugged. "They can try."

Sam spoke next. "You need to watch out for them. Especially Ulric and Ivy, the King and Queen of school, or so they'd have you believe."

"We're not doing anything to threaten the school hierarchy, so why do they have beef with us?" Marlon asked.

"Our school is an elite academy. We have the odd prince come for a term. Now, no disrespect, but rats are coming into school," Sam said.

I wasn't sure how he expected me to not feel disrespected, but I did understand what he was trying to say.

"They think it cheapens their worth to have to be in the same building as you. You'll be treated like the shit on their shoe and they will do everything they can to discredit you and to humiliate you, so just be careful."

"It's them who should be careful," Marlon said. "They don't know what we're capable of."

The two riches looked uncomfortable at that, as if Marlon had just declared we'd pull a knife. Which might back at Sharrow, but here, we'd have to be a lot more cunning with how we handled our enemies. And part of me welcomed the challenge. To show the riches who thought they were so high and mighty just how far they could fall.

The doorbell rang, followed by a knock, and for a

moment I wondered who it was and then I remembered. Skye. I'd forgotten all about her.

"I'll go," Phoebe said.

I mouthed back, "Okay."

The two girls walked back in together a few minutes later. I watched from the back of the room as Skye's eyes sought mine out first. She looked out of her depth here. I saw Lucie go get her a drink and she sat down. The boys looked her over and I wondered what they thought of her pink buzz cut hair, the tattoos she had down one arm, and the black corset, thick black tights and pink tutu she was wearing. It was one thing I admired about Skye Drummond. She knew who she was at heart and she dressed for herself. Her favourite battered Doc Martens were on her feet. The Ivy's of this world were going to have a coronary when Skye walked in, and I would make sure that my own buzz cut was freshly shorn ready for my own first day.

Skye seemed to relax once she'd had a couple of beers and got to know the girls a little better, and as the evening wore on, where increasing amounts of alcohol had been consumed and we'd eaten, a more chilled atmosphere took over the house. I opened up the patio doors and switched on the lights and patio heaters and small groups spilled out over the space.

And then Renee decided it was party games time.

"Oh God no. Renee, I told you no games this time. We've only just all met," Phoebe yelled.

She pouted. "So we can't play spin the bottle?"

"No!" Phoebe looked like she might pass out.

"Can we play the sausage game then?" Renee begged her friend.

"What the hell is the sausage game?" Marlon asked.

Renee looked triumphant that she had managed to potentially engage another person into her schemes. "Well, you see, you tie a sausage to your waist and let it dangle down your back and then you put a toilet roll on the floor beneath your legs and you have to get the sausage into the tube!"

"Absolutely not," Phoebe shrieked. Such was her discomfort that I stood up.

"Sounds like fun. I'll just go get a loo roll, you sort out the sausage," I winked.

Renee beamed while Phoebe looked like she wanted the earth to swallow her up.

16

Phoebe

A nice, sedate little introductory gathering.

That's what I'd anticipated.

But no, currently we had people pretending to put a dick in a pussy, via sausages, string, and toilet rolls. I had to admit, it had broken down the barriers between everyone. There wasn't a single person who hadn't creased up with laughter at the attempts.

And now it was my turn.

"Does anyone want anything from the kitchen?" I asked, trying to escape before Wayne worked out there was only me left to have a go.

"No, Phoebe, we just all want to watch you wiggle your hips and get a sausage in a hole," Liam announced loudly, taunting me.

"I—"

"Phoebe. Phoebe. Phoebe." He clapped his hands

along with the syllables he sang until soon everyone had joined in.

"Sssh," I placed a finger over my lips. "I don't want my parents coming down here."

"Fifi, they were young themselves once you know. They're not going to come here, and even if they did we're playing with sausages not having an orgy," Renee rolled her eyes.

"Yeah, that's at half-ten," Daniel announced, creating a fresh round of laughter.

The chanting started again and so huffing, I let Lucie tie the string around me.

I was hopeless. No matter how much I lowered myself or moved my hips, the sausage missed the inside of the toilet roll tube. Inside, I was praying to God to let this ordeal be over sooner rather than later, but no, it seemed my embarrassment had to continue.

My so-called best friend was pointing at me and laughing so hard, I watched her wipe tears from her eyes.

"I think it's time I gave you some assistance," Liam walked up behind me. "You'd never make a guy, Miss Ridley. Now let me help you."

I didn't know what I expected, but it wasn't for him to slide in closely behind me, moulding himself to my body and putting his hands on my stomach. I froze in place and he leaned forward and whispered in my ear. "I'm not fucking you, Phoebe. We're just playing a game."

He was toying with me. Teasing me and tormenting me. Well two could play at that game. I let myself relax and let him guide me. I moved my hips as directed until eventually the sausage met its destination. Then as everyone cheered and got up to get new drinks, the game over, I made sure to roll my hips again and push back into Liam, and what was evidently his rock-hard dick. I heard the small groan escape his lips.

I moved myself. "Thanks for the help," I whispered. "I'm sure I'll have a much better idea of how to direct a sausage to a hole from now on."

Then I walked away and into the kitchen, while the smirk on my face got wider.

Renee was in the kitchen talking to Skye and so I went up to them. "Hey, Skye, you all ready for next week?"

"Not really," she said. "I'm worried about how people will treat me while I'm there. I mean," she looked over at the others. "They have each other. I'm the only girl."

"I'm sure they'll look out for you too, but we'll be around. We'll do our best to make sure people treat you right."

"Thanks, that's appreciated."

"Look, why don't you come up to my house for half-eight next Monday and we'll go into school together? Then that gives a clear message that the Ridleys are supporting your placement.

"Oh, that would be amazing. Thank you."

"Not a problem," I replied. I looked at Skye and tried to imagine how Liam had seen her. What it was about her that had made him sleep with her. Was it the vulnerability she displayed that he'd preyed on? Her body? The corset showed she had an ample amount of cleavage. Did that mouth suck him off just right?

Why the hell was I thinking these things? I knew it might have a lot to do with the fact that his hard cock had been up against me not ten minutes before.

We all exchanged numbers and told Skye to ring us if she needed anything before she started school. Then I excused myself to visit the bathroom.

After yet more drinking and some dancing, the party eventually wound down. Brett hadn't touched a drop of alcohol so that he could drive the others home. Stefan had ordered a driver for himself and his mates. We stood at the door and waved them all off.

"I think this evening was a success in terms of our introductions to the boys," Lucie whispered. "We all know which one is ours, right?"

"Damn straight," Renee acknowledged.

"Daniel is lovely," Flora said dreamily, and we all turned to her. "What?"

"You. You still think Disney Princesses are real. Let the stars fall from your eyes, babe. He might be nice but remember he's a rat."

"That's not nice, Lucie," Flora huffed.

"But true. Just get to know him a little better before you start imagining he's going to transform like Cinderella, because the reality is life after midnight, babe."

I turned around to ensure that we were definitely out of earshot, but Liam and Skye were nowhere to be seen. My teeth ground as I wondered if despite what he'd said, Liam was about to fuck her in his brand-new bedroom.

Cars came to pick up my friends and I waved good-bye. I wasn't sure whether to go in and say goodbye myself, or to walk up home.

Oh, who was I fooling? I needed to just take myself off home, but... the front door had been left open and so I could excuse my behaviour if I happened to walk in on something I shouldn't. I just needed to know.

My feet trod lightly on the flooring, and as I got closer to the kitchen, I heard Liam.

"Skye, you knew what you were signing up to coming here. If you can't handle it then withdraw."

"I'm just asking if you'll..." her voice trailed off.

"You want me to say that if anyone gives you shit, I'll step in and sort them out. Sorry, but will I fuck. I'm not doing anything to jeopardize my place here. Any shit that comes your way is yours to deal with. You're a big girl now. An adult. Act like one."

"But doesn't what we had count for anything?"

"What we had?" He scoffed. "What we had was my cock in your mouth and pussy. That's what we had. I've fucked a lot more women than you, Skye, and most of them were better."

I heard her sharp intake of breath.

There was a phone bleep. "The Uber is on its way up the drive. Like I said, either stand up for what you want to get out of your Richstone place like we're all going to, or stay in Sharrow, but you are nothing to me, remember? Nothing. Now get out."

ANGEL DEVLIN

My legs hurried to carry me back outside, where I took a seat on a bench outside the front, pretending to enjoy the crisp air.

Skye exited, sobbing.

I stood up. "Skye, are you okay?"

She turned to me. "Yeah, I'm fine. Just starting to feel a little overwhelmed by it all. It's a big step. But I'll manage."

I hugged her to me. "You will. You'll be fine. You have me and the girls and we will look after you. Don't worry." I passed her a fresh tissue from my bag.

"Thanks."

She blew her nose and then the headlights of the car came into view.

"See you at mine, next week. Ring if you need me in the meantime."

"Thanks, Phoebe. I really appreciate it."

I smiled and then watched her get in the car and it drive away.

A slow clap sounded out from behind me.

"St. Phoebe of Richstone."

I turned around, a sneer on my face. "Your behaviour towards that girl is disgraceful."

"Why? Because I call a spade, a spade? She's a leech. You'll soon find that out for yourself."

I walked past him and into the house. "I'll help tidy up and then I'll head on home."

He followed me into the kitchen where I pulled out a couple of black sacks. "I don't need you to help me tidy

172

up. I'm perfectly capable of sorting out rubbish. I can even recycle. I'm *poor*, not *dumb*," he snarled.

"Really? Because your behaviour towards that girl sounded pretty dumb. Pretty disrespectful and dumb." I flushed as I realised I'd just outed myself.

He stalked towards me. "So you were listening at the door? Well, Miss Ridley, I didn't say anything to Skye that I wouldn't say in front of anyone's face. She knew the score when we hooked up. It was just fucking."

"Yeah, yeah, yeah. You're a cold-hearted bastard with no soul. Blah, blah, blah. Sounds like a great excuse to allow yourself to be a dick."

Before I could acknowledge my body moving, I was up against the kitchen wall, Liam's hand around my throat. But instead of feeling fearful, like my father made me feel, I felt triumphant. Something about having gained this reaction from him meant I'd hit him in his feelings. That he did have some. He dropped his hand quickly, but his eyes still raced with stormy waves.

"I am not a good man. I've already told you that, Phoebe. You can challenge me all you like, but we both know I'll win, because I can't afford to lose anything else. You can't save me, because I don't need rescuing."

His face lowered down to mine and his lips crushed against my own. I paused for a second, maybe only a split-second, before I answered his kiss with a hungry one of my own. He thrust his tongue inside my mouth and lifted me up. As I wrapped my legs around him, he took me over to the kitchen island. I heard rubbish: paper plates covered with food remains, and paper cups swept to the floor and then my backside was on the worktop.

He fisted my hair as he carried on kissing me and he ground his erection against my core. I groaned with the friction he was creating, needing more.

And then he pulled away and stopped.

I opened my eyes and looked up at him.

"Two can play at being a prick tease. That's for what you did after the game."

"You're such a dick," I yelled, humiliated at the fact I'd let him kiss me and dry hump me.

"So, I keep telling you, Phoebe Ridley. I'm a bad *bad* boy."

Jumping off the island, I stomped towards the door. "You can clean all this shit up yourself now."

He curled up his fists and put them in front of his eyes and twisted, "Boo hoo."

I took off down the hall, opened the door and then slammed it behind me.

I'd just almost turned the corner when the door opened.

"Hey, Phoebe?"

I placed my hands on my hips. "What?" I snapped.

"I'm gonna have a rest day tomorrow, but I'll see you Tuesday."

"Go to hell."

His laughter sounded out into the quiet night and then he blew me a kiss, turned around and closed the door.

By the time I'd marched back to my own house, my

mood was foul. I went straight to bed where I threw myself down on the mattress and kicked my legs like a three-year-old.

The alcohol had helped me sleep and after a brief rundown of the events I felt I could share with my mother while she ate her breakfast, I hopped in the car and went to meet the girls at Café Renzo. The little coffee house was situated on the corner of a street and was our main hangout. The others were already there when I arrived, and a black coffee was on the table in front of my seat.

"Everyone feeling a little delicate today?" I looked around at my friends.

"I'm not too bad," Renee said, and Flora is fine, but Lucie, well..."

Lucie groaned from behind dark glasses. "It must be because I switched to vodka. Shouldn't mix."

"It's more like the six vodkas you had after the beer," Flora pointed out.

"Shut up. Every word you say hurts my ears." Lucie pulled her polo neck up over her ears to prove her point.

"Okay, we'll just have to pretend she's not here," Renee shook her head and tutted. "So, operation BLDM. Next moves?"

It would appear that Lucie could hear perfectly well, despite her ears being covered. "BLDM. Is this some new kind of sex thing?"

"You're such a ho. It's their initials," Renee huffed.

"Oh. Shame."

"So, I managed to chat to Brett a lot last night. Largely superficial, but it's a start. Now, I can see him at school and say hi. Maybe we could sit with them in the canteen at lunch?"

"You just need to sleep with the guy. Send him a pic of your boobs and a time and place," Lucie rolled her eyes.

Renee leaned in closer to Lucie. "Okay," she yelled, making Lucie wince and clutch her right ear.

"Son of a bitch, I think I'm going to hurl."

"What about you, Fifi? Update."

"I've already told Liam about Ivy. I need for him to witness her for himself. She's bound to be vile, and then I think it'll be a cake walk."

"And we know Flora is already picking her wedding dress out, so she's on track to make over Daniel. Does he know it'll be a tux?"

"Oh, hush your mouth. He's just fun, that's all. I enjoyed his company. I know I'm a hopeless romantic, but even I can see there's unlikely to be a happy ever after with this pairing. He'll be going home in a few months' time and then never the twain shall meet." She sighed.

"Just all make sure you take your pills, and that it's wrapped so there are no diseases," I reminded them.

"Erm, yeah, okay, mother. I think we know that," Renee scoffed. "You got that, Flora, in your romantic dreams? To not wind up with crabs?"

"Ewwww."

"So, Lucie, how d'you get on?" Renee shoved her in the shoulder.

"Lucie is about to poke you in your eyeball." She took a drink of her coffee and then pulled a face like she was drinking cat sick. Her hand came to her mouth, and she gestured for a minute. "Marlon will be my willing slave, my robot. Just not today. Excuse me." Her chair scraped against the floor as she pushed it back and dashed in the direction of the female toilets.

"You seen anything of Liam today, to see how he thought it went?" Renee asked.

"No. I'm hoping I don't have to see him for the rest of the week."

"Why? What happened after we left?" She looked me over closely. "Do you have something to tell me, Fifi?"

I shook my head. "No. It's just my head hurts with booze and my brain hurts thinking of a week today when they start school. Though its selfish, I'd just like as much of this week to myself as possible before my babysitting duties start."

Complete lies, when I'd always told Renee the truth. Well, about everything but my father. What had happened with me and Liam would now stand side by side with my covering up of my father's abuse. I just had to hope it didn't create a distance between me and my best friend.

177

17

Liam

Liam: If you don't answer my fucking texts I'll just come up to the house. I'll only have to say 'Mrs Ridley, is it okay if Phoebe shows me around Richstone?', and she'll make you.

I sat back against the sofa, my arm behind my head and waited.

Read.

Dots appeared across the screen.

Fine. I'll be outside yours at eleven. Be ready.

I laughed to myself. I could just imagine her now, muttering to herself about how much of a dick I was. How much she didn't want to show me around. I bet she'd been tempted to send me an expletive-laden reply; but wouldn't, just in case I showed her mummy.

She had sass, but I didn't believe she truly had the balls to back it up. I'd continue to toy with her and then, when the time was right, Phoebe would be putty in my hands and I'd score the winning goal. Which would more than likely be a positive pregnancy test. I couldn't see Daphne Ridley's offer amassing me as much money as my own idea. The Ridleys were extremely rich and wanting Phoebe to marry a rich man from a 'good' family. I'd be paid off to disappear faster than a reluctant business owner paid up when looking down the barrel of a gun from their 'protection'.

But all in good time. Today, Phoebe could show me around Richstone. It would be people's first glimpse of the rat living in their nest. Let's see how Phoebe handled it when everyone stared at her being out with the trash. Wherever the main hangouts were with the riches, today I would be there.

A car beeped from outside at ten minutes after eleven. I'd taken a bet of her leaving it until quarter-past before arriving, just to show me how she wasn't my slave. Wrong. Huh. She would be eventually. She'd be begging for my orders before long.

I took my time locking up my front door and then I sauntered down the path. I walked around to the passenger side of the car and went to open the door, only to find it locked, so I knocked on the window. Phoebe turned around to me and smiled, but she didn't make any effort to unlock the door.

I banged harder with my fist. "Open the door."

This time she smirked.

Like that, was it? I showed her my house key and indicated to her that I'd key it down her door.

Huffing, she unlocked the car, but as I went to get in, she pulled the car forward slightly.

"Motherfucker."

She wound the window down and smiled sweetly. "That's just to let you know that you might threaten people and act like a dick, but if you try to fuck with me, when you least expect it, I will surprise you."

My dick hardened in response.

I turned and lowered myself into the passenger seat. "Looking forward to your attempts, *Fifi*."

She exhaled in a large huff, her nostrils flaring. "Do *not* call me that. Only Renee calls me that."

"Not anymore, Fifi."

"Fine, *William*. If that's how you want to play it. Now, where do you want to go? The sooner this trip is over with, the better."

"Oh, Fifi. Did I not explain? It's going to take allllll day. Now where do the riches mainly hang out? The ones I'll be going to school with, like this Ulric guy?"

"They'll be in the lounge at the sports club, but there's a dress code." She looked at my clothes. "You'll need a polo shirt, and you'll need plain trousers, no jeans."

My right fist clenched. I didn't want to have to change any aspect of myself for these people, and yet I

181

was already being controlled by their stupid rules. "Just a minute. I did bring something. I'll go change."

"Okay."

I stared at her, waiting for the smug grin I expected to appear across her face, but she just sat back, waiting.

No, the smug grin came when I got back in the car dressed in my dark navy polo shirt and black suit trousers. The ones I'd just had to pull the new tags off because I didn't wear things like this. I'd had a feeling it might be necessary at some point. I just hadn't expected it to be so soon.

"My goodness, if it weren't for the permanent scowl etched on your face, I might think a whole different person was in my car."

"Fuck you. Now drive, Fifi."

"Okay, William." She set off.

I quizzed her about the riches on our way there, while I also looked at the gorgeous car she had but didn't appreciate. I could perve over the bodywork and interior of this Audi as much as I could a supermodel.

We passed buildings that Phoebe pointed out and described: the coffee shop she said was her hangout with her friends, a few restaurants including a seafood restaurant she said was extremely exclusive, the country club which was the main hangout of the elder riches. There were designer shops, niche boutiques and businesses. We passed high end jewellery stores and car showrooms where you'd need to book an appointment, everything behind blacked out windows.

Eventually, Phoebe drove the car through gates that

led to a large white building next to the river. The river widened at this point and I could see there were boats moored up at the side.

"That's the sailing club. There's a separate bar around the other side of it. Very exclusive for the dads. All the yachts are usually named after their wives. They do that to placate the wife while they go pratting about on the water."

"You sound bitter, Fifi."

"My friend's father entertains his mistress on the very yacht that's named after his wife and no one acknowledges it. I've told you, most of the people here are fake as fuck."

She pulled the car into a parking space and cut the engine.

"But not you? You're telling me how it is, are you?"

She sighed. "I'm beyond giving a toss, William, and that's the fucking truth."

I could hear the frustration in her tone and in that one moment I decided to try to call a truce for the rest of the day.

"Hey. I know you don't want to babysit me, and you probably don't trust me an inch, but how about we just try and make the best of the situation and see if we can enjoy the day?"

Her face turned towards mine. "That works for me. Okay, let's go face the firing squad," she said, and suddenly I didn't feel so keen to go inside. Phoebe stepped out of the car. I closed my eyes for a moment, remembered who I was and why I was there, and then I climbed out, stretching my neck from side to side. At six foot two, and with my history, I knew I could create a presence in a room, and wearing these ridiculous clothes or not, I was Liam Lawson, and they'd be fools to mess with me.

Phoebe greeted the reception staff and booked herself in as herself and a guest. None of the staff there batted an eyelid at me, past asking me to show them some I.D. to prove I was over eighteen. I was treated politely and the same as Phoebe. But that all changed as we walked into the sports lounge.

For a start, 'sports lounge' had made me think of football and Formula One. But here it was the riches style: cricket, polo, Wimbledon. The music was low and ambient, with people standing around the bar, some chatting, others waiting for service. Others sat in booths: some large and open, some small and intimate. One booth held around a dozen older teenagers and every head there was turned towards me and Phoebe.

"Let's get you a drink. You're going to need one," she said, "Because Ivy and Ulric are over there."

"No. I think we'll head straight over to their booth," I insisted. She had to swallow her protest because I was already making my way over.

Every single one of them stared at me, so I let my eyes trail over each of them in return as I said, "Hey. I'm Liam Lawson. I start at Richstone Academy next week."

A too thin blonde, pretty, but with a scrawny neck and fake teeth smiled witheringly at me. "Yes, it's pretty obvious that you're one of them." She looked me up and down, and then turned around to the others and picked up whatever conversation they'd already been having.

"Or it could be that you remember from sitting on my cock last night," I winked in her direction and watched as her head snapped back to mine and her horsey mouth dropped open.

"I wouldn't touch you if my last breath depended on it. I'd be scared of what you were riddled with."

"Well, a large cock and the ability to use it, mainly. Anyway, see you all around on Monday. I'm sure it'll be fun."

An athletic looking dude with blonde hair and glasses leaned over and held out his hand. "Ulric McDowell. Welcome to Richstone." I shook his hand, thinking that at least one of them was acknowledging me. "I have to say, you're braver than I am. I wouldn't transfer to Sharrow Manor if the opportunity rose. Then again, who would?" He paused for a few seconds. "*Oh*," he said the 'oh' dramatically as if he was having a lightbulb moment. "I see now why you'd come here. Delusions of grandeur. Do you think you might become one of us if you hang round with us enough? That we might become friends and your sad little life will suddenly improve? Is that your angle? Oh, how very amusing and... pathetic."

The rest of the table tittered.

I breathed deeply through my nose, trying not to show my annoyance. If anyone talked to me this way at Sharrow Manor, they'd find themselves fucked up with my blade, but here I had to think of the long game. Drawing myself to my full height, I crossed my arms.

"Oh, I don't want to become one of you. None of you have anything in your own right. You're all just spoiled little rich kids. I want my own wealth, and to keep my personality. One thing I'm rich in and you're not."

I turned around to Phoebe who'd stayed just behind me. "Let's get that drink now," I told her.

We took seats at a table that Phoebe picked out. One for two people, but one that wasn't intimate or hidden. She settled in and picked up a menu. "I did warn you what they were like, but I guess it was better that you got that first meeting out of the way today. Now you have a flavour of how they're going to be in school. My guess is they'll oscillate between derision and pretending you don't exist at all."

I shrugged. "They don't bother me. Acting all superior and showing off in front of the others. One on one, I'd bet they'd shit themselves." Looking up to see Phoebe's face at my crude retort, I found worry there rather than disgust.

"Liam, people like Ulric don't dirty their hands in fights. They pay someone to take care of things. You must remember to think like a rich person. To anticipate their moves, ask yourself what you would do if money was no object. These people never have bruised knuckles, or a trace to the people who appear and then mysteriously disappear having left an enemy beaten up in a car park with no witnesses."

"Yeah," I drummed my fingers on the table top. "But

I'm the sort of person they usually hire. And they need to ask themselves, what would a rat do."

A server brought our drinks and Phoebe picked up the coke she'd ordered herself as she'd said she didn't drink at all when driving.

"I just get the feeling this can't end well," she said, taking a sip and then putting her glass back down.

I already knew it was unlikely to end well for Phoebe Ridley.

And as for Ivy and Ulric. They would get theirs at some point. The last laugh would be mine as I took my leave of Richstone.

"So how about we get out of here?" Phoebe said. "I'll take you to my favourite place for lunch instead, and then I'll push you out of your comfort zone this afternoon. I promise you'll have fun. What do you say?"

"I say let's go. I'm done here." I quickly drank down the rest of my pint of beer.

We stood up. Phoebe threw some notes at the server who approached, telling her to keep the change. I didn't look behind me to see what the riches were doing and neither did Phoebe. She'd stood by me today. Maybe she'd done it quietly, but she'd done it all the same.

I actually felt a little tiny raindrop sized piece of guilt for what I'd do to her. But just like rain, I knew it would evaporate.

18

Phoebe

Liam Lawson messed with my head.

He had more personalities than a travelling circus.

But he had my interest.

In a world of golden statues, he was a sculpture carved of hard granite.

I knew nothing really about his life in Sharrow Manor. He could tell me stories of drug dealing and fights, but I'd only ever be able to marry it up in my head to things I'd seen on films and TV. So I tried to tell myself it was the same for him. I doubted he'd ever watched Made in Chelsea, but I'm sure he'd heard of it. He'd think us all the same. Idiots with more money than sense.

But I wasn't.

So, for whatever time he was here, I would let the river that ran between us sweep me along and see where I ended up.

I'd brought him to a bistro for lunch and he'd been having a love affair with a burger and fries thanks to aioli and brioche.

When he'd finished, he sat back and patted his stomach. "Now that was good. That was a part of Richstone I've enjoyed." He picked up the dessert menu, but I shook my head.

"That wouldn't go well with this afternoon's activities." I called over the server. "Could we have the bill please?"

Liam went in his pocket and took out his wallet, but I shook my head. "These can be courtesy of my father."

"Yet another thing I have to thank your father for then."

I'm sure my returning smile came out more as a grimace, so I pretended to have a touch of cramp.

While we'd sat in the bistro, no one had treated Liam any differently. Hadn't stared at him, made fun of him, or looked down on him, and I'd seen him slowly start to relax. Yes, he was still looking around astutely though. His eyes seemed to take in everything.

"You're staring at me."

"I'm just wondering what you're thinking," I replied truthfully.

"I'm thinking I might end up fat if all the food I get to eat in Richstone is as good as that burger. I'm also wondering what we're doing next."

I signed the meal slip and said, "Let's put you out of your misery then."

· · ·

"Fuck me, you really do have a pony! Where are you hiding your handbag dog?"

"No dogs, but we do have four horses. So, you're about to have your first riding lesson."

Liam stood still looking out over my estate. "I'm going to be honest with you, Phoebe. I feel like I must be asleep or having a breakdown because I'm from a place called Sharrow. I do not ride fucking horses, I ride women."

"Charming."

"It's weird though isn't it? I mean, I'm a rat and you're one of the riches. What the fuck is happening here? How did I get here?"

"Here in Richstone or here about to ride a horse?"

"Both. I mean this is all because of your mother's offer."

"Yes, well, we'll never probably know what was behind that idea really."

"What do you mean?"

I debated telling him the truth.

"You can't say that and then not tell me anything else. What do you mean, Fifi?"

I blew out a breath that rattled my lips. "My mum made her announcement about the scholarship at the Barratts' house one evening over dinner. Said she'd been considering it for a while. Stefan and I believe she thought about it about three seconds before her announcement as she wanted to get one over on his mum, but who knows? Maybe she had been thinking about it for a long time, since her psychology days. Without lie detectors or being able to mind read we'll just have to assume it did have some basis in doing good. As for why you're here horse-riding, well, I figure you should try every opportunity you're offered while here, and also it will give me a much-needed giggle to see the drug dealing bad boy atop a horse.

Liam playfully clipped the back of my head with his hand, "Hey. I might be really good."

I felt sick, it hurt so bad. I took deep breaths in through my nose, trying not to let it show.

"I hardly touched you, you wimp, but sorry."

I shook my head. "It's fine, just must have caught on a weird bone or something. Let's walk on up to the stables and Grayson will help get you kitted up."

Ten minutes later, Liam was sitting on a large brown gelding called Alto and I was on my own filly called Bonny. The difference was that while I trotted Bonny around with the confidence of someone who'd been riding almost since she could walk, Alto's reins were being held by Grayson as they walked around the yard.

I'd already been in fits of laughter just watching him try to get on Alto in the first place. Liam had scowled at the helmet, scowled at trying to mount a horse when wearing slacks and now scowled at the very slow plod he was engaged in. I stopped Bonny and snapped a few photos of him from behind on my iPhone, and a quick video clip.

"Okay, Liam, let's try a trot. Gently squeeze your legs so Alto knows that's what you want him to do. Hold onto the front of the saddle to steady yourself if needed because you're going to move in your seat more. That's good. Keep going. Relax those legs, Liam."

By the end of the hour, Liam was managing to trot around the field with Alto on his own with Grayson keeping a short distance between them, and I'd been out in the main field cantering with Bonny.

After more hilarity watching Liam dismount, we left the equipment at Grayson's insistence that he'd put it all away and walked back towards the house.

"Oh my fucking god, I can hardly move my legs."

"Yep, you were all about how good you were at *riding*, but you don't have as much stamina as you thought, do you?" I mocked.

"Sod off."

"Get back to the house and grab yourself a long, hot soak in the tub. It'll help. Oh and make no plans for tomorrow other than more hot baths."

"I didn't realise how much of a sadistic bitch you were. You're enjoying this, aren't you?"

"Immensely." I smirked.

"Well, I've tried horse-riding now, but you can definitely put that one on the list of things I never plan on doing again if I can help it." He rubbed his thigh.

"What a wimp."

"Oh, like that is it? I'll have to think of something to challenge you at in return."

"Bring it," I teased.

"I will. When I've had a good long think of what would make Little Miss Ridley look less smug."

I didn't want to like Liam. He'd treated Skye like absolute trash last night, but there was just something about him that drew me in. Like as if underneath all the hardship of his life was a good guy trying to get out and prove his worth.

Or maybe that's just the story I wanted to believe.

Maybe this was the persona he was showing the people of Richstone.

Because he'd said he wasn't a good guy at all.

We reached my house.

"You need to go grab your bathing suit now, Fifi."

"What?" My head snapped to his so fast I didn't know how I'd not given myself whiplash.

"Yes, it just came to me. The hot tub. How I can relax my weary thighs. So you can come along too. I want to ask you more about Richstone."

"If you make one suggestive comment about me in my swimsuit, I'm out of there," I warned him.

"Out of the hot tub, or the swimsuit?" he quipped. He tipped his head towards the house. "Chop, chop, Fifi. I don't know how much longer I'll be able to actually stand up."

"You go to the house and I promise I'll be there shortly, along with my swimsuit. Only, I can't carry you if your legs give way."

"Okay. Don't be long." He headed off down the drive and I went inside and to my bathroom because if I was wearing swimwear, I wanted to shave my legs first.

Looking through my swimwear I snorted. If Liam thought he was going to perve over my body, he was shit out of luck. I'd managed to find my bodysuit that covered my arms up to my elbows and had shorts to the knees in a pink/black combo. As I was coming back down the stairs, I found my mother at the bottom.

"Hello, darling. I saw you in the yard with Liam. I have to say, I was most surprised to see him on a horse. That's very unlike the boy I interviewed in my office."

I smiled while I thought about him sat on the horse again. "I've told him he has to try everything Richstone has to offer. All the experiences. He didn't like horse-riding and he swore a lot, but he's willing to give things a go. It's a good thing you did. People like Liam are getting to see a whole different side of life."

"That's good. Are you going to the pool now? Wasn't the riding enough exercise for one day?" She shook her head. "I wish I had the stamina of a teen again."

"No. I'm going down to the guest residence. To the hot tub."

"Oh." My mum's face suddenly wore a mask of disapproval. "I hope you know not to get over-involved with this boy, Phoebe."

"Mum!" I scolded. "I'm going in the hot tub that's all. We've both said how much our thighs hurt. I'll be right at the other side of the tub, believe me! Plus, look at what I'm wearing! I'm hardly flirting with the guy in this get-up, am I? He wants to know more about Richstone, that's all. I may as well enjoy myself while I talk to him about school. Let's not forget the reason I'm doing all this is at *your* request. I'd much rather have met my friends today."

"Okay, darling. I'm sorry. I trust you implicitly, but I don't trust him."

"I'm eighteen, Mum. Loosen up a little. Trust that I know what I'm doing."

"Fine. I will relax. It's just we need to keep your reputation pristine. Otherwise, your worth to the Richstone heirs will lower."

I blinked slowly. "Maybe you should have thought of that before making me babysit someone from Sharrow Manor."

"Babysitting him is fine. Just keep a respectable distance between the two of you at all times."

I groaned. "Yes, *Mother*."

"You are putting a coat on to go out, aren't you?"

I sighed. "No, Mum, I'm going to walk out in the middle of February in just my swimwear. I'm—"

"Eighteen. I know. I also remember what I was like at eighteen." With that, she turned and walked away, leaving me wondering what my mum had been like when she was younger.

By the time I'd escaped the embarrassment of my mother virtually asking me to protect my honour as if I was going to deliver my virginity as a gift to my new husband, I was ever so slightly tempted to go to the guest residence and let Liam have his way with me just to spite her. Did she really think I was still a virgin at eighteen? I'd rid myself of that back at a party just after my sixteenth birthday to Alfie Denan, who had been in the same predicament of wishing to get it over with. We'd done it a few more times after for practice until he'd used his new-found experience to move onto someone who could teach him a few more things. Then he'd moved on, out of Richstone, which pleased me no end as I didn't have to see him anymore and be reminded about all the awkwardness.

My phone pinged.

Liam: I've left the front door unlocked. Just come straight through to the back. I've just got in the tub. It's fucking awesome. I'll hold off with the bubbles until you get here. For now, just the warm water is as satisfying as a BJ!

I typed a quick text.

Phoebe: I may forward this text on to your friends, along with the video clip of you walking a horse I took earlier…

Liam: Don't you fucking dare…

I giggled, and then I put my phone in my bag and carried on down the drive. A few minutes later I was walking through the hallway and through the living room doors that led out onto the patio. Liam was indeed in the hot tub and had snacks and cans of coke on the side.

But it was hard to focus on the snacks. I was forcing myself to look at his smiling and welcoming face, because all I could see was his bare chest.

"Come on. Take your coat off," he demanded.

When I slipped it off, his mouth fell open, and not because he wanted to drool.

"What, for the love of God is that you have on?"

"It's February. I'm not wearing a bikini. We're not in Ibiza with foam."

"More's the pity."

I climbed in.

"Want a drink?"

I nodded. "Yeah, I'll have a can." I lowered myself into the water, welcoming the heat against my body and my newly worked out thighs.

As he turned to pass me a drink and then opened the large packet of crisps and dips, I took the opportunity to let my eyes rake over his chest. Ripped, there wasn't an ounce of fat on him. He was all defined pecs and abdomen. A small smattering of dark hair ran across his chest and down in a trail that finished somewhere below the waistband of his shorts.

"I can take them off if you're after a look at the goods."

My eyes shot back up to meet his and my face heated.

"I wasn't—"

"Yes, you were. But it's fine. I've also been wondering what your tits look like under that fucking travesty. It's perfectly natural to be inquisitive. Doesn't mean we have to bone... unless you'd like to...?" he teased.

"I think maybe I should go," I lifted myself back up from the small lip I'd been seated on in the tub.

"Sit back down, Fifi, for fuck's sake. We're just going to enjoy the warmth of a hot tub on a winter's day." He switched on the jets.

I moved so one was hitting me squarely in the tightly knotted muscles in my neck and I knew then I was going nowhere for at least the next twenty minutes. It was just too nice.

"So, I'm sure you're dying to ask me questions about life as a rat. Fire away," he said.

So I did.

19

Liam

"What's it like where you live? Describe your house to me. I want to picture it," she said.

"Well, currently after the fire, I expect it's still covered in soot and scorch marks, but if I say that our whole downstairs would fit into the living room just through there..." I pointed through the doors.

"The whole of it?" she repeated.

"Yep. I mean, it's not even our house anymore. My ma's waiting to be rehoused now. But I'll describe it to you as if you've just walked in through my front door and it's before the fire, shall I? Let you know what is was like."

"Okay."

"For a start we didn't own our house. It was rented off the council, so we didn't pay the bank, we paid the council. That means you don't pay off the house and eventually own it. It always belongs to the council."

"Oh, right. There are some private rentals here. Sounds like that."

"Yeah, it's exactly like that," I scoffed.

"Oh, shut up. Carry on, describe your house. I'm going to close my eyes so I can imagine it." She did indeed close her eyes, and she looked so fucking innocent, eyes closed, trusting me when I was so very near to her. Part of me wanted to lean over and kiss her. Put my hand straight between her thighs over that suit and rub. Watch and see whether her blank canvas of facial expressions would turn to lust or hate. But instead, I carried on talking. That bathing monstrosity material was that thick she'd probably not feel me anyway.

"So straight off the street. There's no front garden or anything. Our downstairs window is square and has a net curtain up against it. It's dirty because my ma doesn't notice the grime because she's always in an alcohol-induced haze. I try to keep the place clean, but between school and trying to earn money to pay the bills, net curtains aren't my priority."

"I get that," she said. "So... I've just knocked on your front door." She banged the side of the hot tub three times. Her closed eyes didn't see my amusement at her behaviour.

"You've stood in front of and knocked on our battered and white paint-peeling, wooden front door. I've opened it and invited you in. There's no entrance hall, you walk straight into our living room. There's a dark grey doormat for you to wipe your feet on and then you'll see brown carpets and an old, worn brown leather sofa. There's a door to the stairs, that leads up to two bedrooms and a bathroom. Front bedroom is my ma's, a double. The back bedroom is mine, a single. Still, I raise my brow at you as I gesture to the bed. I don't need a lot of room to rock a girl's world."

She opened her eyes and then rolled them at me. "I've just told you 'in your dreams' and asked where the bathroom is." She closed her eyes again.

"The bathroom barely fits in a bath, sink, and toilet. We have a shower over the bath. After you've been in there, saying you wanted a wee, when really you needed a minute to gather yourself from resisting me and wanting to jump my bones, we come back downstairs. At the opposite side of the stairs, walking over the small square of what you'd call a hallway, you're through to the kitchen/diner. That's it."

"Do you have a garden?"

I shook my head. "We have a small concrete yard. There's a cracked plastic flowerpot out there from the summer my mum decided she'd grow some bulbs. She didn't get that far and the flowerpot's been knocked over so many times it's broken beyond repair now. But if I try to throw it out, she tells me she's going to get around to sorting it and to leave it." I let out an amused huff. Wonder if she'll go and collect it to take to the new place.

Phoebe's eyes are back open. "Being here just must seem completely alien then?"

I sucked on my teeth for a moment while I considered my answer. "It's beyond anything I could ever have imagined. Like I'm in a dream. I really want to be grateful for the opportunity, but like at the party when I could hazard a guess as to how much people's watches cost, there's resentment there for how hard we have to work and how tough even existing there is. I'm not so dumb as to think you've never had a problem, Phoebe, but fuck, it's..."

"All you can see is the privilege?"

I nodded.

"So you sell drugs? All drugs? Who do you sell them to? Where do you get them from?"

I laughed. "Let me answer some of them before you ask me any more. You're sending me dizzy."

"Sorry. I just want to try to understand what you've come from, rather than what the riches imagine."

"I sell cigarettes and weed. I'm very small time. Mainly it's to people I know from school. I buy what I need from a guy who's more of a proper dealer. I'm small fry to him. I could make a hell of a lot more money upping my game and dealing the harder stuff, but I don't want to. It's only ever been a way for me to keep the roof over mine and Ma's head."

"So what happens now you're here?"

"I'm going to pop back on Thursday. Get people what they need and take it from there. I can't give it up while I'm here because I'll still probably need it when I get back, unless some other less criminal opportunity comes my way."

"How do people know where to get the weed from you?"

"I'll set up at someone's house for a while. Sell from

their place, then move on. The pigs tolerate it unless you take the piss, so I keep moving my yard on and then they're happy, because crime tends to follow where you deal. They'll go rob someone on the way if that's the only chance they have of affording their bud."

"I'm following. Just. Although it's like you're speaking a different language."

"We can't all talk like the Queen herself taught us."

She stuck her tongue out. The jacuzzi stopped and I reached over and pressed the button again.

"You're supposed to get out after twenty minutes," she protested.

"What's going to happen to us?" I popped the top of another can. "Live on the wild side, Fifi, and stay in the tub."

She settled back under the water.

"Your turn now. How do you usually spend your days? Is it all parties, fine dining, and shopping?"

"Mainly. I go to school, come home and do home-work. Sometimes we go straight from school shopping, or out for a meal. I chat to Renee a lot on the phone. I go see the horses. Weekends, my mother usually has us having dinner with someone she wants to impress or whose son she wants to marry me off to."

"Like Stefan?"

"Yes. I have French lessons, which Mum actually cancelled this weekend as you'd just arrived, so thank you for that one, because it's beyond tedious, although I like France."

"How many times have you been?"

"A few. Shopping trips to Paris. Holidays in the South. God, I sound so terribly spoiled. Anyway, sometimes on Friday and Saturday nights there are parties, or drive-in movies outside the concert arena, or I meet my closest friends for a bitch about Ivy."

"Having met her I can see why."

"I hate her," she said looking into the distance. "She does her best to make my life miserable and I never did anything wrong to her. It's all because I'm the principal's daughter. One day, I'll wipe that smug grin off her face."

"The one I saw for myself today? One day I might help you," I replied.

Phoebe's face broke out into a smile that lit up her whole features.

"Ah. Now I've discovered the secret to making Phoebe Ridley happy. It's not offers of sitting on my cock and it's certainly not cars. But taking her enemies down a peg or two? That's the secret."

When the jets went off a second time, Phoebe insisted on getting out. "I'm tired and I want to get showered for dinner. You've been babysat enough today. Did you order a meal from the house for tonight?" she asked, wrapping a towel around her and drying herself down.

"I did."

"Good. Then you're all set. I'm just going into the guest room to change into some dry clothes I dropped in the hallway and then I'm going home. You can text me if you need anything, but I'm telling you that tomorrow, all you'll want to do is groan and rest your legs."

"Great. I can't wait," I said sarcastically.

"I'm sure you'll be okay, stuck in this house for a day."

"I'll somehow manage."

"Right, thanks for the company. Bye."

She left. I tried to get up on the pretence of seeing her out and the reality of trying to sneak a peek watching her get changed, but the pain in my thighs made me wince. I lowered back down and switched the jacuzzi jets on for a third time.

When I woke the next morning, for a few minutes I tried to recall what fight I'd been in. My abdomen hurt when I moved, and my balls were sore like I'd been kicked in the nuts. Remembering where I was, and that it was all due to my horse-riding experience, I groaned out loud as I tried to move my legs.

"Fucking holy bastard. What the actual fuck? Owww."

I was desperate for a piss, and half considered using the litter bin in the room, but the hotness of a bath meant I slowly hobbled and whined all the way to the bathroom.

Things felt a little easier after an hour in the tub. By then I was ravenous, so I fixed some lunch. I'd just swallowed the last of my sandwich when there was a knock on the door. I'd bet this was Fifi, here to laugh at my expense.

So when I swung the door open with a shit-eating grin on my face, I didn't expect to be looking down at Daphne Ridley. I quickly recovered myself, pasting the smile back on. "Hello, Daphne."

"Hello, Liam. I probably should have called ahead, but I was on my way out and I just thought I'd see if you were available for a very quick chat. Mind if I come in?"

Like I could say no to the person who was letting me stay both in the house and in Richstone itself. "Sure, come through. You'll have to excuse my slow walk. I'm not used to being astride a horse."

She spoke but carried on walking ahead of me. "Yes, I saw you were riding yesterday. It is quite a workout. Maxwell also has some protective shorts he wears underneath his jodhpurs. A future recommendation."

"Well, I don't imagine getting back on one anytime soon, but yes, in order to protect my future children, I would need some of those." I wondered how I'd managed to be talking about my balls in the space of a minute of Daphne being in the house. "Would you like a drink?" I offered.

"No. No. I'll just have a quick sit in the living room with you and then I'll be on my way. Lots to do."

I followed her into the room. Daphne sat on the three-seater. I sat on the sectional diagonal to her.

She carried herself just as you'd expect a headteacher to. Straight backed, she wore tailored clothing, and her hair didn't have a strand out of place.

"Phoebe seems to be having fun and I know you're spending a lot of time together. I wanted to remind you about showing her more about the world outside of Richstone and taking her with you to Sharrow Manor at some point."

"I've not forgotten," I replied.

"Phoebe likes you I think, and that's good. I'm glad you get along, but I don't want her wearing rose-tinted spectacles as to who you are and where you're from. I think if you took her there just briefly. Maybe a quick tour of the place or something, it might just let reality sink in a little for her. Do you understand what I'm getting at? It's simply that Phoebe has lived an extremely sheltered life and is probably wrapped up in daydreams because you're a good-looking boy."

"She said something?" I hoped she didn't pick up on my interest in her answer.

"No, it's just a hunch I got from watching the two of you together yesterday."

"We're just friends."

"Good. Well, in any case, I'll leave the overall decision of when you visit to you. I trust you'll keep her safe over there. I'm aware she'd stand out like a sore thumb, but you're more than capable of protecting her, I'm sure. You'll have planned to pop back from time to time to see your mum, yes?" She stood up without waiting for a response. "Oh look at the time. I'd better be going. Charity dinner planning. Boring, but necessary. I'll see myself out so that you don't have to move your legs."

Daphne exited the room and I felt like I'd been hit by a mini tornado. She'd blown in, warned me about getting close to her daughter, reminded me about why she'd let me stay here—me showing Phoebe my shit life—and then left as fast as she'd come. I was under no illusion that she was leaving it up to me. It was an order.

Put my daughter off you because you're not good enough for her.

I'd do as she'd asked in taking Phoebe to Sharrow Manor, but when I was ready. Because if Phoebe did decide she wanted one of the riches, I'd no longer be useful. No, right now, I'd carry on getting Phoebe to want to be with me. I'd just have to attempt to keep one step ahead of the woman who seemed to run Richstone.

Somehow...

20

Liam

After another hot bath and an afternoon dip in the hot tub, I'd decided on another night on the sofa with Netflix and snacks.

As I woke Thursday morning, I actually gave thanks to a God I didn't believe in as my legs moved with only a dull ache.

After my new morning routine of a shower and a good breakfast, I dressed and left the house ready for the walk back across the river and into Sharrow Manor. I had business to attend to and then I was meeting the rest of the lads. I wished they'd been able to stay in Richstone too. It was stupid, but somehow I felt on the 'outs', like those three were still there together and I was on my own and was missing out on stuff. Potentially important stuff. I could just imagine me getting there and whining. All three would punch me in the face.

I skipped around to the back of the pub where Shaun, the guy I bought my supplies from, was an assistant chef. Yep, I'd never eat there. Not with what I knew about him. Those hands were dirty in more ways than one. I knocked the 'code' on the back door.

Eventually Shaun opened it. He looked at me and tilted his head. "What you doing here, mate? Got lost on your way to Tiffany's?"

"Funny. I've come for the usual."

"Sorry, I don't do that no more." He went to close the door in my face, but I put my hand out.

"What the fuck are you talking about? Shaun, what's going on? I'm here for my regular order."

"Yeah, that's not going to be possible." He folded his arms across his chest.

"Because?" I was pissed but was trying not to show it. This guy could have my face redesigned with fists or a scalpel.

"Because you crossed the road to the other side. I've given your patch away. See you around, Liam."

With that he did actually shut the door in my face.

I knew I should have called around to see my mother, but if I found out she was on the sauce still I'd go insane, so I'd made excuses about not going to Uncle Karl's this week.

I made my way into a pub I would be having a beer and a pint in with the lads. I'd arrived first and headed straight to the bar. The barmaid had questions on the tip of her tongue. Let's face it, most rumours started in these places. But I thanked her and walked off before she could ask them. I sat nursing my pint, thinking about how my trip to Richstone was already changing things and I'd not been there a week yet.

The door banged and Daniel walked in, grinning at me. He made the sign for 'did I want a drink' by tipping a pretend one towards his mouth and raising his eyebrows. I shook my head. I was good for now.

"So how goes it on the other side?" He said as he sank into the seat opposite me after being served.

"I'll tell you when the others get here, because they'll ask the same question, and I don't want to repeat myself."

"Fair enough. I'll just sit and enjoy my pint then. So strange to think that next week we'll all be at Richstone Academy."

The door opened again, and Marlon and Brett strolled in. They did the same hand motion before getting a drink and sliding into the other two seats.

"So, what's occurring?" Marlon asked.

"Nothing's fucking occurring. Shaun wouldn't give me any of my regular order. Said I was done, and he'd given away my patch. Looks like we'd better make Richstone work because it seems Sharrow Manor isn't all that supportive of what we're doing."

"It doesn't surprise me. I don't think you can have a foot in each camp unless you're one of the Richstone people's staff and therefore still know your place in the hierarchy. We're about to become anomalies," Brett announced.

"Well, I have a good feeling about it all." Daniel grinned at us.

"Would you like to tell us all why?" Marlon raised an eyebrow at me and shook his head.

His eyes sparkled. "I've been texting Flora all week since the party. We get on really well. I don't think I'll have to trick her into anything. I think we're going to fall in love anyway."

I hit him around the ear.

"Ow."

"Are you fucking stupid? No fucking way is her family going to let her be with you, in love or not. You need to tie her down, so make sure you stick to the plan and stick pins in the condoms or whatever you need to do to get your girl, and the money. Unless you think she'd be happy to move to Sharrow or somewhere else cheap as fuck while you either continue your education or give it all up and become just another Sharrow loser."

"Hey," Brett snapped. "Not everyone in Sharrow is a loser. Is that place already turning your head?" He turned to Daniel. "He's right about one thing though, mate. Don't let a girl crush or getting your dick wet get in the way of using this brain." He poked him in the forehead.

"Will you all leave my fucking head alone? Okay, okay. I'll stick to the plan. But at least I found myself a good one. Someone I actually like."

I'd have to keep an eye on Daniel. His heart could rule his head and at Richstone, we couldn't afford for that to happen.

As we sat chatting and I sipped my pint, I pondered over why I'd been so dismissive of the place I'd called home for all of my life. Then I realised why.

I no longer had a home here.

No longer had a job.

I didn't go to school here anymore.

There was nothing for me in Sharrow Manor, other than my friends, my mother and my uncle. And they would benefit from me bettering myself. I had nothing to lose by turning my back on this place and everything to gain.

I said goodbye to my friends, knowing the next time I saw them would be at our new school.

Knowing I'd see a lot more of the boys around the house once they crossed the river, I made the most of the rest of the week enjoying my home comforts. I didn't contact Phoebe, other than to answer her texts saying I was fine when she checked in with me.

Before I knew it, Monday morning had rolled around.

Now, the reality would set in, and the games would properly begin.

I met the other three at the bridge. We'd decided to meet there and walk over to the academy together.

"Well, that was pleasant... not," Daniel said, through panting breaths.

"Oh?" I queried.

"We all just managed to avoid being egged by pupils who weren't impressed by the 'scabs'." Brett explained.

"So they think we're traitors. Like the bridge is the picket line and we've decided to cross it," Marlon added.

"I'll come meet you further in tomorrow and let them know what they can expect if they do that again," I threatened.

"Don't sweat it. They'll be bored and onto something else by tomorrow. I might wear a bigger coat though just in case," Brett said.

We chatted on our way there, preparing ourselves for shit when we arrived at the academy. We no longer fit in at either side of the river.

When we walked through the school entrance, all heads unsurprisingly turned in our direction.

"What the hell are they wearing?" I heard one shout to another.

"Goodness knows. Even our recycle stores wouldn't stock that appalling attire," said another.

And then the music started. My head whipped around to follow the sound. Ulric stood there with a recorder in his left hand. He laughed and then beckoned us forward with his right hand, "Come on, rats. This way." His faithful followers all fell about laughing.

Brett grabbed hold of my arm as I started forward. He leaned closer, his mouth near to my ear. "Don't give them what they want before you even get in school. This time you have to fight them their way. Be better than them."

I looked him in the eye. "What? I don't get you."

"We need to make them look dumb as fuck, not fight

them with our fists."

"Not in public anyway," Marlon added.

Daniel looked over my shoulder and waved with too much enthusiasm for first thing on a Monday morning. "Flora!"

I turned around to see the four girls walking up towards the front of school. Of course, my eyes fell straight onto Phoebe. She wore a short, black, knee length skirt; a cream blouse; and had a black and cream polka dot scarf tied around her neck. Her hair was poker straight. She looked every bit the Richstone girl. As she approached, I saw the polish on her nails and the gloss on her lips. She looked pretty, but I much preferred the pared back Phoebe who'd been in the hot tub.

Daniel and Flora had walked in through the entrance already chattering away. Phoebe addressed the rest of us. "You remember Renee and Lucie," she gestured to the others. "Shall we go in? Do you know where your first lessons are?"

I shook my head. "We have to report to reception, and someone will escort us to our first class."

"Okay. Come on then, best not to be tardy on your first day."

We all walked inside. Phoebe said bye to the others and then hung around the reception with us. "We're fine here. You don't need to hang around."

My words seemed to amuse her. "I'm not here for you. I'm here to meet Skye. Make sure she has someone seeing as she's the only girl. You lot have each other. She doesn't have anyone. Not really."

"Doesn't being so helpful and good get boring?" I asked her.

"Doesn't being so snarky and bad get boring?" she quipped back.

"Never," I smirked. "It's always so much fucking fun. You should try it sometime."

"Maybe I will," she folded her arms over her chest. "Maybe you'll become a good boy and I'll become a bad girl."

I huffed. "You don't have it in you, Miss Ridley."

"I could have it *in me* if I wanted to. I have no doubt." She looked directly down at my groin.

My mouth fell open in shock.

She sniggered, and then stepped past me. "Skye! Good morning and welcome to Richstone Academy. Let's get you all your passes and into your first class."

She left me standing there as if she hadn't just made a provocative comment that had spoken straight to my dick. I placed my book bag over my hard-on and stood behind Phoebe and Skye at the reception desk.

We were furnished with lockers, lunch passes etc, and taken to our first class. Mine was history. Daniel was in the same class and so we were both introduced by the teacher, Mr Garamore, to the rest of the students. Lucie and Flora were in the class, but there was no sign of Ulric and Ivy for which I was grateful, and no sign of Phoebe, which disappointed me.

There was no such luck in my maths class after

break. Both Ulric and Ivy were present. We'd been sitting working for around twenty minutes when the rotten smell of sulphur permeated the air. A stink bomb. I felt my mouth form a sneer while I waited for what came next. Really? This was the level of them? Juvenile.

"What is that smell?" A male voice said. "Has someone brought shit into class?"

A female voice replied, "It certainly smells like it. I think you should go find it so we can have it removed."

The teacher got up and left the classroom. I couldn't fucking believe it. Footsteps got audibly nearer to me until a head came near to my ear and the red-headed guy who hung with Ulric made a loud sniffing sound.

"Found it."

More tittering followed. Oh, how amusing it was. I stared into the guy's face and kept my expression dead. His mission done, he walked away. He'd have been the one shitting a brick, not me. He'd have been hoping that I didn't break his nose for what he just did. I'd get the fucker, but it wouldn't be in a classroom full of witnesses.

For now, I'd let them think they had the upper hand. Let them get too comfortable on their high pedestal. Then the fall would be further and the landing harder.

At lunchtime, I met up with the rest of the guys in the canteen.

"So how's your morning been?" I asked the others.

Brett shrugged, "Nothing I can't handle."

Daniel smiled, "I got some name calling, but I also sat with Flora in one class, so it wasn't all bad." He looked over into the dining room. "Oh the girls are there. They're waving us over and have saved us some seats."

The rest of us exchanged exasperated looks, but we took our food over to the table. Skye was there. Her eyes were puffy like she'd been crying, but I didn't ask. I didn't want to get involved. Phoebe and the rest of them could look after her. Of course, Daniel immediately began chatting to Flora. I noticed that Renee engaged Brett in conversation too. Looked like Brett might be having some fun sooner rather than later.

"Could you pass me the salt please, Marlon?" Lucie asked.

Marlon looked at the table where the salt was as near to Lucie as it was to him.

"Why? What have you done to it?"

Lucie pulled an overly bewildered face. "Nothing, it's just polite."

"I thought you women wanted to be equals, so get your own salt," he said, spearing a potato croquette with his fork and biting off the end.

"I could have been eating your potato croquette, but now you can suck your own dick." Lucie got up and moved to the other end of the table with her food while Marlon almost choked on his. I saw Phoebe's upper lip quirk to the side, but she kept looking down at her dinner.

There was a shout of, "Now," and as I turned around to see what was happening, two guys rushed to our table, lifting Marlon out of his seat. All heads turned to watch as they dashed with him to a large open refuse bin in the dinner hall where they dropped him in it.

My poor friend sat there for a moment, his legs dangling over the sides while the guys who had dumped him in there sniggered and the rest of the dining room either laughed or looked at each other in anticipation of what would happen next.

Ulric walked over to the side of the bin and said loudly, "That's where the trash goes."

Marlon pushed himself out as Ulric walked away. His hands scrunched into tight fists, and I watched as he strode over to behind Ulric.

"No!" I yelled out, but it was too late. Marlon pulled his fist back and punched Ulric straight in the kidneys.

Ulric bent over, doubled in pain. Staff ran over and Marlon was dragged out of the room. I put my head in my hands for a moment because I knew that Marlon had lost his school placement already, if not all of ours. He'd managed a morning before Ulric had won.

"I need to follow him. You all stay here while I find out what's happening," I instructed a shellshocked Brett and Daniel.

"I'll come with you. It'll no doubt be my mother who he has to report to," Phoebe said, getting to her feet.

I didn't say no. She might be able to save the day being the principal's daughter. Right now, Marlon needed all the help he could get.

The three of us sat outside the reception area. Ulric had been taken to the matron's office and then we'd watched as he'd walked past us, his teeth gritted, straight into Principal Ridley's office.

"What do you think will happen to me?" Marlon

asked Phoebe.

Phoebe shrugged. "I honestly don't know. I mean, he provoked you. He was asking for it in my opinion. I only wished I could have done it myself."

"It doesn't matter that he started it," I said. "There are rats in Richstone and they want to cleanse it of us. That much is clear."

Twenty minutes later Ulric exited, uttering, "You're fucked," to Marlon out of the side of his mouth while Phoebe's mother glowered in our direction.

"Marlon," she said and all three of us stood up.

Sighing, she let us all through.

Once we'd taken a seat, she stood by her window and looked at Marlon.

"What happened?" She looked from me to Phoebe. "I'm asking him."

Marlon relayed Ulric's Pied Piper act before we'd come in and then how his friends had dumped him in the trash can and Ulric had called him trash.

"I appreciate that is inflammatory, Marlon, but you can't go around punching people for these things. You come to me. We have a zero-tolerance policy for such things."

Phoebe snorted.

"You have something to add, Miss Ridley?" She tilted her head at her daughter.

"Ulric got what he deserved."

"His father doesn't think that. Mr McDowall is coming to see me this afternoon demanding answers, and I only have one for him, I'm afraid."

"No." I snapped, guessing what it was.

"It's fine," Marlon threw his hands up in the air. "I'm out, right?"

Daphne nodded. "I'm sorry, Marlon. I have no alternative. You assaulted another pupil. I will make sure no charges are filed against you, that I can guarantee."

"How?" Phoebe asked and then she waved her own hand. "Oh, of course. Through some negotiation. A new wing in the McDowall name, or Head Boy of the Year for Prince Ulric."

"There must be something we can do." I banged my hand down on my lap.

"It's fine, Liam, honestly. I almost said I'd changed my mind when we were at the pub. Then I'd decided to give it a go. See what the first week brought. Well, I've managed the first day and that's enough for me. I want to go back to Sharrow Manor. I know what to expect there. I'll still get my education and I intend to work hard until I get a decent standard of life, but I can't be among these people. There has to be some midway point and I'm going to find it." He stood up. "Thanks for the opportunity, Principal Ridley, but I'm going to go back, so I accept the suspension."

"I won't suspend you. I'll just say we came to a mutual agreement that you'd return to Sharrow. No need for anything to mark your record; though if Mr McDowall asks, I did. You are welcome to join your friends here at the guest residence at any time Liam sees fit. Just keep out of the line of fire of the Ulric's of the school, okay?"

"Thank you. That means a lot."

"Okay, well you're all dismissed. Mr Rowe, please sign out and return to Sharrow Manor. Miss Ridley and Mr Lawson return to class."

I opened my mouth, "As soon as you've seen your friend safely over the other side, Mr Lawson."

I nodded. It felt like Principal Ridley could read me like a book and I wondered what her own background was, because she was the first to do so. It was unnerving. I'd have to watch myself around her. I wasn't used to being on the backfoot.

We signed out of school and took the walk back over to the bridge. I bro-fisted my friend who had repeatedly kept saying he was fine, and this was what felt right for him. Phoebe formally shook his hand and wished him well. Typical riches. Telling him I'd text him later, he was gone out of sight with a last wave.

I took my book bag off my shoulder and thrust it with force onto the ground over and over. "One morning. One fucking morning was all it took."

Phoebe tried to get hold of my arm. "No. Get off me. Leave me the fuck alone." I shook her off.

She squealed as she slipped, falling onto the pavement. "Ow. Oh fuck. Ow."

Though I could feel her eyes on me, I left her there while I kicked a lamppost. If the princess thought I'd help her to her feet and make sure she was okay, she was fantasising. No one had asked her to come calm me down. I wasn't some kid having a tantrum. I was a mightily fucked-off grown man.

"You're a fucking dick," she yelled.

My eyes moved to her. She sat there looking at her hands. Her eyes flashed up to mine and I could see tears in the periphery. I still left her there, though I could see the skin scratched off the heels of her hands and the darkness of stones still embedded. The red of the blood starting to flow.

Fuck it. Grabbing her arm, I pulled her up to her feet roughly.

"I will make him pay for this. One day I will make him fucking pay," I uttered through gritted teeth.

Phoebe gingerly began to move, rubbing her right hip with her fingertips.

"You just have to be patient," she said, starting to make a move back towards school. "The tortoise and the hare remember? You bide your time and then you go for it when they least expect it."

Then before I knew what she was doing, she'd taken her elbow and dead-legged me in my left thigh. It was agony, coupled with the fact I still had the slight ache from the horse-riding.

"Like that," she said. "That's for being stabby when I was only trying to help."

"I'm teaching you independence," I gasped out, still recovering from her attack. "I thought that's what you were all about? Not wanting to be married off to some rich boy."

"Well, I'm teaching you patience, Liam Lawson," she flounced off in front of me, and I let her, because her arse looked amazing in that tight skirt.

21

Phoebe

The already pale-skinned Skye had come into school looking like a ghost. She'd not travelled in with me as originally planned as she'd said she was running late. I wondered whether the truth had been more that she'd been running to the loo a lot or thinking about not coming at all. It had to be rough on her, being the only girl.

"You look nice," I said, admiring the black and white striped dungaree dress she was wearing over a white polo neck.

"Thanks." She smoothed the material over her stomach and I saw her hand shake.

I squeezed her shoulder. "Hey. You're with me. My mum said I was to shadow you in your classes all day, so don't be so nervous. I'll take care of you."

She visibly lowered her shoulders. "Really? All day? That makes me feel a little better." She exhaled loudly.

"Hey, where are the loos? I could do with going before class."

Yeah, nerves.

After collecting her passes and class timetables from reception we went via the ladies toilets and then into our first class: English. "I'm in this class anyway. Renee's moved to another seat so that you can sit behind me." I paused. "Now, just to warn you that if anyone says anything mean, ignore them. Queen Ivy is in this class. Ulric too."

"Oh God." I saw her look back down the hall, so I put my arm through hers and took a step forward. Luckily, she followed me in.

Although the Poisons looked, no one said anything and the lesson progressed as normal. Or so I'd thought. Towards the end of class Ivy suddenly stood up and said, "What are all these dark little droppings?" while looking at the floor. She slowly followed the trail of what were clearly chocolate drops she must have put there while I was deep into analysing the text we'd been given to study, ironically on how an author addressed an audience. Now, Skye had her own audience. The rest of the class, who were watching Ivy.

Ivy's heels clattered on the floor until she came to a stop at the side of Skye's desk. "Oh, I know what these are. They're rat droppings," she said smugly, "and look who they lead to. A real life rat."

Skye swallowed, looking down at her text as if she'd not heard her.

"Miss Sackville, please return to your seat," Mr

Gallagher, the English teacher instructed. Though we knew if Ivy wanted to, she would stay where she was.

She turned to the teacher. "I really think you need to get pest control in here, sir. Rats breed prolifically. Otherwise, before we know it, we'll be overrun with them." She walked back to her seat and sat back down while titters of laughter and sniggers sounded out around her.

The rest of the class passed without incident, but once we were outside of the classroom on first break, two of Ivy's friends knocked into Skye, taking her down onto the floor. They then stepped over her, making sure their feet brushed her body on their way.

"What the hell are you doing?" I yelled, grabbing hold of Skye and pulling her back to her feet.

"Sorry, we thought she was a zebra crossing," Ivy scoffed as she walked past us.

It was plain to see that Skye was about to burst into a flood of noisy tears and so I headed her back to the reception and with a nod at the receptionist, went into the staff bathroom near to my mother's office.

"I'm so sorry. Ivy is a complete bitch. I said I'd look out for you and I will. I'm going to report her behaviour to my mother now."

Skye shook her head. "No, don't. Then she'll just think I'm a snitch. There's only one thing to do if I want to be part of Richstone. Will you help me?" she asked and then she laid out her idea. We agreed she'd come to mine after school, and I'd rope the others in.

It had been my intention to talk about it with the girls

over lunch, but that got derailed when Ulric's minions picked Marlon up and dumped him in the bin.

One thing about that incident was that other than low murmurings about 'one down, four to go'—it seemed Mr Billings wasn't included in the great plan—the rest of the afternoon passed off relatively quietly.

Walking out of the doors together, the five of us: me, Skye, Renee, Flora, and Lucie, got in our cars and drove back to mine. Skye came with me. She still needed to get to know us all better and hopefully this could be the start of it.

"So you want a makeover?" Flora clapped her hands with glee. "Oh, Skye, that is like my dream job. Can I be your stylist this evening? You know, just advise you. You make all the final decisions."

Skye gave a half-smile. "I think what I actually said was I wondered if you had any spare clothes and that I was going to dye my hair a more normal colour."

"Potato-pohtato. It'd be much more fun if you'd let us spoil you. I promise we're not treating you like a doll. We do this all the time when one of us fancies a change of image or has a date."

"Yes, but you all have the money to do that."

"I have too much money," Flora announced, and Lucie groaned. "What? It's true. So I want to spend some of it on you, Skye. Pretty please? I promise I'll also look through my clothes to see if there's anything for you. We look a similar size."

That was one thing in Skye's favour. She was slim. The Poisons were 'fattest' but couldn't bitch about Skye where her weight was concerned. I felt sad that she felt she had to change herself to fit in, but no one was forcing her to do it. She could have stuck it out or walked away. Anyway, making herself look like one of us was no guarantee they'd let her off the hook, a fact I'd told her when she'd originally suggested it.

"Okay, so which boutique shall we hit first?" Renee asked.

Lucie shook her head. "None. She needs expensive but not one-of-a-kind."

"Why?"

"Think like a Poison."

"Oh," Renee answered. "Of course. Spilled drinks is the most obvious, but yes. She'll need a change of clothes."

I called Bells to see if she could come over. She said she'd make an excuse to get away from her current appointment and would be straight over once she'd got some items selected. I ordered food to my room for us all and we snacked and chatted until later when Bells arrived.

"Thank you for coming at such short notice," I told her, air-kissing each cheek.

"I couldn't miss such an exciting opportunity. Tell me all," she asked, and we filled her in on how wretched Ivy had been.

Bells looked at Skye. We'd sent her some snapshots. "I have some amazing clothes for you to try on. And I know you want to fit in, but you can still have your own signature style: a little black lace here, a little tartan there. We'll not make you lose your whole identity, okay?"

"Thank you," Skye said on a happy sigh.

A selection of outfits tried on and discussed later and Bells went off to get everything sorted and delivered. Meanwhile we went off to *The Look Book*, our go-to hair and beauty salon.

Emily smiled in greeting as we walked in. "So this is the young lady you were discussing on the telephone? Come in and take a seat and let's see what we can do." She escorted Skye over to one of the chairs in front of a mirror and started lifting up her bobbed hair. "While pink suits you, you've not helped your hair's condition by dying it." She frowned. "I can run a bleach bath through this to lift out the pink and get it stripped back to the blonde underneath. Then I can use extensions to make your hair longer and more luxurious looking, though there's nothing I can do for the buzz cut. Or... and this would be my suggestion, we cut the rest short and I take you darker, almost black. It'll bring out those gorgeous brown eyes and then you can grow it out if you wish stage by stage." She looked at Skye through the mirror.

"That please. Short and dark brown."

"Excellent. And while we're doing all that, we'll do your mani-pedi, brow and lash work in between. You'll leave here a new woman."

Skye beamed. "That's what I'm hoping to be."

And she did indeed leave looking like a different person. Our new friend had a short, funky, chocolate-brown pixie cut, along with on point eyebrows and dyed lashes. Her nails were done in a 'sand' shade. While she'd been undergoing her treatments, Flora and Renee had gone to the local MAC counter and bought Skye a complete new set of make-up to complement her new hair colour.

An applied fake tan and several hours later, and she was all done.

"Who is actually excited for school now tomorrow?" Lucie quipped.

After a call home to my mum and one to Skye's, it had been agreed that she'd stay at ours just for one night. It was getting late by the time we got back so I arranged for hot chocolates and said goodnight to her.

By the time I finally fell to sleep I was exhausted from all the day's events.

The faces of the Poisons was worth every penny spent. The five of us walked into school and at first Ivy and her friends didn't even realise it was Skye. Not until she sashayed past them, in her new short black pleated skirt, peach blouse, and a black tie and winked at Ulric.

Ulric's eyes widened with realisation and he licked his top lip. Clearly the new Skye agreed with him. Although he and Ivy weren't together relationship-wise, she clearly didn't approve of his new eye candy and moved to stand in front of him.

He wasn't the only one taking note. Maybe none of the riches would entertain a pink-haired punk girl, but a sassy and confident femme fatale? Tongues were hanging out everywhere we went and as the number of admirers went up, the number of bullies went down. By lunchtime there was only Ivy and the rest of her Poisons chipping away saying things like, 'You can't make a silk purse out of a sow's ear'.

And predictably, Ivy 'accidentally' fell with her tray of spaghetti Bolognese, which landed all down Skye's front.

"Oh God, I am so, so, sorry," Ivy fake-apologised.

Skye held a hand up. "It's fine. No biggie." She went off in the direction of the bathroom, Lucie accompanying her. She then returned only a few minutes later looking spotless, making sure to walk straight past Ivy.

"What the fuck?" Ivy spat out.

"Looks like your mean girls act is getting old. Like it needs retirement. Or they need another leader. One that's not so pathetic," I told her.

"You think you're so clever, just because you brought her a change of clothes. I'll show you why I'm where I am in this academy," she snarled before exiting the dining room.

My laughter accompanied her until she was out of earshot.

2 2

Liam

Skye was the talk of the Academy.

"Did you see the new girl today? Wow. We need to throw a party and invite her, like yesterday." I'd been hearing guys saying this kind of thing all morning.

I turned to Brett. "These are the same people who said she was vermin and needed to be exterminated just twenty-four hours ago, right?"

"All it took was for her to change into one of them," he said.

It had pissed me off when I'd first seen her. The fact she'd given her identity up so easily to blend in, instead of fighting for herself. But she was alone, her only friends here Phoebe and her rich friends and so she had a harder fight than us.

"Mr Billings quit yesterday," Daniel said walking up to us.

"He did what? On the first day? Stupid fucker." All the fucking work I'd done to get him here. Well, having a word with Mrs Whitstable. As long as they didn't let the bitch who screwed my mother over in here though I didn't care, and that wouldn't happen, or I'd buy a wall projector and play her fuck show on it to the pupils and teachers.

"Flora said that Phoebe said that her mum said he looked around and changed his mind. Said he got a bigger sense of satisfaction working at Sharrow Manor. So they agreed he'd go back."

"The girls all went out from school, didn't they? When did you chat with Flora?"

"This morning when I woke up. I missed her."

"Fucking pussywhipped by one of the riches. Disgraceful," Brett tormented.

"Apparently, Renee said you were like Nutella, Brett. Dark, tasty and needed spreading, only all over her body, not on toast."

"I think we should maybe double-date later, my man? What do you think?" Brett put his arm around Daniel's shoulder, and they walked off to class together chatting away. At least they were on plan. I'd got some ground to catch up on after my temper outburst yesterday.

The day's 'taunts' were yet more juvenile behaviour. They played UB40's *Rat In Mi Kitchen* on their iPhones, knocked into us in corridors saying they hadn't seen us there. They put a black bin bag over Daniel's head to 'tidy up the trash'. But it was nothing we couldn't cope with.

By the time we got to lunchtime and sat with the girls again, it appeared Skye's day had gone downhill. She'd had to change her clothes twice.

"So how many changes of clothes do you have?" Brett asked her.

"Everyone brought a spare, so I'm on three of five, but still, I can't do this every day, so I'm going to have to think of something to stop Ivy."

"Do it back. She won't have a change of clothes, will she?"

I looked around for the ketchup to put on my chips. "Where's the sauce gone?"

"Sorry, mate. I borrowed it," a guy at the next table said.

He handed it back to me. I shook it and popped the top ready to put it on my chips. The sauce exploded. It was on me, Skye, Phoebe, and Brett. It had shot in the air and all over the floor. It looked like a massacre. Ulric walked over and high-fived the kid who'd passed me the sauce.

"I see you like your ketchup with a spot of baking powder," he said, laughing as he walked out of the dining hall.

"I'll bring every one of those fuckers down," I declared. "But I don't play parlour tricks."

Phoebe stared at me, but she didn't say anything.

I was too angry to even eat.

Not having a change of clothes myself, I cleaned up the best I could in the male bathroom and headed to class. I got angrier with every step I took. Once again, I found Ulric coming to stand next to my desk and I wondered what was going to come out of his mouth next.

"You, me, racing. Saturday morning at the arena track."

"Is there not an event on?" I queried.

"No, and in any case, we'll be meeting at one am. Unless you're scared of the dark?"

"I'm scared of nothing," I told him. "I'll see you there."

Tonight, I needed to talk to Phoebe. To find out about past races and plan to win.

Walking to the car park after school, a gang of girls starting running towards Skye, Phoebe, and the others. Some girls held the others back while a few grabbed Skye and set off, heading behind the trees with her. "What the fuck are they doing now?" I said to Brett and Daniel. "Come on, let's go and help her."

By the time we got to the woods the others were running out laughing. Ivy walked out with clothes in her hands. She dropped them at our feet, grinding her foot into them and coating them in mud. The sounds of sobbing came from the trees.

"I reckon that should be enough to get the second of you out of here, but if not, there's lots more where that came from." She stalked off.

The clothes were covered in mud. There was no way Skye could put them back on. "Pick those up while I go see what's happening. You keep back because Skye won't want you to see her like this."

They nodded and I set off into the wooded area.

"Skye? It's just me, Liam."

"L- Liam. They t- took my clothes."

I walked towards her voice to find her huddled behind a tree. On her knees, she was bent over like a small child, her arms around her knees.

"Skye, I'm going to give you my shirt and jacket. They'll cover you to your knees, okay? Then we can get out of here."

"P- please don't look at me. I d-d don't know why I thought they'd l- leave me alone if I tried to f- fit in."

"We're only on the second day. They'll get bored, Skye, or we'll get even." I took off my jacket, putting it over the branch of a tree and then lifted my shirt off. "Stand up so we can get this on you. You must be freezing."

She stood and she looked so vulnerable, stripped back. Naked, muddy, and defeated. Ivy had just lined herself up for some of the same treatment. Ulric had it coming, but Ivy had just gone to the top of my shit list.

I pulled my shirt over her head and like I'd thought, because she was small it came past her knees. I held out my jacket while she slipped her arms in.

"Thanks, Liam," she said, looking at me like I'd hung the moon. I thought of the video of her on my phone. I was really no better than the people who'd just stripped her. I decided to delete it. New battlelines had just been drawn and I was now on Skye's side, not against her.

"Come on. I'll drive you past the bridge," I told her.

When I got back to my own place, Phoebe was sitting on my doorstep. She jumped up as I turned off the engine.

"H- how is she?" She enquired, her eyes wide, grazing over my bare chest as I exited the car and started moving towards the entrance, the gravel crunching under my feet.

"Destroyed. Devastated. Defeated. Talking about not coming back to school. I've tried reasoning with her and maybe you can too, but I honestly don't expect her to come back. It looks like Ivy's done what she said, got two of us out. Two days ago, including Mr Billings, there were six people from Sharrow Manor in Richstone Academy. Now there are three."

"I'll talk to Skye."

"What can you do? Throwing money at the situation didn't help, did it? You're the principal's daughter. You can hardly challenge Ivy or punch her in the face."

"I can't do anything *publicly*, no. Doesn't mean I can't do anything at all. I just need help."

I opened the door. "Are you coming in?"

She nodded and walked inside, heading straight for the kitchen. Her confidence amused me. She didn't hesitate and wait for me to ask her to go in a particular room. She just walked in like she owned the place, which I guess she kind of did. It should have pissed me off that she hadn't deferred to me, but for some reason it didn't.

She started fixing coffee. "You want one?"

"Sure."

"You can be going to put a shirt on."

"Do you truly want me to put a shirt on?" I queried. She stared at me. "That's why I said it."

I moved up closer to her. "I know that's what your words say, but your eyes say something else entirely, Fifi."

She swallowed and her lips parted as I moved my head down closer to hers, nearer and nearer, and then I reached past her for a mug.

She immediately sprang away from me as if I'd burned her. "Actually, I've got what I came for. To find out about Skye. I don't need a coffee after all." Her feet took two steps towards the door, but I intercepted her and this time I backed her up to the counter and crashed my lips to hers.

She took a couple of seconds to respond and then she kissed me back just as hard as my lips had met hers. Her hands roamed my back, feeling my muscles as they moved. My own hands tangled in her hair, until I broke the kiss.

"If you want romantic love making from a boyfriend you know where the exit is." My hand trailed down the side of her face.

Steely determination hung on her own.

"I just want you to fuck me, Liam." She trailed her hand down my chest, squeezing my nipple. Her hand trailed lower until she cupped my junk. "I want to know if you're as good a fuck as I'd imagine you'd be, so don't hold back. I want everything you have to give."

My cock got hard under her hand. My mind swirled

with the fact we could dirty up the good girl, lust surging through me, while at the same time I also needed to consider my other goal. A trapped rich girl. I needed my doctored condoms.

"Let's go into my bedroom," I told her.

She nodded and so picking her up and holding her under her arse, her legs wrapped around me, I stalked from the kitchen to my bedroom where I laid her down on the bed. Suddenly an opportunity to relieve myself of my frustrations of the day had been presented to me, and I would make the most of it.

She wanted my all? She couldn't have all of me, because my heart was cold and dead, and my conscience black and sullied, but my body? I'd gladly give her that.

Phoebe sat up and shuffled to the edge of the bed.

"Changed your mind already?"

"No. But I'm not going to just lie back and think of England," she quipped, her hands coming to the waistband of my trousers. She popped the button and then lowered my zip. Grabbing the material, she pulled my trousers down and I helped by stepping out of them. She did the same with my boxer briefs, except as she freed my cock she paused, taking the size of me in.

"It'll do," she said. That earned a growl from me as I picked her up and threw her back on the bed. I pushed up her skirt, uncovering her white cotton panties, and then I dragged them down and off her legs, leaving her clearly waxed, bare pussy on show. Pushing her knees up, I settled within them, my tongue diving straight into her wet heat. She groaned with desire as my tongue flicked through her wetness and I fastened onto her clit, biting and sucking. Her hips thrust up to meet my endeavours and her hands fisted the sheets while she called out my name, "Oh, Liam. Liam. Yes, like that, don't stop."

But I did. I stopped and she looked at me, lazy lust in her eyes, lying like pools of runny honey.

"See, you're not thinking of England. What are you thinking of?"

"You," she husked out.

I went back to my pussy buffet until she came apart, screaming my name.

Standing, I went over to my bedside drawer to get out a condom.

"Are you clean? I'm on the pill," she said, and my heart went cold. I smiled though I felt anything but happy.

"So who were you seeing before?" I questioned.

"Oh, nothing like that. It's for my periods," she said.

"Right."

"Is there a problem?" she asked.

There was. This meant that Phoebe might not be my golden ticket to my own riches after all and I may need to change to another rich bitch. But right now, while my cock was so hard I felt I might die, and this gorgeous woman laid bare before me, wanton and willing, I wasn't going to give it any more thought.

"No problem. And yes, I'm clean." I shuffled onto the bed and pushed Phoebe's thighs apart, splitting her open and feasting my eyes on her glistening pussy with its pink folds. Grabbing my cock, I lined up and thrust straight inside her, hard. Her eyes closed and she gasped.

"Look at me while I fuck you," I demanded.

Those honey eyes met mine. Her hands moved to fasten on the cheeks of my butt.

I smirked and grabbed one and then the other, lifting them above her head until I had both hands held down with one of my own.

I began to thrust within her again, not keeping a regular rhythm at first, so she didn't know when to expect it. It meant every thrust was met by a moan or a gasp. As her breathing quickened and her cheeks flushed ever redder, I hurried my pace, still being relentless in taking her roughly. Her head was almost hitting the headboard with our movements. Her eyes closed and I let her lose herself in sensation. I let go of her wrists, but she left them there. Instead, I brought my hand between her legs and pinched her clit hard.

"Fuck, oh fuck," she mewled through laboured breaths. "Liam, I'm going to—"

I thrust against her again as I rubbed at her clit and her core exploded against me. Her pussy milked my cock, but I wasn't ready yet. I wanted more time buried deep in Phoebe Ridley.

As she laid back recovering, I once more began slow movements.

"Did you not come?"

"Not yet," I winked, "but I will, and you will too. My lips hovered above hers. Over and over," I spoke into her open mouth before claiming her lips with my own again.

23

Phoebe

Liam was fucking me, and I was enjoying every minute.

It wasn't how I'd expected this day to end, but I wasn't complaining.

The man knew *exactly* what he was doing and as I'd just come for the second time, I decided that while ever he was still here, choose however I felt about him, I would do this with him anytime I could.

Because holy hell fire, he was the spark setting off my firework display. Change my name to Catherine Wheel.

I'd hung around the house only to find out what had happened with Skye. I'd never have foreseen that not twenty minutes later I'd be in his bed.

Liam was moving within me again slowly, waiting for my body to once again align with the tune he was playing on it and work its way towards a crescendo. Pulling up my knees, I twisted and moved my body until I had him on his back. I laughed at the, "What the fuck?" uttered from his shocked mouth.

"I have thighs of steel. I ride horses remember?"

"You just caught me unawares, that's all. But by all means take over, Miss Ridley. Ride me."

His hands reached out to cup my breasts through my clothing and he teased my puckered nipples.

I felt my hair fall over my face, covering one eye as I began to circle my hips. I lifted myself up and down on his cock. My eyes had been closed but I opened them to see Liam's were shut, him concentrating on my movements while stroking my tits. As I quickened my pace, his hands dropped from my breasts and came around to my arse. I could feel I was getting closer and so I bucked and writhed. Liam's fingers dug into my arse so hard I knew it would bruise, but this pain I welcomed because it was accompanied by pleasure. I placed my hand between us, my finger and thumb meeting around the base of his girth like a real-life cock ring, and I pumped hard.

"Fuck, Phoebe." He stiffened and then jerked within me. He carried on pumping and I came myself. I felt weightless, like I was floating on air.

Liam pulled out of me and sank onto the mattress at my side. He pulled the duvet up over the two of us, but didn't pull me under his arm, or kiss me and nuzzle me like a lover would post-sex. Rather he placed a hand behind his head and smiled a slow, lazy smile, before saying, "You're welcome."

"You're a twat."

"Never professed to be anything else."

I sat up straighter. "Liam, you don't have to keep telling me what a badass you are. I get it. No relationships, heart encased in thick ice, yada yada yada. I'm not going to fall for you, and neither am I going to do anything to complicate your life in Richstone. We can do what you did with Skye. Be fuckbuddies. Then when you leave here at the end of term, no hard feelings, because there won't be any feelings at all, right?"

"Deal. But not fuckbuddies, because I do actually see you as a friend, Phoebe. So friends-with-benefits?"

I placed my hand to my chest. "I am truly honoured for the position you bestow upon me, Mr Lawson."

"Why, Miss Ridley, I think your mouth needs occupying with something more than sarcasm," he said. "Wrap your lips around my cock."

Part of me wanted to refuse him because of the way he'd ordered me to do it, but the other wanted to command power over him as he gave himself over to the swirl of my tongue and the suck of my mouth.

I lowered myself down the bed, enveloping his cock in my mouth, and I kept my eyes open watching as the man who told me he would never be mine, gave himself over to me, even if it was only for a little while.

"I'd better get home. I have homework to do ready for the morning." I rubbed at my eyes. "That's if I can keep my eyes open."

"All this activity has made me hungry, not tired, so I'm going to send out for pizza."

My tummy rumbled in response and he laughed.

"Want to share a pizza, friend?"

"No. I'll get Marjorie to fix me a sandwich or soup while I do my work. But I'll take a shower here first if that's okay? The last thing I want to do is go home reeking of sex."

"Go for it," he gestured to the en suite.

Even though I was sore between my legs, part of me had hoped he'd come in and ravish me in the shower, but he didn't.

When I exited, I found the hairdryer left on the bed for me, but Liam was gone. Taking my phone from my bag I called Marjorie and asked her to prepare me some food so I could take it straight up to my room.

Walking out of the bedroom, I shouted to Liam that I was leaving. He sauntered out of the living room, now fully dressed in dark jeans and a skinny fit ice-blue t-shirt that clung to his torso. "You were saying that you couldn't do anything to Ivy publicly. Don't worry about her. I'll take care of it." He said it casually, but I was beginning to see more of Liam than he wanted me too. It made me wonder if he cared for Skye after all and that made my stomach twist even though it shouldn't.

"What if I want to be involved? I want to watch Ivy get what she deserves."

"It's better you're not. But as much as Skye was only a fuckbuddy, she deserved a chance at Richstone, and

Ivy, Ulric, and the rest took that away from her. But it was Ivy who directed most of it, and so she's the one who I'm going to make pay for it."

I smiled. "Will you at least tell me what you do? I want to know she suffered."

"Why, Fifi," he smirked. "I do love this bad side of yours. Oh, by the way, I'm racing Ulric in the early hours of Saturday morning, so I need you to tell me more about race nights. Same time tomorrow?" He arched a brow.

"You tell me now that he's challenged you to a race?"

He shrugged. "We've had a full schedule with first Skye and then fucking."

"I'll see you at some time tomorrow evening and we can talk about race night, but I'm not sure of my plans for tomorrow yet."

"Your plans for tomorrow night are being fucked over the living room sofa by your bad *bad* boy," he drawled.

I opened the front door and walked outside. Liam stood in the doorway. "You know you're already wet thinking about it. I'll tell you what you're going to do now. You're going to eat, do that homework in super quick time, and then you're going to finger fuck yourself over and over while you replay what happened here tonight."

"You flatter yourself."

He shrugged. "Know I'll be jerking off thinking of being back inside that hot, wet pussy," he whispered and then he closed the door.

As I walked up the drive, I made myself think about

other things than Liam's cock. I managed to get through a parental quizzing of my day, which meant I ended up eating my food in the dining room with them, before escaping to my room.

But Liam was wrong in what he assumed I'd do. Because for the first time in my whole life, apart from when caused by illness, I didn't do my homework at all.

Instead, I replayed the evening over and over going between bringing myself off and wondering what on earth I was getting into with Liam Lawson.

This wouldn't end well.

But I didn't need to worry about that right now, did I?

Right now, I could enjoy fabulous sex and hopefully soon claim a winning entry into our bet, because Liam had agreed to deal with Ivy Sackville.

I wasn't sure which would give me the greater satisfaction.

Skye didn't return to Richstone. It meant that Ivy was even more insufferable in class. But my mind also ran to other things. Like how easily Liam just treated me the same as if he hadn't made me have multiple orgasms the night before.

Lunch talk was about the upcoming race, and Renee, full of her usual exuberance, did my job for me, telling of how things went down at the track.

"There will be a bet, for sure. Ulric wants you to race him because he's unbeaten and he thinks he's unbeatable.

So then you'll owe him. Just be careful of what you agree to because they want you out. That's their main aim with everything they do."

"I'll be ready for him. I just need some practice out there, so who's up for a meet tonight out at the arena? Say eight pm? I checked and there's nothing on."

Everyone said they were on for it. I wondered what had happened to his plans for fucking me over the sofa. I wouldn't allow myself to be disappointed. I had my own agenda here after all. And beating Ulric would be another jewel lost in the crown of the king.

After school I drove everyone to Café Renzo. The conversation was of course on the rats. We ordered drinks and macarons to accompany the gossip.

"I can't believe I have no one to win the competition with now. Unless I set my sights on the remaining three too?" Lucie teased.

Flora's mouth opened on a gasp and Lucie fell about laughing.

"Oh my, dear Flora, you seem to have it bad."

"Daniel is amazing," she sighed.

"Flora, he does seem to be as keen on you as you are on him, but please keep your wits about you. What if he's just trying to score himself a prime piece of pussy and a way out of Sharrow?" I warned her.

Flora's eyes narrowed in my direction. "He's not like that."

"You've known him just over a week. You don't know what he's like."

"And how's Liam?" Lucie asked in a swift change of conversation. I tensed at the mention of his name.

"I'm not sure what you mean."

"Really? Because the two of you were eye fucking each other all lunch time."

"Don't be ridiculous," I answered defensively.

"Fine. If you don't want to confess now, I understand. There's something hotter about a dirty little secret. Anyway, I shall now judge the winner of our little competition given I'm on the outs, so progress report please. I ordered a trophy for the winner last night. It's a rat trap made in bespoke silver. Also, the winner gets a small boat moored at the marina. Let's wind up the old men by sunbathing down there and showing them what they can't have."

"You're buying a boat?" Flora asked Lucie.

"No, all three losers are. I mean, we'll all be on it, so really there are no losers." Lucie grinned. "Okay, time for an update. You first Renee."

Renee finished eating her macaron, making Lucie wait. "I've been chatting to Brett and we seem to be getting along, but he's quite reserved. Sensible. I need a party again, where I can get some booze down him and have him lose some of his inhibitions."

"In other words, you're getting nowhere so far and need to get him pissed to get in his pants. Bravo." Lucie slow clapped. Renee gave her the middle finger.

"Flora, apart from your huge crush on Daniel, have you managed to get him to agree to a makeover yet?"

"No. I've not even started. We're just getting to know each other."

"In other words, you have such a crush you forgot about the bet."

"I like Daniel. I'm not all that interested about changing him."

"Someone pass me a vodka to deal with her," Lucie rolled her eyes.

I was worried about Flora. Despite my warnings she was just jumping in with both feet.

"Don't forget what I said to you about protecting yourself, sexually, and your heart, Flora," I told her. "Please, for me, keep your wits about you."

"I'm not some silly little girl, you know?" she snapped. "Just because I like him doesn't mean I'm an idiot. Stop treating me like some halfwit."

Fuck. Flora very rarely lost her temper. She was right. I had to trust she and the others knew what they were doing. It was their lives.

"I'm sorry. I just worry about the effect the rats will have on us all."

"Huh, at the moment it's been the effect the riches have had on them," Flora stated. "I mean half of them are gone already, thanks to Ivy and Ulric."

"Your turn to update us," Lucie said turning back to me.

I smiled. "After what Ivy did to Skye, Liam said he

253

would take care of Ivy. So my plan is completely on track."

"Ooh, it would appear we have a leader so far," Lucie turned to the others. "You two need to up your games."

Renee's eyes met mine. "So what's he going to do?"

I shrugged my shoulders. "I don't know, but I should imagine it will be spectacular, and everything the bitch deserves."

24

Liam

I told Brett and Daniel my plans and then I put them into action. Then I texted Phoebe, who I'd heard at lunch was going to a cafe after school with her friends.

Liam: I need you to anonymously send a large bouquet of flowers to Ivy asap. So extravagant it couldn't possibly be from a rat. Put 'from a secret admirer'. Then arrange something else for tomorrow, a pendant maybe, and put 'from your secret admirer. Wear me and I might reveal a clue as to my identity'.

She sent a text back.

Phoebe: Will do as soon as I'm home. Intrigued.

I didn't like the fact that her intrigue pleased me. I

needed to not give a fuck what Phoebe thought about anything I was doing except for if I was doing her. Now I'd found out she was on the pill, I might need to move on, find a new rich bitch. Like Ivy. Part of Ivy's downfall could be revenge and maybe part of this could be my new plan? If I fucked Ivy, I could kill two birds with one stone...

But you want Phoebe, my mind announced like a bucket of ice-cold water. This was dangerous thinking. I had to remember why I was here, what it was I intended to do. So I couldn't get her pregnant, but I still had the option of blackmail or her mother's proposition.

The arena was deserted as I pulled into the car park with my friends. The grounds were vast and wrapped the whole way around the arena.

"So, you're just racing around and we're timing the laps? Make sure you get faster." Brett asked.

"Yeah, I guess so."

Phoebe's Audi pulled up, Renee getting out of her passenger side. A few minutes later, another car pulled in: Lucie's Mercedes-Benz CLA coupe, Flora waving at Daniel from her seat.

I walked towards Phoebe as the girls came towards us. All I could think about was being balls deep inside her. An opportunity lost by my needing to practice racing.

"So, as Renee said at lunchtime, the races are usually

three laps of the stadium and are timed. The fastest wins," she said.

"How do you decide who gets pole?"

"No one gets pole. You toss a coin to see who goes first," Phoebe's brow creased.

"You mean you race alone, but it's timed?" I was clearly hearing things.

"Yes, otherwise it would be ridiculously dangerous."

"Are you fucking kidding me?" I shook my head. "That's not a race. A race is where you go head-to-head to see who crosses the finishing line first."

"Not in Richstone."

"Fucking pussies." I turned to Brett as Daniel was distracted by Flora. "You'd better time me then and we'll see how much I can improve."

We'd been there about an hour when a Mercedes AMG coupe whizzed into the car park. Ulric hung out of his driver's side window.

"Yes, get as much practice in as possible, loser," he yelled out. "You'll need it for when I destroy you. Oh, and the bet. If I win, you and your other two friends leave Richstone. You can think about what you want as your prize if you like, but you'll be wasting your time, because I never lose."

I walked over to his car. Ulric smiled like a psychopath, the smug and sadistic smile of someone who wanted to win and liked seeing others suffer. I wanted to punch his glasses straight into his eyes. But there were other ways to triumph over Ulric. He'd not raced me before and I had no intention of leaving Richstone.

I lowered my head and stared directly into his eyes. "We race properly, unless you're too scared against a real rival. Head-to-head. I'll even give you pole position, and a ten-second head start. We do six laps of the arena, because it's a race, not a fucking beauty pageant, and when I win, *when*, you back off and you let us rats get on with it. We're not here to affect you. We're here to say we attended Richstone, to get it on our CV, so that we can make something of ourselves in life." I straightened up. "So this race is simple. You win and we go. I win and you back the fuck off."

"We don't do head-to-heads."

"You want us out of Richstone you do. You said a race. That's a race. Unless you're not the amazing driver you say you are, pussy boy?"

Ulric squinted at me, a hard smile on his lips. "A proper race it is. You'd be better off spending the time packing your belongings though ready to get the hell out of here than practicing." He put his window up and drove away.

With fire in my belly and a determination to do whatever it took to beat Ulric into submissiveness, I began to do my practice laps. Losing was not an option, but even if somehow, I did, I knew we wouldn't leave Richstone. I'd just have to find another way to deal with Ulric.

"I'm cold now. Shall we go somewhere for hot chocolate?" Renee said after another half an hour's practice.

"I'm staying," I told her.

"Oh, come on, man. My fingers are freezing. You've shown you can handle it no problem," Daniel whined.

"We don't want to time you anymore. We want to defrost."

"You lot go. I'm staying," I insisted.

"Don't be such a fucking idiot. We've frozen to death on your behalf, now come buy the hot drinks," Brett looked like he might strangle me if I refused.

I sighed. "Fine, once more, and then we'll go for hot chocolate."

I had to admit it was good hot chocolate and it came with whipped cream, marshmallows, and a dusting of cocoa. But the best bit of the experience of being here was that we were just hanging out. Three guys and four girls, just chatting and laughing and right now there were no barriers. No one putting the river between us. Phoebe had sat next to me, but also hadn't said a word to me since. Fuck knew why.

And you shouldn't care.

"So, shall we have another party at mine this weekend?" I asked around.

"There's a party at Jolene French's house on Saturday night. I'll make sure you're all invited," Lucie said. "It'll be a wild one. Jolene's parties are something else."

"And you think she'll let us attend?"

"Jolene will salivate at the thought. Three hot boys from the wrong side of the tracks? I'm surprised you've not had her prowling around you already."

"It'll be because of Ivy," Renee added.

"What about Ivy?" I bristled.

"The queen has decreed that no one go near you or they'll face her wrath."

Yet another reason why I would destroy the bitch.

My fists curled where they sat on my lap and then I startled slightly as a small, warm hand landed on top of my right hand and squeezed slightly. Phoebe's reassurance, or her reminding me of the upcoming revenge?

Unfolding my fist, I moved my own right hand off my lap and onto Phoebe's left thigh. She dropped the last piece of cookie that had been on her way to her mouth.

"Let me get that for you," I said, and I trailed my hands across her pelvis, reaching down to between her thighs where it had fallen on her skirt. I lifted it up.

"That's okay. It's touched my clothes now, so I don't want it," she said.

"Oh, do you want anything else instead?" I asked.

"I don't think so. I think my appetite has been satisfied now," she answered, and she turned away to talk to Renee.

I moved my hand back and while I fixed my attention on the talk at the table, I pulled up the side of Phoebe's skirt.

Her hand came down on it, holding down the material.

I waited until it was almost closing time and then Phoebe made her excuses to go to the bathroom. I was amazed when none of her friends went to join her. I thought they did that shit together? As I got up myself to head out there, Lucie's gaze met mine, along with a smug grin.

"Hey, I could do with a breath of fresh air before I get in the car home. I'm starting to feel a bit queasy. We can show you around Richstone a little if you like," she said to the others, and then she looked back at me. "Liam, can you hang on for Phoebe? We'll meet you back here in say, twenty minutes?"

Well, well, well. Had Phoebe been confiding in her friend?

"Sure."

Renee got the bill and then they all left. Meanwhile, Phoebe was still in the bathrooms. I headed back there.

Pushing open the door of the ladies bathroom, ready to say, 'Oh my mistake' should I come across anyone else, I found Phoebe standing staring in the mirror. Her hands were gripping onto the countertop as if her life depended on it.

"You can't be in here," she whisper-shouted.

"The others have gone for a walk at Lucie's insistence. Did you tell her about us?"

"No, but she suspects something."

My brows pinched. "Why are you in here, staring at your reflection?"

"I'm angry and trying to calm down."

"Oh," I laughed.

Her eyes narrowed to tiny slits. "Amusing is it, Liam? Did you find it hilarious trying to get your hands under my skirt in the coffee shop where I spend most of my time? I know we're friends-with-benefits, but do you think that means you can arrange a fuck for eight pm and then change it on a whim? Or suddenly reach under my skirt at a coffee shop in order to play some kind of game with me?"

"I still don't understand why you're so mad," I replied honestly.

"Because you're the person I thought I could count on to just be straight with me. If you make an arrangement you should keep it. I'm not at the end of some leash waiting for you to pull on it, William."

"We have twenty minutes. There are no other customers left and the waitresses are clearing up. Soon they'll come check the bathrooms ready to close up for the night. Take your panties off and lean over the sink."

"No. Get out." She squared up to me in the mirror, where I now stood right behind her. "You missed our sofa appointment and now you have to wait for a new space in my schedule."

I wrapped my hand around her hair at the base of her neck and I tugged it towards me hard. "You'll make space for me right now, Fifi, because I'm hard as fuck, and although you're pissed because you wanted me and didn't get me, your panties are wet and your pussy desperate. Better late than never, right?"

Her head was pulled back, revealing her throat, and I trailed kisses down her neck. Phoebe shivered beneath me.

"Pleasure and pain, Phoebe," I said, pulling her around to face me by her hair. I saw tears form in her eyes from the pain. Then I kissed her, hard and bruising. I yelped as she bit my lip.

"What the fuck?" I wiped my mouth and looked at the small drops of blood there.

"Pleasure and pain, you said." Phoebe grabbed my shirt and pulled me towards her, and she ran her tongue over the bite.

I pulled up her skirt above her waist and thrust my hand inside her panties. She was soaking wet. I speared her with two fingers. "You like it rough, don't you, Phoebe?"

"Yes," she hissed with lust. Those amber eyes were like flames as she grabbed my hand and guided me in thrusting even harder. "Flick my clit with your thumb," she demanded. I did, and before long she came apart, her body shaking against me.

"I want to fuck you, but not here. We need to get out while we can and take the others home. Come straight to mine after."

"I won't be able to stay long. I'll be expected back."

"We'll just have to make the most of what time we have then."

We met the others, Phoebe pretending she wasn't feeling so good, and then we said our goodbyes. Phoebe had to drop Renee off first. I left the front door unlocked and went through the house, turning the lights on dim and closing the curtains, before finally sitting down in an armchair, waiting. The thought flashed through my mind that she might not come here after I'd changed our arrangement tonight, but then I remembered how wet she'd been. She'd be here.

Around ten minutes later I heard the front door open. "I'm in the living room," I shouted.

She pushed open the door and began stripping out of her clothes, discarding them to the floor until she remained in a black lacy bra and G-string. My eyes soaked up every inch of her skin.

She walked over to the sofa and put her hands on the back of it.

A slow, lazy smirk came over my face. "How wet are you for me?"

"Soaking. I need you inside me right now."

"Bring yourself off."

"What?" Miss Feisty was back.

"Bring yourself off."

"No. Get over here and fuck me already."

Standing up from the chair, I slowly walked over to her, standing behind her.

"Now strip," she commanded.

I went in my pocket, took out the switchblade I carried around with me and I flicked the lever. I showed her the knife before holding her hair in my fist again, pulling her head back and holding the blade to her throat.

But she didn't scream or beg me to let her go. She just stayed there, her breathing heavy.

"Still think you're in control?" I asked.

"You're going to fuck me. We both know it. So, yes, I still am." She defied me with her words. I moved the knife and slit through her bra strap, so it fell off her shoulder. Then I did the same to the other. Finally, I turned her to face me, slitting through the centre of the bra, so the material fell onto the floor in a drift of lace. Turning the knife around, I ran the end of the handle down between the valley of her breasts, trailing it down to her panties. Over her mound. Her breath hitched as it dipped between the valley of her thighs, touching her most intimate places. I turned the knife and cut through both sides of her panties, so the material fell away, leaving her completely naked. Then I pushed the handle of the knife into her wetness and inside her. I could only do it slightly, an inch or so, because I didn't want to cut myself on the blade, but there was no fear on Phoebe's face, just complete wanton lust. She was delirious with it. I trailed it over her cunt, in and out, and then I threw it to the floor, freeing my cock from my trousers and boxers. Turning her once more, I bent her over the sofa. I slammed into her so hard her feet came off the floor, and that's how I continued. Every fuck a punishment and a reward. My left hand held her hip while my right hand squeezed her nipples.

Her breath was almost musical in its exertion, like the beat of a drum.

Pant, pant, pant, pant, pant.

"Don't hold back, Fifi. There's no one here to hear you scream but me. Give me everything and I'll give it you right back."

Her own hand dropped between her thighs and she rubbed her clit hard. Knowing she was fingering herself almost drove me insane and I pounded into her harder and faster.

"I'm coming. Oh my god, I'm coming," she screamed as her climax took her. She came so hard it finished me off and I spurted inside her, grabbing my cock and making sure she got every last drop of my cum.

I took her down onto the carpet. Lying beside her while we both caught our breath.

And I knew I was in trouble. Because in all my plans for Richstone, I had not anticipated the power and persuasion of Phoebe Ridley.

She took my depravity and enjoyed it like the finest caviar.

She accepted me for who I was, not where I was from.

She could become an addiction and we all knew most of those didn't end well.

25

Phoebe

When I'd first been told I had to babysit whichever students came to Richstone, I'm not afraid to say I'd had my own judgements about what they'd be like. Never in a million years would I have anticipated the things happening between Liam and me.

I knew there was no future in it. Liam was here to improve his chances of future success, and my own plans were to escape Richstone. Somehow, I would get myself away from here. Away from the diamond encrusted lead my parents had around my neck.

But every time I saw Liam's eyes filled with lust for me, it made me feel powerful. He said he had no heart, but I couldn't help but tangle myself up with him anyway.

He would leave and I didn't want to stay, so why not continue to enjoy the great sex and adventures I was participating in while I waited for an opportunity to get out of here?

He was going to deal with Ivy and help me win my entry to the bet, but I didn't care about a boat. Not unless it could sail out into the sunset with me on a one-way trip out of here.

Also, every time I fucked him it was a huge 'fuck you' to my parents. To the mother who'd brought him here as a project, but abandoned her 'test subject' on me, and to the father who wanted me seen and not heard, except on society dinners where I could be shown like a prize pig while they waited for me to choose a husband.

But something else was happening. While I lay on the floor next to him gathering my breath, I told myself it was sheer lust. But the fact was he excited me, entertained me, exhilarated me.

When he'd put the knife against my neck, I'd known he wouldn't harm me with it. And he'd known I needed it. He didn't know the reasons why I enjoyed pleasure and pain in perfect harmony, but he gave it me anyway.

"I need to go," I murmured.

"Do you want a quick shower first?"

"Yeah."

He pulled me to my feet.

"Might not be as quick as last time." He smacked my backside as we walked out of the room.

. . .

My intentions had been to go straight to my bedroom, but my father stood outside of the sitting room, a glass of whiskey in his hand.

"You're late home, Phoebe. It's a school night. When we say eleven, we don't mean midnight."

"I sent Mum a message. She said it was okay because I was with my friends."

"It's not okay with me. Eleven pm on a school night is late enough. Now come here, I have other things to discuss with you."

Oh God. No.

I yawned. It was fake in the fact I'd thought about it to bring it on, but I was genuinely tired and ready for bed. A bout of sexual exertion would do that to you. I'd been utterly relaxed and ready to sleep until my father had appeared. "Daddy, could it wait until the morning? I know my being late is my own doing, but really am so very tired."

"Do I have to drag you in there, Phoebe?"

I froze. No, I did not want him dragging me in there. He might use my clothes to do so, but he might not and hands in my hair were now the domain of Liam, not my father.

I walked towards him and followed him into the sitting room.

He took a seat on the sofa, but when I went to sit, he shook his head. "You can stand. I shan't keep you long. I just wanted you to know that on Saturday evening we shall be dining with the Pembertons. I think their son, Nigel, would be a perfect husband for you."

My mouth dropped open. "Daddy, Nige Pemberton is five foot one and has terrible allergies."

His cheeks reddened. *Fuck.* "So? He comes with a huge fortune to inherit. Our families aligning would be incredible."

"I'd look a joke, Daddy," I said quietly, "please can you choose someone else? I promise to marry someone you choose, but please, not him."

He threw his glass. I watched as it sailed through the air. I tried to escape it, but it bounced off my collarbone before landing on the floor. The sumptuous carpet meant it didn't break, but it did leave a large stain. My father took a handkerchief out of his pocket and passed it to me. "Get that up."

I took it, my hand shaking, and I began to mop up the spill, watching the white handkerchief turn brown from the scotch it was absorbing.

"It's funny how you can hang around with Sharrow scum and yet not Nigel Pemberton. You judge him for his looks. Do you know how shallow that is, Phoebe?"

I desperately tried to reason with him. "Please let me choose someone who I might have a good pairing with. What would our children be like with his height and allergies? We need a healthy man for good heirs, don't we?"

His foot came down on top of my fingers and he pressed down. It hurt under his weight, "Ow, Daddy, please, you're hurting me."

He pressed harder. "Even the most robust stock can

collapse under pressure, daughter. Do I need to remind you of which of us is in charge?"

"No, Daddy. I'll be there, Saturday, to meet Nigel," I said.

"Good." He took his foot away, and I breathed a sigh of relief, until he swung it back and kicked me straight in the back with it.

"Oh God." I fell to the ground, clutching at my back and trying not to be sick, or pass out with the pain.

"That's your place, Phoebe. By my feet, and you'd do well to remember that. Now finish clearing up. There'd better not be a stain there tomorrow."

He left the room, closing the door behind us and I laid on the floor and wept, staying as quiet as I could. I knew one thing. Tomorrow I needed to tell my mother what was happening, because this time he hadn't cared that he could have broken my fingers, and she needed to get him help, or get me out of this house.

The next morning, I ate breakfast alone and then travelled to school. My first class had Ivy in it. She was already going on and on about her flowers and secret admirer, while trying to guess who it could be.

Later, I'd need to sort today's gift. But right now, I had other things to attend to. I needed an audience with my mother and the only way I could get one was to make an appointment with the principal.

Or so I'd thought.

"She's busy all day. I'm sorry, Phoebe, but she can't

be disturbed," the receptionist told me. I'd had enough, anger coursed through my veins. One parent was too busy to see me, and the other abused me. Looked like I needed a different plan.

"Stefan." I hurried over to my friend. "I need you to do something for me, because I need to speak to my mother urgently and the receptionist won't make time."

"Is it that urgent?"

"It really is."

Stefan tipped my chin up and stared directly into my eyes. "What is it, Phoebe? I've known you forever. Is it connected to Liam?"

"No, No." My eyes began to swim with tears. Frustration about not being able to speak to my mother had them spilling from my cheeks.

"Phoebe, Phoebs." Stefan pulled me into his arms and hugged me tightly. Then he extended his arms and ran his thumb under my eye to wipe away the tears.

Just as Liam walked out of the nearby classroom.

He stopped still in his tracks. His face a mask of deadly composure and then he walked away.

"Are you sure this isn't connected with Liam, Phoebe? Because I need a knife to cut through that sexual tension."

The connotations of the word knife brought back memories of the previous evening, but it wasn't those I needed to address right now.

"You mustn't say a word, Stefan. I just need to tell someone. As a friend, but not my inner circle. The girls wouldn't understand."

"Sssh. Just tell me. I'm here for you. You know that." He ran a hand over my hair.

"It's my father. He hurts me. Hits me. Kicks me."

Stefan's eyes widened in horror.

"Nowhere obvious and not often. Just when he thinks I've stepped out of line. He wants me to have dinner with the Pembertons, Stefan. He wants me to marry Nige Pemberton." Tears rolled down my cheeks.

"No way." Stefan shook his head. "We will deal with this, Phoebe. Whatever you need me to do, I'll do. Then we can both talk to your mother, and if it comes to it, Phoebe, I'll marry you. We don't love each other, but we are friends. Maybe love would come, and if not, then just fuck someone else and carry us an illegitimate heir. I bet half the kids here belong to the gardener anyway."

He made me giggle.

"That's better. And I'm not joking. If we can't find another way out of this, then you can become Mrs Phoebe Barratt."

"I don't know what I would do without you, Stefan." I sniffed.

He went to pass me a handkerchief and I backed away. He looked at me weirdly but didn't ask further. "Without me you'd be Mrs Nige Pemberton," he mock-shuddered. "Now come on, let's do this."

And so we staged an argument and Stefan let me slap him across the face. Teachers stepped in to stop our slanging match and we were sent straight to the principal.

Result.

. . .

"Do you have any idea how busy I am today? And I find out not only that my own daughter was brawling, but it's with Stefan. Explain yourself before I bring Stefan in." My mother was furious.

"I know you're busy. You're always busy. You were busy and gone before breakfast. I couldn't even get an appointment with my own mother." My hands were flying all over with dramatic flair. "I had to fake a fight with Stefan to get to see you when my texts went unanswered."

"You did what? What on earth could be so important as to do that, and I didn't answer your urgent text because usually it's just a request for a late pass to stay out with your friends."

"Daddy has been hitting me." I told her and I watched her face pale. She looked over to her door, then lowered her voice.

"What are you talking about, Phoebe?"

"Daddy. He gets frustrated with me and he attacks me."

She steepled her fingers. "Parents do discipline children. But I understand you're eighteen now. I'll have a word with him because a smack is no longer acceptable."

"You think a smack is acceptable to a child?"

"Phoebe, never mind that right now. I'm not starting a debate with you on child discipline. I've told you I'm busy. I'll speak to him, now off you go."

"He isn't smacking me. Last night, he stepped on my fingers. He threw his whisky glass and it hit me here." I touched my collarbone. "He kicked me in the back. He bangs my head into walls."

She exhaled slowly. "Where. Show me."

"I don't think I have anything to show you. He's very careful. Just take a look at my back in case there's a bruise." I lifted up my clothing.

"I can't see anything, and, Phoebe," she says as if she's talking to a toddler. This just doesn't sound like your father at all. In all of our years of marriage your father has never laid a finger on me and he adores you. Always has. Even though he had a son and heir, you've been the apple of his eye."

"Until I had my own opinions maybe," I said.

"Oh," Mum touched her forehead. "Of course. He's spoken to you about Nigel Pemberton and the dinner, hasn't he? It's just a dinner, darling. We won't announce your engagement there. Just see how you find him out of school and give us a chance to get to know the Pembertons better. There's no need to make up such dramatic stories."

"You think I'd do that?" I tilted my head at my mother. "You think I'd make up such lies, just to get away from meeting the Pembertons?"

"Oh believe me, Phoebe. I've heard much more outlandish untruths from the pupils here when they want to get out of something."

I stood up. "But I'm not just a pupil, mother. I'm your daughter."

"I will speak to him."

"Don't." I shook my head. "You'll make matters

worse. Just forget this conversation ever took place. And you can cancel the meal with the Pembertons. Stefan and I have agreed that we will enter into an arrangement."

"You have?" Her face lit up with delight.

"We will have a courtship first. Do not start planning engagement parties or weddings. I want a year to get to know him better as a romantic partner. That's my final offer."

"Of course, of course. And if your father has been a little *volatile*, I'm sure this news will settle him right down."

She looked at me with an expectant gaze. Expectant in my leaving now. I walked out of the office and up to Stefan.

"So what happened?"

"She didn't believe me. Not one word. We're fake dating, Stefan, until I can think of a new plan."

He put his arm around my shoulder and pulled me in tight.

26

Liam

The fuck?

Why was Phoebe in Stefan Barratt's arms? His fingers tracing down her cheek. I'd thought they were just friends.

And then by lunchtime they were the main topic of conversation as people gossiped in the lunch queues about why they'd had an argument and got sent to the principal's office. It made no sense. Just before that I'd seen them share an intimate moment.

They walked into the dining room hand in hand. It shouldn't have bothered me so much. Shouldn't have made me feel like I wanted to go over there, pull him away from Phoebe and beat him to a bloody pulp.

But it did.

I couldn't stay. "I need to get out of here a while. My head's banging. I'm going to step outside for ten," I told the others and I walked out of the dining room. I didn't go back in. I slipped out of the grounds and grabbed a sandwich from the local deli.

On my way out, I bumped into Ivy. "Oh no. Have you been in there? In my favourite deli? Maya won't pass the food standards agency inspections if you infect the place. Stay away." She paused on the step. "Oh, but actually by the early hours of Saturday morning we'll be rid of you all anyway, won't we?"

I completely ignored her and walked away.

After eating my sandwich, I took my phone out of my pocket and texted Phoebe.

Liam: If you've not sent the jewellery yet, don't bother. Change of plan.

Phoebe: Oh, okay. Shall I pop by later?

Liam: No, I'll be busy. You spend time with Stefan.

I couldn't bring myself to type the word 'boyfriend'.

Phoebe: Okay. See you tomorrow.

I'd actually thought she was different to other women, but no. Somehow, she'd changed her mind and decided she'd become a society wife after all. Had she decided this after we'd fucked? Had it made her feel dirty and so her response was to go get together with Stefan? Daphne wouldn't need our arrangement if Phoebe was serious about Stefan now.

Hatred filled my veins, but I didn't know who it was for. Phoebe who'd disappointed me, Ivy who continued to bait me, or myself, who'd discovered he had mixed up feelings about the girl with amber eyes, who'd gone straight from his bed to start dating a riches.

One thing was for sure. Tonight, I would delight in taking down Ivy Sackville because she'd poked the bear once too often, and now it would tear her limb from limb.

The good thing about the bitch giving everyone her complete life story was that she was too busy talking to see what happened in front of her face. She was drinking her juice drink when I walked past her. I turned back to look at her and smirked.

"Hey, pretty lady."

"What do you want, other than a lice bath?"

"You're too quick to discount me, Ivy. I know I'm poor, but I sure am pretty." I came closer to her, "and I can show you a real good time." I placed my lips on hers, taking the drink out of her hand and meeting my other behind her back where I dropped in the sleeping pill. Of course she fought against me but I'd only needed those few seconds.

"Get off me. I bet I have a disease now. You're done here, rat. I'm going to have you arrested for assault."

I put my hands up. "I'm sorry. I'm sorry. I thought you'd been treating me mean to keep me keen. I get the message. I won't bother you again."

I walked away and sat in my car, watching through the rear-view mirror as her friends drove away. Ivy stayed behind after the others and I wondered why. I'd parked my car in the furthest car park this morning and so I watched from the corner of the building. I couldn't let her drive out of school in case she hurt anyone else. The pill would take up to an hour to work and so I waited for a chance to make a move. When there was barely anyone else around, I watched as Ivy got out of the car, looking around her. She went into the boot where she took out a brown paper bag and then got back in her car. Fascinated, I stared as she began cramming cake into her mouth. Easily more than one piece at a time. Here was my opportunity. While she was gorging herself, I dashed across the car park and opened the passenger door she'd left unlocked.

She almost choked on her cake. It was a shame she recovered as I couldn't have thought of a nicer ending for her.

Ivy wiped her mouth down and jutted her chin up in the air. "What do you want now? Don't you think you've done enough, kissing me?" She reached for her phone, but I grabbed her hand.

"I don't think so, Ivy. I think I'll sit here, and you can eat your buns and cakes while you tell me just why you hate all us Sharrow people so much."

"I don't need that long," she said and then she went woozy. "Fuck, I need to stop doing this. I feel bad. Must be all the sugar." She started to look a bit panicked.

"Okay, I know we're not friends, but just sit back and I'll hang on until you feel better. Then I'll go."

Ivy sat back with her head against the rest. "I've gone really tired." Her eyes widened for a moment. "What if I'm going into a diabetic coma?"

"Swap seats with me," I told her. "I'll take you

through to the hospital and you can get checked out just in case."

I helped her move into the passenger seat and by the time I was out of the school gates, Ivy's eyes were closed.

"You good?"

"I just f- feel s- sleepy. W- weird."

She was out of it enough to not know where I was taking her.

I pulled her car into the garage and pulled the shutters down. I'd told the others I might need them and that I'd left a key under the front mat. When I walked inside they were all in the kitchen.

"So what's going on?" Marlon said.

I hugged him. "I've missed you, my friend."

"It's only been a few days. You grown a vagina?"

I smirked. "What's going on is I have Ivy Sackville drugged and in my garage in her car."

Daniel leaped up from his seat. "What the fuck? Are you crazy?"

"She needed dealing with. She wants you out of here, Daniel. Do you want to go? What if she realises you're with Flora and she starts picking on her? The woman is poison and all I want is some insurance. Just to know that she'll keep her mouth shut and leave us the hell alone."

"So what do you want us to do?" Marlon asked.

"Video her sucking my dick."

"But you said she was drugged."

"She won't be in a few hours. She'll be ready and willing then. She can suck any of yours too if you fancy it. I need one of you to help me bring her inside while the others watch for anyone showing up here. I'm not expecting anyone though. We can grab a few beers and catch up with Marlon while we wait."

Four hours later, and with lots of begging and wailing, I'd had enough, and I took my switchblade out of my pocket. I held it to Ivy's face and watched her go still.

"What would everyone think if the perfect Ivy Sackville's face was all carved up? Worse than the kids with acne you pick on, or the ones with birthmarks. I could carve 'bully' right into your cheek. Or maybe 'bitch' on your forehead. The pupils at Richstone would laugh, not only at your horrendous face, but also because you got payback."

"P- please, l- let me go." One lone tear ran down her cheek.

"All you have to do, Ivy, to protect your face, is to suck my cock. That's it. You don't even have to bring me off; just look like you're enjoying yourself and basically begging for it. Then afterwards, why not just make yourself sick? I mean I'm guessing that's what you do after you've eaten all those buns and cakes. Oh, oops. This time you'll have digested them while you were out of it. You might put a pound on, the shame."

Ivy shivered. "J- just put it in and then I can go?"

"Yup. And you can even still be mean and bitchy to all us rats in public. You just can't do anything that could lead to getting rid of us. We have a pass to stay in Richstone or your daddy gets the video of you giving head."

"Ulric won't stop just because I have," she said.

"You don't breathe a word of this to Ulric or anyone. I'll be dealing with him next."

"O- okay. I'll do it. Can we just get this over with, please?"

"You stop directing your shit at my friend Phoebe too."

"Okay, okay."

I took the knife away and just for one second, seeing Ivy Sackville looking vulnerable, I felt like letting her go with a warning. Just for one second, because then I remembered what she'd done to Skye and then I didn't feel sorry at all.

I pulled down my trousers and my pants.

"Open wide, Ivy, and make sure you look enthusiastic."

Ivy drove out of the gates herself with a warning not to look suspicious or race home.

"Wow, remind me never to get on your bad side," Daniel said, "Cos I don't want to have to suck your dick."

I pushed him in the arm.

"Another beer, to celebrate a job well done?" I asked the others.

We chinked our tins together in a toast to a slightly easier time in Richstone. Then I called them a taxi to take them all home.

As soon as they were gone, I stepped straight into the shower where I scrubbed my dick to rid itself of all traces of Ivy's mouth. I thought about how strange it was that a weapon like my knife could be used to torment one minute and tease the next. As my thoughts changed from Ivy's mouth to Phoebe's, I imagined her taking my cock in her mouth. Imagined her here in the shower like last night. I fastened my hand around my cock and started pumping my hand up and down it. How can it have been just one evening before? Her enveloping my cock with that wet and willing mouth, sucking, licking, flicking, taking me all the way to the back of her throat until I came down it. My hand moved faster and faster while the palm of the other rested against the shower wall. I thought about Phoebe's open legs, an invite for me to plunge my cock between them. I came, streams of cum washing down the shower drain, along with regret that just hours later she'd started dating someone else.

Sleep was hard to find that night and in the end I swallowed one of the sedatives I'd given Ivy. I just had to keep remembering that whichever way we did it, one of the three of us needed to secure a financial fortune. And we couldn't let anything stand in our way.

Anything at all.

27

Phoebe

I had no friends-with-benefits situation happening this evening and so I used the time to get caught up on school-work because tomorrow night I'd meet my friends for something to eat before the race.

I had Marjorie send my food up to my room because I wanted to avoid my parents at all costs. I needed a way to get money of my own in order to get out of here. I wasn't marrying Stefan Barratt or any other Richstone heir, and although Stefan had bought me a little time with our current arrangement, it hadn't brought me the assurance my dad wouldn't hurt me again. I knew now that my mother was no help. I needed my own financial security. A nest egg.

Any savings I had, like the money my granny had left me were locked up in trusts I couldn't access until I was twenty-one. My father wasn't stupid. He knew I'd be even less likely to rush to marry if I was financially self-sufficient.

The only thing I could think of doing was starting to sell some of my things through a secret account on eBay or a similar site, but even then, girls like me didn't trundle off to the post office with parcels and there was no one I felt I could confide in, not even Marjorie.

I was stuck, and for now I'd just have to pretend with Stefan until I could think of a way out of Richstone.

Our year was full of talk of the race the next day. I noted Ivy's absence though. She hadn't made it into school, and I hoped that meant she wouldn't be at the track later either.

"Are you fake-meeting Stefan later?" Lucie asked me at lunch.

"No. He hates racing."

"You shouldn't have to fake-date anyone," Flora huffed. "You should be able to marry for love."

"Well, I can, as long as I meet them by a certain date and they're rich and successful enough," I said with heavy sarcasm.

"So you need to meet someone else while publicly fake-dating Stefan? Good luck with that one," Lucie patted me on the back.

I'd not told any of them about my plans to escape Richstone and I didn't intend to. Depending on how it went down, I'd either be able to invite them to visit or I'd have to cut off all ties. I would hate to lose contact with my friends, but if that's what I had to do to gain my freedom, I'd just have to suck it up. I'd meet new people and so would my friends. If it came to it, I would eventually leave with the clothes on my back and start again somewhere else.

I wondered if Liam would be able to help me? Was he in touch with people who could get you a new identity? I inwardly laughed at myself. He was from Sharrow not the Mafia.

"You pissed Liam off?" Lucie studied my face.

"No, why?" I looked up to see Liam standing in the food queue talking to the others.

"He keeps glaring in this direction."

I shrugged. "I don't know why. We haven't fallen out or anything."

"Maybe he's not keen on your fake-dating Stefan? Maybe he's jealous?" She arched a brow.

As Liam did look over in my direction and then looked straight away from me, his eyes cold and hard, I had a thought.

"Did any of you tell the boys about my fake-dating?"

They all shook their heads.

"If you do, then obviously they need to keep it to themselves," I said.

"Well, duh," Lucie replied.

But her sarcasm was lost on me because I was trying not to break out in a shit-eating grin, because could it be that Liam Lawson was jealous?

They came to sit with us, and Liam sat at the farthest seat away, with Brett next to him and no one facing him.

Renee was at Brett's other side though and distracted him with talk about the race. Liam spent most of lunch staring at his phone, until a shadow crossed the table and I turned around to see Ulric had come over.

"Not changed your mind then about the race?"

That icy gaze settled on the cocky guy standing in front of him. "Why would I have done that?" Liam said coldly.

Being up this close to Ulric I could see his bottom lip give one quiver, showing he wasn't as brave as he was acting. "Just thought I'd give you the chance to forfeit."

"Don't eat too much this lunchtime," Brett eyed Ulric. "You'll need space for the humble pie you'll be eating later."

"It'll be so nice not having to see your face again around here," Ulric sneered, and he stalked off.

"You'd better bloody beat them," Renee told Brett. "He needs that smug look wiping off his face."

"It'll happen," Liam answered, and then he allowed his eyes to meet mine fleetingly before looking away.

Before I knew it, it was just before one am and we were all at the track. It was a cold night, but luckily not icy. Ulric was in his Mercedes waiting for Liam to turn up. We heard an engine and then watched as a beaten-up BMW drove into the arena.

"What the fuck?" Renee said, walking in the direction of the now stopped car. Brett stepped out and walked over to her. I'd followed along.

"Where's the Porsche?" I asked.

Brett looked at me like I'd just asked him to show me his dick.

"He couldn't race that. What if he damaged it? In fact, I'd take bets that Ulric planned exactly that. Why race when you can side swipe a car and have the driver thrown out of Richstone for ruining a classic?"

"I'd never thought of that," I admitted.

"Yeah, well we've been brought up on looking at every angle and around every corner, so he's racing in my BMW."

"I like it," Renee said, putting her arm through his. "Can I have a closer look?"

I walked over to Liam who'd just stepped out of the car. Ulric was on his way over, so I didn't have long.

"You can borrow my Audi if you like," I told him.

"The BMW's fine. It's as good as an Audi any day of the week. Plus, if it gets trashed, I don't have to rob a bank to pay Brett."

"Is everything okay? You seem a little off?" I asked.

"I'm about to have a race where if I lose we're supposed to leave Richstone, so maybe I'm just a little tense." Ulric had almost reached us. "Where's your boyfriend? Why don't you go annoy him instead of me?"

"You about ready?" Ulric queried.

"Ready when you are, mate," Liam said.

"I thought we'd up the stakes a bit," Ulric smirked.

Liam's chin set taut, "We already made the rules."

"We did, but how about we both take a girl each

riding shotgun? We each choose the girl for the other car?"

I looked around and saw that Ivy had arrived and was approaching us all.

"Well, Ulric," she air-kissed him on both cheeks. "Break a leg, and I don't mean good luck. I mean crash his fucking car off the road and break his leg, or his neck. I'm not particular."

Liam grinned and as his gaze settled on Ivy, I noticed she blushed a little and looked away.

Why would she do that? My suspicions rose. I'd never seen Ivy blush before in her life.

"Suck it, Ivy. The only thing I'm gonna break is whatever speed record pretty boy has set on this track."

"So, what about my idea of girls riding shotgun?" Ulric fastened his arms around his chest.

"I don't understand what purpose it serves," Liam scrubbed a hand through his buzzed hair over his right ear.

"I'm banking on it putting you off, because I vote for Little Miss Principal's daughter sitting at the side of you. You'll have to drive extra carefully then. Can't risk hurting a hair on her head, can you?"

"You up for it?" Liam said in my direction. His words sounded as if it bored him to even speak to me.

"Sure."

"Phoebe!" Renee said. "Don't be ridiculous. It's dangerous. I don't know what's got into Ulric, but he seems to be desperate to push the boundaries."

"You'll be fine," Brett told me. "Liam's an amazing

driver and he wouldn't put you in danger in order to win a bet. He's not like that. Whereas it looks like Ulric's losing his sanity."

"Okay, you take Ivy, I'll take Phoebe," Liam and Ulric shook hands and then it was time for the race to begin.

Crowds of teenagers stood around the arena building and people who had been standing in groups to the side began to move to join them as I walked over to the BMW and opened the passenger door.

I climbed inside.

"Drive as you intended to do. Pretend I'm not here. Don't let me being in the passenger seat put you off," I instructed.

"Who said that?" Liam replied still in his 'give no fucks' tone and he started the engine, slowly driving up to the starting line.

Engines revved and Ulric jeered from his Mercedes before putting the hood up. Brett had taken command of the starting flag. He waved it and Ulric set off.

I counted the ten seconds down in my head and then with another flag wave, it was our turn. Liam floored the car, and we were on our way.

It was the first time I'd been a participant in a race, and at first, I clutched the door handle like my life depended on it. But as my stomach and equilibrium acclimated to the pace, my adrenaline soared, meaning that by the time we were on the second lap, a beaming smile had broken across my face. I turned to Liam, but his own face was a mask of concentration. He looked straight ahead and it struck me how composed he was, his mind on the task in hand, no distractions. I might as well have not been there. Disappointment sunk in my belly like a stone. I wanted to shriek. To scream with pleasure about how much fun I was having, but I knew that was what Ulric was banking on. Ivy had ridden in the cars before. I hadn't. He'd no doubt thought I'd scream with hysteria and put Liam off.

But I wouldn't. I'd sit tight in my seat and let the main driver concentrate while I enjoyed the heady rush of speed, better than any fairground ride I'd ever been on.

28

Liam

I had just one goal in my mind. One target. There could be no distractions. And the girl sat by my side belonged to someone else anyway.

Hurtling around a bend on the third lap I tried to overtake, but Ulric blocked my move.

"Fuck." I yelled out, frustration feeling like it was biting me with a shark's sharp teeth. As I continued onto lap four, I was conscious the opportunity was waning and I was going to have to make another move, even if it was a reckless one.

"If you win, I'll let you fuck me over the car bonnet," Phoebe yelled.

"Won't Stefan have a problem with that?" She shouldn't be talking, and I shouldn't be replying. I was already falling further behind. I put my foot down, trying to block out her voice.

"Of course not. He's my fake-boyfriend. He couldn't care less," she announced.

"What did you just say?" Had I heard that right? She wasn't dating Stefan?

"I'm not dating Stefan Barratt. So... you going to win that alfresco fuck or what?"

She didn't need to ask me again. As we headed into the fifth lap I dropped back for a minute, acting as if there might be a problem with the car. Praying it would make Ulric lose concentration for a moment, I then put my foot to the floor, pedal to the metal.

And of course there was the other thing I'd not anticipated. Not considered. Ulric was used to racing laps on his own. As I pulled up alongside him and knocked into his ridiculously expensive Mercedes, I could imagine the horror on his face as he had to tell Daddy what he'd done to his car. Just that little nudge and he lost concentration, enough that I sailed past him.

"Hell yes," I yelled as we got through to the final lap.

"*Floor it*," Phoebe yelled. I could hear the exhilaration in her voice and with what she'd asked me to do after, the endorphins were obviously running rampant around her body.

As we sailed through the finish line, I came to a screeching halt and then did a donut around the track. Ulric came in behind, but I wasn't interested in gloating over him. I just wanted everyone to leave so I could sink into Phoebe's pussy.

Phoebe was squealing with delight. She exited the car and jumped up and down. The others came over and both Brett and Daniel body slammed me. "You fucking did it, man." Daniel rubbed the top of my head.

Lucie brought over a bottle of champagne.

"Here, Champ," she said.

I shook it, popped the cork and sprayed it over everyone.

Ulric got out of his car and I heard him telling Ivy to go fuck herself and get lost. She screamed back at him, slapping him across the face and then stomped off, the other poison girls running after her. Not two minutes later she left the arena.

"What's that all about?" Renee nodded over in their direction.

"Not so cocky now, is she?" I chin tilted towards Ulric who was talking to his friends while looking in our direction. "Ivy just realised we're allowed to be around school now without any hassle at all. She'll be livid."

Eventually, Ulric made his way over. He held out his hand. "You race well. Next time I'll be on the side-lines placing money on you, while some other punk takes their chances. Best fun I've had in ages," he said.

I shook his hand. "That's it. No trying to renege on the bet?"

"I don't do that. We bet. You won. If you'd have lost, I'd have been helping you pack."

"I wouldn't have left."

"Just remember I'm not the only one trying to get you out of this school," he challenged back. "Party at mine, Sunday afternoon until late. Gives you chance to recover from Jolene's on Saturday." With that he walked back to his car chatting to his friends and then he drove off.

I'd be at that party. I still had other scores to settle with Ulric McDowell. But right now I had other things on my mind...

Taking my phone out of my pocket I texted Phoebe.

Get rid of your friends and meet me at mine. The Porsche is in the garage waiting...

I watched her take the phone out of her pocket and I swear she purposely swept her tongue around her top lip and then bit on her bottom one.

She typed into her phone and I watched, waiting for the message to appear on my screen.

See you there.

The guys couldn't believe I was blowing them off without celebratory drinks. I told them we had two days of partying ahead and so tonight, I wanted to crash. That the adrenaline was leaving my system and taking me down. They gave me shit for it, but went on their way when Renee and Flora asked for a lift home. "You mind?" Brett asked.

"Nah, get to it." I wondered what the girls' parents would think to them being driven home in a beaten-up BMW.

I walked over to Phoebe. "Could I have a lift? The guys have taken the girls home."

"Home, right?" Lucie said, with a smirk. "Well, I'm

going to get my driver to come for me," she took her phone out of her bag.

"I'm taking you home, Lucie," Phoebe protested.

"Nuh-uh. I'm not sitting in a car with you two getting wet for each other. I'll see you tomorrow night at the party where I am going to get myself a guy because you two are making me horny."

"TMI!" Phoebe shouted at her friend's retreating back. Then she turned to me and smirked. "Let's go."

Phoebe seemed to do her own version of the race to get us back to my house. I wanted to devour her, to trail my hands all over her while she attempted to drive, but I'd have been tormenting myself as much as her. The minute she pulled up outside my garage I was out of the car, and around to her passenger door. I unlocked the garage with the electronic key and revealed the Porsche. Picking her up and putting her over my shoulder I carried her inside.

She giggled as I placed her down on the car bonnet. "It's cold. My bum cheeks are cold," she protested.

"Pain and pleasure, Fifi," I teased. I slid her off the bonnet and pulling her to her feet, I stripped her of all her clothes. I drank in every inch of her, running my hands down from her throat, down her breast and to her pussy, where I pushed a finger inside her.

She groaned.

"You want my fingers inside you, Fifi?"

"Mmmmhmmm."

I gripped her chin and tilted her face up to mine.

"Look at me, Phoebe. Do you want my fingers fucking you?"

Her amber eyes stared back. "Yes."

I pushed three fingers inside her, stretching her. She pushed back, taking all I was offering. I could feel her excitement dripping onto my hand. My cock was punching against my jeans. Stopping playing with her, I quickly undid my jeans, pushing those and my boxers down and off, after kicking off my trainers. My top came next until I was as naked as she was. I placed her back on the bonnet and laid her back. Parting her legs widely, I settled myself between them and pushed inside her. Pulling back out, I allowed myself to look at the sight before me for a moment. Phoebe's hair fanned out over the car behind her, her pale skin a stark contrast to the black exterior. But she shone more than the paintwork as the lust flushed her cheeks.

"Tell me what you want me to do," I ordered her.

"Fuck me," she replied without hesitation.

So I did. I plunged into her again and again. Holding one of her ankles behind my own arse, getting deeper and deeper into her. As she got closer to coming, she tilted her hips up to meet me harder and harder, desperate, needy, and begging for release.

I felt my balls tighten and a tingle at the base of my spine and with a grunt I spilled my cum within her as her pussy contracted and pulsed and she shook with the ferocity of her climax.

Little aftershocks pulsed around my cock. It was sensational.

But I realised I was fucked in more ways than one. Because only two weeks into my placement in Richstone, I was falling for Phoebe Ridley.

I told myself it was fine. I could do this, have amazing sex and a good time for a few more weeks without thinking too much about it, but then I'd have to revert to the plan, even if it meant breaking her.

She'd recover. Mummy could buy her a new pony.

But right now, all I would think about was fucking Phoebe into a zoned-out state of bliss, while taking myself along for the ride.

After letting her warm-up in the jacuzzi, I bent Phoebe over the patio table and took her again. My hand fisted in her hair, pulling it back as I play bit her neck. I'd leave no visible marks on her, but she'd know I'd been there.

Eventually, I carried her into the shower where we washed each other's bodies before I had to take her all over again.

Damp and exhausted, I fell onto my bed. Phoebe picked up her clothes but then sat against the side of the bed.

My eyes were closed but I could feel her looking at me.

"What is it, Fifi? Want me to fuck your arse?"

"I- I can stay. Lucie said I could say I was staying over at hers and she'd cover."

I opened my eyes. Fuck. That was another level. I didn't do sleepovers.

My answer must have shown in my face.

"That's okay. It was just an option, if you wanted to wake in a few hours and carry on where we'd left off."

"It's better you go home."

She nodded and began to get dressed.

I could see I'd fucked up. Phoebe clearly felt I'd treated her as some side piece, fucked and discarded. But even though I watched as tears swam in her lower eyelids, she kept it together, stiff upper lip and all that, until she told me she was leaving.

"I'll see you out."

She nodded.

I fastened a robe around myself and walked her to the door.

"Night, Liam," she said, walking to her car. She climbed inside and then pulled up her Audi in front of me. Lowering her window, she leaned her head over to see me. "I would have let you fuck me in the arse, preferably while my hands were tied behind my back and I was blindfolded and gagged," she pouted and sighed. "Oh well, have a good sleep, won't you?" She drove off, leaving me knowing there'd be no sleep, not until I'd rubbed one out on my already sore dick, while I played that scenario she'd just described out in my spank bank.

Every time I pushed at Phoebe, she pushed me right back. It was intoxicating and dangerous to my plans.

I'd made the right decision to send her home, even if my dick didn't agree.

29

Liam

I fucked Renee last night. Mission started.

Brett's text set the show completely on the road. It was time to up my own game, and I had two parties to help with that. But before then it was time to finally do what Principal Ridley had asked me and take Phoebe to my side of the river. Not to remove her rose-tinted glasses about me though, but to lead her even further down the 'wanting to save me' path.

I got out of bed and stretched. My body felt tense and so I decided that before I did anything else, I'd go work-out and try and move some of the kinks. Working out just made me more frustrated if anything. I didn't want to push myself too hard as I didn't want sore muscles at the party. I wanted to be able to move freely. Banging one of the riches was the plan. Renee and Flora were out, so that left Lucie as an opportunity.

But you want Phoebe.

It was like my brain had decided it wanted to torment me. I switched the treadmill up faster and ran until sweat poured off my body and then I hit the shower.

I picked up my phone.

Liam: Hope you're not cross with me for sending you away last night. If it's any consolation I thought about you all night and couldn't sleep.

That should be the right amount of grovelling, I hoped.

Phoebe: Good. I hope you feel like crap.

There was that sass I loved.

My heart thudded in my chest at my internal thoughts.

I didn't love Phoebe. I was incapable of such emotion, but I'd definitely started feeling a fondness for her. That was dangerous. Tonight, I really must remember the plans and forget the fact that Phoebe was an intriguing and beautiful woman.

Liam: I'm going back to Sharrow today. Want to come? See my side of the river?

The dots appeared across the screen.

Phoebe: Sure, what time?

She waited for me outside of the house. Standing there, hip tilted, staring at her phone. She'd tried to dress down in jeans, a sweater, and a thick coat, plus winter boots, but she was so perfectly polished, her hair in a shiny, sleek ponytail, that she'd still stand out a mile in Sharrow Manor. Oh well. It was what it was. Just as I had turned up here and faced the wrath of Richstone, I couldn't predict how Phoebe would be treated at Sharrow Manor.

"Are you sure about this?" I queried as I walked outside and locked the front door.

"I wouldn't be standing here otherwise, would I?" she sassed, making me smile.

We walked down the driveway and all the way over the bridge. It was a long walk, but the day was bright if cold, and Phoebe quizzed me about the place she was about to visit.

"I need to see my mother," I confessed. "I've tried to put it off, but it's been over two weeks now. I'll call my uncle in a bit, but for now I'll show you all the places I hung out and take you to lunch."

"Oooh, you spoil me," she grinned. "Will we see Marlon?"

"I'd not thought about it. We could do. I could call and see if he wants to meet us in the pub."

"It's up to you," she shrugged. "He's your mate. I only met him twice."

I brought out my phone. "He'd have my balls if I visited and didn't let him know."

That made her smile.

I called my friend.

"Hey, I'm almost at the garage. Fancy a pint and some lunch in about thirty?"

"Make it forty-five. I'm not showered yet. You could have given me a bit more notice."

"Just thought about it. It was Phoebe who suggested it."

"What's Phoebe got to do with anything?"

"She's with me. I'm showing her Sharrow."

There was a silence at the other end and then a raised voice. "Are you both out of your goddamned minds?"

Phoebe clearly heard him from where she stood. She looked startled.

"Some Sharrow fuckers robbed Skye's house two nights ago. Took all the nice things she'd been bought. You can't bring anything to do with the riches here and certainly not one of them."

"We'll be fine. We're only having a quick walk around, visiting my ma, and having lunch with you. So get your arse in the shower and come meet us."

I hung up on him.

"I gather he didn't agree with my coming here?"

"He'll be fine."

We walked around Sharrow and I took her to my uncle's garage. Of course he hadn't been expecting me and so when I called his name and he wheeled out from under a car, he already looked surprised and then did a double-take when he saw Phoebe.

"Could have bloody told me. I'd have made sure to wash my hands and face." He looked at Phoebe. "I'm Liam's Uncle Karl. I'd shake your hand, darlin', but you don't want this on ya." He held up a greased palm.

"That's okay. Nice to meet you. I'm Phoebe. Phoebe

Ridley. Liam's living in our guest residence at the moment."

"Oh, you're the principal's daughter? Thanks for taking him off my hands for a bit. He's a handful. Been nice to have a bit of peace and quiet."

"Ha ha," I replied.

"If I had some money myself, I'd rent the place so you could keep him past the end of the school year." He stared at me. "You've got your head down at school, right, to pass those exams?"

"Yes. The exams and studying I have no problem with."

I met his look of concern.

"And any problems at school have hopefully now been dealt with."

He gave me a chin tilt.

"Is Ma home?"

"She should be."

"And dare I ask how she's doing?"

"She's been okay. Had a drink or two of an evening, but I've removed the bottle after that. She's on a waiting list for treatment now. Six months plus though. Reckon we can sort it ourselves by then. I'll cut her down bit by bit."

I didn't have the heart to tell him I'd tried that many times before.

"We're going to walk to The Crown now to meet Marlon. Good to see you and thanks for looking after my ma."

"She's my sister too at the end of the day. Gotta look

out for your own." He went in his overall's pocket. "Here, take my key to the house. Leave it under the mat outside, okay?"

"Thanks." I took the key from him.

"Take care, my man. Once again, nice to make your acquaintance, Phoebe."

She raised a hand at him, smiled, and then said, "Same to you."

We walked off down the street. Someone came zooming past on a motorbike, laughing and shouting. They'd clearly stolen it. Phoebe was taking in all her surroundings.

"I see what you mean about how crammed in things are around here. Your streets aren't very far apart and everything is right next to each other. And there's litter everywhere."

We walked past a bus stop where cigarette butts were strewn all around the shelter. I saw her mouth pucker up. "Your mouth looks like an itchy anus," I commented.

"Ew," she wrinkled her nose. It was too cute.

"Your first look at the differences between where we live. Why a postcode deems how wide your pavements are I don't know." Except I did. Money dictated everything and small pockets of council housing had every square inch milked.

"Show me more," she put her arm through mine. I thought about unlinking us, but then I just went with it. What was it going to do? It didn't mean we were engaged for fuck's sake.

I took her to where I used to live. They'd not done

anything with it yet other than put a large fence around with a 'Danger: keep out' sign.

"It's so small," she observed.

"And there was only me and Ma, and of course Vin when was he was around trying to milk every penny out of my mother."

"It makes me feel guilty about what I have."

"That's good, isn't it? Your family supports charities, don't they?"

"They do, but there's nothing ground level like here."

"Your mum offered the scholarships. She's making a change."

"Maybe. The jury's still out until we see the outcome."

A small pang of guilt hit me because the outcome was unlikely to be good.

"I'm starving. Is it time for lunch yet?" she asked, and I turned my mind to that instead of the coming weeks ahead.

"Hey, Phoebe." Marlon got up to greet us from his seat. He shook Phoebe's hand and then bumped knuckles with me.

"Hi, Marlon. How's it going?"

"Good. Surprised to see you here though. You're a brave woman."

"It's been fine so far," she shrugged.

Marlon looked around. "Don't turn around, but you're being stared at in here. It might be the clothes. It might just be they know Liam's been in Richstone and they don't know you." He kicked me under the table. "Incoming."

"Hey, Liam. Marlon." I turned to see one of the women we'd gone to school with. Lizzie had her hair scraped back in a tight ponytail, and the classic overdone eyebrows, fake eyelashes and trout pout look. Her eyes looked over Phoebe.

"Lizzie. You okay?"

"Good, thanks. Heard you were in Richstone on a scholarship. Is it true?"

"It is. Popped back to see my mum. I'm there until the end of my exams."

"Fancy." Her eyes went back to Phoebe. "You gonna introduce me? I don't think we've met before."

"Phoebe. Lizzie. Lizzie, Phoebe," I said.

Phoebe smiled. "Hi, Lizzie. Nice to meet you."

Lizzie smiled back but it didn't reach her eyes. "Wow, you're one of them."

"One of who?" Phoebe shot back at her.

"The riches."

"My name is Phoebe. If I said, 'oh you're a rat' you'd be insulted."

"Phoebe." Marlon said under his breath as we saw Lizzie's mouth curl into a sneer.

"Sorry," Phoebe looked up at Lizzie. "I didn't mean to be rude. It's just that when you call me one of the 'riches', it makes me feel how you'd feel if I called you a rat. I'm not a 'riches', I'm just Phoebe."

"I don't think you feel like I feel for a second," Lizzie said, "because I had to suck a guy off last night to pay my electric bill and you're walking around with earrings that I bet could pay off my whole years rent and bills."

"Lizzie," I warned.

"She's not welcome. Get her the fuck out of here," she snarled.

I got to my feet quickly. "She's with me, Lizzie. Take your threats and fuck off. We'll be eating here, and we'll leave when I fucking say we're leaving."

Lizzie huffed. "Whatever." As she walked back past us, she spat in Phoebe's face.

To my surprise, Marlon leaped up before I did. He grabbed hold of Lizzie's arm. "You make sure Phoebe's okay," he said. Then he yelled for the landlord and a kicking and screaming Lizzie was thrown out of the bar by the two of them. Apparently she'd been drinking neat vodka for the last hour. So much for paying her electric bill, or maybe she'd sucked more than one cock.

Phoebe had headed for the bathrooms with me in close pursuit. When the next chick went to use the toilet, I stopped her. "Just be a minute. They're being cleaned," I lied.

"You seem different," Marlon said, standing beside me. "If I didn't know any better, I'd think you actually liked the girl."

"Phoebe's okay," I admitted, much to his surprise.

"I think I'd better sit down. You actually sound like you... respect a female, other than your ma."

"She's not scared of me and she doesn't act like I'm the shit on her shoe." It was the first time I'd voiced how she made me feel out loud. "It makes a pleasant change."

"So what about the plan for Richstone then?"

"All still on."

"You're going to trap her?"

I shook my head. "Found out she's on the pill. I'm thinking of trying my luck with her friend, Lucie."

"Mate. I know money can make a huge difference, but you're doing your studying at Richstone which will already help you in the future. What if you had a chance of romance with Phoebe?"

I let out an amused chuckle. "I don't do romance, Marlon, you know that. I said I liked her, not I wanted to marry her. And as if that would happen. Could you see one of the riches letting their daughter date a rat?"

"No, but I also couldn't see Liam Lawson accepting that decision regardless. The Liam I know would fight the injustice, either dirtily or with his fists."

"I've known the girl two weeks. In two years, she'll be a distant memory," I told him.

"Don't say I didn't warn you, when you fuck her friend and burn your bridges once and for all."

The door opened and a fresher faced Phoebe emerged. Her head held high.

"Mine's a pint of beer," I told Marlon. "What do you want, Fifi?"

30

Phoebe

What I wanted was to get out of there. I wanted to scream. I wanted to cry. I was angry and upset, but most of all I felt foolish. Shouldn't I have expected this?

"I'll have a gin please, if that's okay?" I pulled my handbag towards me and moved my hand to the zip to reach my purse.

"No, I'll get these. You're good. Just go sit back down. Maybe sit in a corner this time, just in case, hey?" Marlon said.

I nodded. "Yeah, okay. Thank you."

Liam came back with me and we moved to a seat nearer the back of the pub and in an alcove. I immediately felt better for being more inconspicuous.

"I knew you might get some shit said to you, but I didn't expect that. You okay?" Liam asked.

"I'm fine. It caught me unawares, but it's done with

now, isn't it?" I picked up the menu from the table. "Okay, what do you recommend?"

When Marlon came back with the drinks. Liam waited while he looked at the food menu and then he went to order. I asked for a coke to go with my meal and that he watched them pour it, so it remained saliva free. He smirked at that comment.

Marlon and I chatted until he returned.

Liam had recommended steak and ale pie and mushy peas. The food was delicious.

"Where has this been all my life?" I said as I heartily tucked in.

Both the men watched me.

"What?" I looked from one to the other.

"I've never seen someone eat so fast," Marlon said.

"I've never seen a girl eat so much. I was hoping for leftovers."

I put the last forkful in my mouth, put my knife and fork down on my plate, and then tapped my belly.

"Are we having dessert?" I asked.

One sticky toffee pudding and custard later. I felt like I might need carrying out of the pub.

"I'm going to get going, things to do and all that," Marlon said. He and Liam did that bro fist thing again, and I smiled, waved, and said it had been good to see him again.

"Think you can manage a slow walk around to my

uncles so I can see my ma? Then we'll get out of here. I'm sure you'll have seen enough for one day."

"It's been... interesting." I replied honestly, "I've learned a lot from it. Though I could have done without being spat at. Lizzie resents what I have, and I get that. My money overrides what anyone thinks of me. It wasn't personal, right?"

Liam gave me a slight headshake.

"No, it's not personal," he said.

Our slow walk revealed more of what I'd seen on my way to the pub. Graffiti on walls and across boarded up windows. The smell of petrol from cars being so near. The noise of car engines. People walked past. There was excited chatter between young teens; mum's looking hassled while pushing prams, a phone in one hand while they tried to steer with the other. We came to a halt outside a large building block. I could see several doors on what appeared to be two levels and balconies ran along both.

"It's called a maisonette," Liam informed me.

We both knew this building was about the same size as my entire house and yet from the number of doors, it suggested it housed ten different people or families.

I followed Liam down the path and through a communal doorway. He pressed a button for the lift. The whole place stank of urine. When the lift doors opened and I walked inside there was chewing gum stuck on the walls, food packages strewn on the floor, and a vague odour of cannabis.

Stepping out of the lift, Liam went through another communal door, passing someone going in the other direction.

We turned left and then walked down the balcony until we reached the last door. Liam put the key in the lock and walked inside.

"Ma?" He yelled out, but there was no response. Then we heard giggling.

Liam's pace quickened and he headed in the direction of the noise. I kept up and so when he opened the door, I saw what he did at the same time. His mother was clearly intoxicated. Although she kept laughing, her eyes were glazed, but she kept drinking from the glass in her hand. She was sitting on the floor against the sofa in just her panties, everything else on show, while the guy standing in front of her was looking at Liam, with his mouth open. The guy's cock dangled above Liam's mother's head.

"Fuck," was all he managed to say before Liam launched. Liam's fist came back and then the sound of crunching bone echoed in the sparsely decorated home. The guy's nose exploded with blood, but Liam's arm was already back and he punched him again, this time straight in the stomach. The guy hit the floor and I ran over to his mother, moving the glass, finding her top and trying to manoeuvre her into it. It wasn't easy. She kept closing her eyes and half falling asleep, her head drooping forwards.

The man was on the floor saying, "Sorry," but Liam just rained blows down on him again and again. He was going to kill him if he wasn't careful. The man's lip was now split, his eye swollen to almost shut and he had another cut on his cheek. As he tried to protect his face, Liam kicked him in the back. It reminded me of my father and a keening scream came from my mouth, stopping Liam in his tracks.

"Please, stop. Please," I begged, placing my head in my hands and rocking back and forth.

Liam came to me. "Shit, Phoebe. It's okay. He deserved it. He's been told to stay away and he keeps coming back to take advantage of her."

"L- Liam?" His mother managed a moment of lucidness. "Hey, son. Do you want a drink? I invited Vin round. I missed him." Her head rolled back again.

Liam sunk to the ground at the side of me.

"Phoebe. Meet my mother," was all he said. We both just sat there for a moment, lost in our own thoughts while his mother laid unconscious and Vin mumbled in pain.

When I eventually got over the shock, I stood and moved over to where Vin was. Liam watched me. "Vin. Do you need a hospital?" I asked.

He managed to sit up. I didn't help him. "No hospitals. A damp towel wouldn't go amiss though."

"Okay." I went in search of the kitchen and found a dry towel that looked clean enough and I ran part of it under the tap.

Vin had got to his feet by the time I returned a couple

of minutes later. He took the towel off me and began to dab at his cuts, smarting when he touched the broken skin.

"Let's go," Liam said, and I followed him out of the house, questions on the edge of my tongue.

As soon as we were outside, the first one spilled out. "Why did you leave her with him?"

His eyes were dulled and for a moment he looked skyward as if he might find answers there. His features seemed to sag in his face. Liam looked world weary, a look I'd seen more than once since I'd walked through Sharrow Manor.

"She asked him. After everything that's happened. He stole from her. He cheated on her. After everything, she called and asked him over, and she's drunk again. I'm done. They're welcome to each other."

Before I could say another word, he took his phone from his pocket and dialled a number. "Uncle Karl," he began. He told his uncle everything that had happened and finished with, "make her homeless. Send her to the council. She's not the sister you remember and if you don't, you'll lose either your whole home or at least anything you own of any value."

When he hung up, he stared off into space for a moment and then he straightened his shoulders, fixed a 'don't fuck with me' glare on his face and said, "Let's go. We're done here."

As he'd phoned his uncle I'd noticed the cuts and red marks marring his fists. "When we get back, I need to sort out those cuts."

"I don't need your sympathy or your assistance," he ground out.

"I-" I started, but he didn't let me finish.

"I stopped doing what I needed to do in there because you panicked. Clearly no-one brawls in your presence."

"That's not why—"

"Save it, princess. This." He waved his hand back in the direction of the maisonette, "is what I am. The man you've met in the guest residence isn't me. He's a person who's trying to make life better for himself, but this you saw just now is me. I fuck people up. I put people in hospital. I give people drugs. The real me threatens to carve people's faces up with knives, and blackmails to survive."

His jaw jutted as he scowled.

"You should be scared of me, Phoebe. You should run far, far away."

He was right. I should. With everything I knew about him, I should kick his arse to the kerb.

But somewhere in there was a man who could do better. Who wanted to. Who had the potential. And it called to me, like a whisper on a breeze, heading my way and making me shiver when it arrived.

"I'm not scared of you, Liam. Give me your darkness. I can take it," I told him.

"You don't know what you're saying," he replied.

"Then let's stop talking. There must be somewhere we can go."

His head hung in defeat. "I can't be gentle, Phoebe.

317

Not right now. I have demons in my soul. They don't feel quenched. They want to win, to own, to dominate. To... hurt."

"As long as pleasure comes with the pain."

His eyes were on mine, wary but predatory, like the demons sat behind his irises, ordering him to take the offer.

"Follow me," he said and started walking towards some boarded up shops. His pace was hurried, and he never looked back at me. Walking around the back of one of the abandoned shops, he messed with the locks and kicked it until the door opened. Liam tilted his head for me to follow him inside. He'd just broken into a store in broad daylight and no one had come to see what was happening. To try to stop him.

Inside, the place was almost pitch black with just a small amount of light coming through from the edges of the boarded up windows. Looking around, I saw it had used to be a shoe shop. There was a square seating area in the middle.

Liam dropped onto it and sat with his head in his hands.

It wasn't what I'd expected. I'd thought he'd push me against the wall and fuck my brains out.

He looked up at me and although I could only see shadows on his face, his voice broke my heart.

"Why am I not enough for her, Phoebe? Why can't she try and stop drinking. For me?"

I sank down next to him. "Because she has an addiction and when you do you crave it and search for it, even when you know it's the worst thing you can do and you shouldn't. Even if it can destroy your life, you can't let it go."

My eyes wavered on his.

"Am I your addiction, Phoebe?" he asked me.

"I think you are," I replied honestly, because no matter what he did, I didn't seem to be able to resist him.

His mouth came down hard on mine, his tongue invading. His hands came onto my clothes and he removed them like his life depended on it. Standing, he stripped out of his own clothes and then he pushed me back onto the seating area, moved on top of me and thrust inside. There was no foreplay, just raw need. My core was slick for him anyway. Had been as soon as he'd started kissing me. He rode my body hard, biting my breasts, one hand in the back of my hair, gripped tightly as he thrust. I wrapped my legs around him pulling his arse towards me with every thrust, tilting my hips up so he could hit me deeper. As I felt myself coming undone, I raked my nails down his back knowing it would hurt, knowing it would draw blood. It took him over and he shuddered deep inside me.

"I will ruin you, Phoebe. No good can come from this," he said as he rolled off me.

I didn't reply.

31

Liam

I was a mess.

I should have known that my mother wouldn't have been able to help herself. Now I'd left my uncle with bloodstains on his carpets.

I'd make it up to him. Once I got my fortune, I'd give him a good lump sum too. He deserved it.

Phoebe and I got dressed and walked slowly back up to the Ridley estate. She went on ahead to get showered and said she might see me at the party later.

She would, but I'd be there with my focus on other things. Like other riches. I had to keep my options open. I couldn't afford not to.

Lucie had gotten us our invite to Jolene's house and as we walked up the driveway I knew we were in for a treat. The lights blared out through the windows of her palatial home and you could hear the bass of the music from the end of the drive.

People milled around the hallway and spilled out of nearby rooms. There were already couples making out and guys cheering while egging others on in challenges. We'd brought a couple of packs of beers with us, so we walked in the direction of the kitchen first, placing the cans down on the worktop counter.

"Everyone has to do a Jell-o shot," a guy said, pointing to a tray, "and then eat a special cookie." We all took one of each, downed the Jell-o shot and then moved on. I deposited my cookie in the nearest plant pot. The others could do what they wanted but I needed to keep a clear-ish head.

There were still people who talked shit to us and looked down on us, but a snarl in their direction soon brought that to a swift end. Then the girls arrived and once again Daniel and Brett were otherwise occupied. I couldn't complain. They were only getting on with their own futures. Daniel had turned up tonight dressed in designer clothes. Flora had dragged him around the shops and insisted on buying him some. I had to admit he scrubbed up well.

That left me with Lucie and Phoebe. "Would you two like a drink?" I asked them.

"Yes, a couple of vodka's would be good, but if you could swipe a bottle that'd be even better," Lucie sounded like she was giving me an order, but I let it go. She was more forceful than the others; it was just her way.

When I brought the drinks back, Lucie looked over my shoulder. "I can see Jessica over there, so I'll leave you two to it."

I put my hand on her arm to stop her. "No, stay," I said. "The night is young."

She frowned but stayed. I continued to ask her questions about herself while largely ignoring Phoebe. She kept looking at Phoebe as if to ask what the hell was happening. It just made it even more entertaining. The problem was I was thinking more of hate sex with Phoebe than I was about scoring with Lucie. After half an hour, Phoebe said she was off to visit the bathroom. Lucie moved to go with her, but again I put my hand out. "Oh don't do the girly thing of going together. It'll leave me on my own."

She sighed, but she stayed, and I continued to ensure I asked about Lucie's favourite subject—herself. Phoebe didn't return, and I kept Lucie going with drinks and fetched her a cookie. The hard-edged Lucie began to soften. Perfect.

Or so I'd thought.

"Phoebe really likes you," she announced.

"And what about you? Do you like me?" I nudged her shoulder to increase our bodily contact.

"No. I liked Marlon, but Marlon left," she sighed. "It's typical. That always happens whenever I like someone."

Who'd have believed it? A stoned and drunk Lucie was a morose and miserable creature. I caught the eye of the girl Lucie had pointed out earlier and nodded for her to come over.

"Hey," she said.

"Lucie's had a bit too much booze. Can you get her a coffee and try to sober her up a little?"

"Sure," she sat beside her. "You okay, Lucie?"

I wandered off leaving them to it and walked through the party. I'd see if I could spot Phoebe now and find out how jealous I'd made her.

"Drink. Drink. Drink. Drink. Drink," I heard chanting and then, "Come on, Phoebe." I hastened my speed to see her down a vodka shot and slam her glass down. She grinned. I listened as the next person had their turn at 'Never have I ever'.

Phoebe was grinning stupidly from ear-to-ear, clearly pissed out of her brains. She saw me and her eyes narrowed in disdain. She turned to the next player who'd also got to take a shot. "Drink, drink, drink," she shouted, smacking her hands down on the table with every word, while Stefan downed his shot.

I stood there taking her in. Her brown hair now held the smallest of waves. She'd turned up with her hair up and some tight curls framed around her face but since then she'd literally let her hair down. Her face was now flushed from the alcohol and frivolity, her body swaying with the looseness of someone who no longer gave a shit. The guy drank their shot and Phoebe screamed, 'Yeaaaasss', and whooped, her hand in the air. And then she leaned in and kissed him. Their mouths were clumsy against each other's. Two people who'd had too much to drink.

I stalked over and the minute they broke apart, I hauled her out of the seat. "Think you've had enough to drink now, Fifi."

She stood there, hand on her hip. "Who are you? The fun police. Fuck off, Liam. I'm not done yet." She grabbed the card off the next player. "I'm having another turn." She held the card up, squinting her eyes to read it. "Never have I ever posed for pictures in just my underwear," she read.

"Well, have you? If not, drink," the girl whose turn she took said.

Phoebe stood up and peeled off her top revealing a white, lacy bra. "Or someone could take some now. Stefan, you got a camera?"

I turned to see Stefan walking over to her. "Think you might have had a bit too much alcohol now, Phoebs. Time to make a move." He came to my side. "Can we take her back to yours so she can sober up before she goes home? I don't fancy handing her over to her parents in this state."

"Sure."

Phoebe had taken off her skirt and was now only in her underwear and high heels.

"How about you, Liam? Do you want to take my photo? Oh no, you want Lucie's picture now. Silly me." She quickly snagged another shot off the table and drank it down.

"Phoebe," Stefan admonished.

"What?" she wiped her mouth off on the back of her hand. "No one took my photo, so I lost."

"Come on, Phoebe. Get back dressed and we're going to take you to Liam's to sober up."

"It's not Liam's. You're not taking me to Liam's. He's just a lodger," she spat out. "A temporary tenant."

Stefan rolled his eyes in my direction. "This is more easily solved. Can you do me a favour, Stefan? Her friend, Lucie. I left her in another room along with another girl. Lucie was drunk too. The girl was going to help sober her up. Can you make sure that's the case, and I'll deal with Miss Ridley?"

"Makes sense. Lucie lives round the corner from me. I'll make sure I drop her off home after a strong black coffee at mine. I'll find her and warn my mother we're on our way. You sure you're okay with Phoebe?"

I picked up her abandoned clothes, and then I picked up the half-naked woman herself throwing her over my shoulder. "I got this," I told him.

He laughed. "You do."

I was glad I'd only had that one vodka jelly. I'd driven to the party and now I could drive back and not need to leave the car behind to pick up the next day. The other guys had got taxis, but to be honest, my mind wasn't on any of them right now.

Phoebe had protested all the way to the car, but I'd

ignored her. I leaned her against the car, holding her trapped between the car and my thigh while I got the passenger door open. Then I put her inside.

Driving back to mine, Phoebe huffed and sighed a lot at the side of me.

"Got something to say, Fifi?"

"Stop calling me that."

"No."

"Why have you just manhandled me out of the party? You were wanting to be with Lucie. Or did she not return your affections?" Her eyes glittered with scorn.

"I just wanted to see if it made you jealous, me flirting with another woman, and it did."

"So you were game playing. Trying to make someone who's already fucking you jealous. You make no sense at all, Liam. And for your information, I wasn't jealous. I moved away from the two of you because I was bored."

"You tell yourself that."

"If I was jealous, I'd have dangled another man in front of your face, but I didn't."

I could feel my jaw tighten.

"When you thought I was with Stefan you hated it. What's up, Liam? Have we found someone you are actually fearful of?"

"What the fuck are you talking about now? You're off your arse drunk."

"You're scared of me, and the fact you like me. The fact you don't want anyone else to have me. You flirted with Lucie because you can't handle the truth."

At the next junction where there was some farmland, I screeched the car off the main road and onto the dark lane.

"What the fuck?" Phoebe screeched. "I banged my head, you bastard."

Flinging open the car door, I walked around to Phoebe's side and pulled the door open. Unfastening her seat belt, I got hold of her hair and pulled her out of the car.

"Owww. What are you fucking doing?"

"Get on your knees, Phoebe," I gritted out. This woman had me in knots, churned up, and I needed to feel in control again.

She looked down. "It's gravel."

"Get. On. Your. Knees." I shouted, pulling her down with the hair still tangled around my hand.

She sank down.

"W- what are y- you doing?" She half-sobbed. "Please don't hurt me."

I let go of her hair and pulled up her chin.

"Have I ever hurt you? Really hurt you?"

"N- no."

"Then you have nothing to fear and everything to enjoy."

I pulled down my jeans and boxers freeing my cock.

"Do you know how much I wanted to beat the hell out of that guy you kissed tonight?"

She shook her head.

"I imagined him like Vin, bloody and useless on the

floor. And then you stripped off down to your underwear in front of everyone." I twanged her bra strap. "This is for me, Fifi. My eyes only. Do you understand?"

"Yes," she said, but this time when her eyes met mine the fear was gone and lust and heat burned brightly behind her amber gaze.

"Open your mouth," I ordered and she immediately obeyed.

We were both past the point of no return with each other now. Resistance was futile. The dice were thrown, the games would play out and I'd find a way where I got my money and the girl.

I didn't know how she'd done it. Whether it was because she concealed a dark side just as black as mine, but Phoebe had made my cold, dead heart flicker with life.

And after seeing her with another man tonight, I couldn't let her go. She was my possession: a mirror, one that reflected back all my darkness, yet brought the light.

She sucked my cock on her knees in the gravel and I pulled out at the last minute and sprayed my cum onto her chest. Opening the car door, I threw her top at her. "Clean yourself up and get in. You can sober up at mine, while I'm fucking you."

I took her in the hallway, the bedroom, the shower. I couldn't sink deep enough into her. She begged me for more, insatiable. Even when she'd had a coffee and I'd

ANGEL DEVLIN

made her a sandwich and she'd sobered up a little, she made me eat out her pussy while she ate her sandwich.

It was just past one am when she got up off the sofa.

She began to wander around collecting her clothing up and as I watched her, I realised I didn't want the night to be over.

"Tell them you're staying at your friends." I said to her back.

She span around. "What?"

"Tell. Them. Your parents. That you're staying at your friends tonight."

"You want me to stay the night?" she queried.

"I thought I'd made that clear."

Her hands came to her hips. She was giving me her attitude while completely naked. She was a walking wet dream. "When I asked you before, you made me feel like an idiot. I walked out of this house, rejected, and humiliated. So, if you want me to stay, have the balls to actually fucking say it."

My nostrils flared. "Stay the night, Fifi."

She smirked. "See that wasn't hard, was it?"

I stroked my cock. "No, but this is. Make the call and then I'm going to fuck your arse."

Those amber eyes glittered with triumph and desire. She made the call, and I did everything I'd promised. I claimed one of her firsts and it was glorious. As she laid in the crook of my arm after, my body pressed against hers as her soft breaths came with her settled sleep, she didn't know she'd claimed one of mine.

The first time I'd ever let anyone stay the night.

She was the closest thing I'd ever had to a girlfriend.

And for a man who had never not had a plan, here I was in unchartered waters, hoping I could find a way to a life-raft that contained both kinds of riches. The money and the woman.

32

Phoebe

I woke up and for a moment I wondered what the hell was going on. My eyes opened to unfamiliar surroundings, and a quick realisation that I was in bed with someone. The memories slowly came back.

Shots.

Kissing.

So much sex.

Liam asking me to stay the night.

His arm was cast around me now, heavy around my middle. It was the first time I'd stayed the night with a guy.

Staying there, wrapped in his warmth, I thought about how this could only end in heartache. I had to remind myself we were just friends-with-benefits, and not let lust trick me into thinking this was or could be anything else.

I was going to leave Richstone and so would he after he'd taken his exams. He'd be moving onto new things.

And then it struck me.

What if I asked Liam what his plans were for after he left here? I doubted he'd go back to Sharrow Manor. So where would he go, and could I hitch a ride?

Maybe Liam was my way out of Richstone?

Needing the bathroom, I moved his arm off me. He remained asleep and I moved into the en suite. After having a pee, I walked over to the sink to wash my hands and caught sight of myself in the mirror. Mascara had run below my eyes making me resemble a panda, my hair gave bed head a bad name, and my lips were puffy from having been kissed so damn much.

I touched them with my fingertips. I was a complete mess and yet there was a frisson of excitement in my belly, along with a spark of hope.

But I'd see where the coming days or even weeks took us before I raised my plan to leave Richstone. To mention it to Liam right now would be to panic him into thinking I wanted his ring and his babies or something. I imagined a trail of dust on the driveway from where he'd run away so quickly which made me smile to myself. Liam had nothing to worry about. I didn't want to tie him down. I wanted to make myself free.

Opening the shower stall door, I turned the dial so the water started pouring out, and then switched the temperature dial onto a nice hottish temp. I let my mind quiet while the water soothed and relaxed me. Let the jets hit hard onto my neck and shoulders, releasing any tension. Goodness knows how long I'd been in there when the bathroom door opened and Liam walked in.

"Morning," he said, his voice loud and gruff, but muffled slightly by the patter of cascading shower water. He relieved his bladder, clearing giving no fucks about personal space and then brushed his teeth.

He approached the stall and slid open the door and for a moment I thought he planned to join me. "I'm going to make some coffee. Figure you need a bucketful after the state you got yourself in last night."

With that he left the room.

If I'd expected a sweet smile and sweet nothings, I was clearly sleeping with the wrong guy. Looked like the loose brick in his wall from last night had been firmly cemented back into place this morning.

Once I'd dressed, feeling a little stupid in my party skirt and jacket, I made my way out of Liam's bedroom and into his kitchen. I perched on the stool at the island. I did have a slight nagging pain at my temple, but I'd had worse. The coffee would help, along with a slice of the toast Liam was fixing.

"You know Brett and Renee are fucking too, right?" he announced.

I startled a little, both at his statement and also in the way he'd delivered it.

"Renee and I haven't had chance for a catch up in the last few days, but I can't say I'm surprised. And Flora and Daniel too no doubt."

"And Lucie told me last night she liked Marlon and was sad he'd left. Quite the little group we have going on right now," his eyes glittered with challenge, but I wasn't sure what it was.

"What about it?"

"Do you think any of these pairings are going to stand up in the cold light of day? The rumour mill will be out in force after last night's party. Lucie left with Stefan, you left with me. I carried you out of that party in your underwear. Brett and Renee, and Daniel and Flora made no attempts to hide their budding romances. I wonder what their parents will think of it when it reaches their ears?"

I folded my arms across my chest. "Well, Flora won't care, because her father's a cheating scumbag. She's all for the love not the money. I'm not sure about Renee. She doesn't take much in life seriously and I doubt Brett's anything more than a fuck." I took a bite of toast.

"Lucie's shit out of luck with Marlon. He's not interested."

I finished chewing and swallowing. "I'm sure she'll get over it."

Liam studied my face for a moment, until I fidgeted on my stool under his spotlight. "And us, Fifi. We're just friends-with-benefits, but what do you think will happen if your father hears about last night?"

I shrugged on the outside even though the inside of me shivered. "I don't know. I guess I'll have to make sure I'm seen with Stefan tonight. I mean, like you said, we're just friends-with-benefits."

We stared at each other but neither of us challenged the other. Even though I'd stayed the night.

Liam took his phone out of his pocket. "I dealt with Ivy. Even though she's still acting like poison at school, she won't do anything to get the rats out of Richstone, and she'll largely leave you alone."

My mouth opened slightly. "You did? When? You never said."

"Thursday night."

"And what did you do? Do I get to know?"

He gave me a curt nod, but he hesitated, the phone in his hand.

"I'm a big girl, Liam, and you've told me the kind of guy you are. I don't expect it to be pretty."

"Don't say you weren't warned," he said, passing the phone over to me. I pressed play on the clip.

I watched Ivy Sackville get on her knees, and although to anyone looking quickly she'd seem as eager as fuck to be unzipping Liam's trousers and putting his dick in her mouth, I knew Ivy much better than that. Her eyes told the truth. That she wanted to close down her mouth and bite hard.

"Oh, baby, yes, just like that," Liam put his hands at the back of her head.

Ivy broke off after a few minutes. "I want you, Liam, so bad. Please."

"Thought I was a rat to be rid of?" he said.

"It's expected I say that. I'm the queen of Richstone Academy. What would this do to my status, but please, fuck me. I need it. I beg you."

"Put my cock back in your mouth and make sure you swallow," he ordered, *"then we'll see."*

She grabbed his dick and put it back inside her mouth again and the video cut.

I handed the phone back to him. The jealousy was eating me up inside, even though I knew the reason why he'd done it.

"So that's why she could barely look at you at the race."

His eyes widened imperceptibly. "That's all you have to say? Not a thank you? I did what you asked after all."

My voice took on a tart tone, "Thank you, Liam, so very, very much. You're an absolute superstar. However can I repay you for what you've done."

He smirked and steepled his fingers. "Are you jealous, Phoebe? Even though you know the only mouth I want my cock in is yours? You get that, right? This was a means to an end. A way to shut up Ivy Sackville. She won't get us rats out of Richstone and she agreed to fake mock you at school but to largely back off. This video is my insurance. The rest of the rats were there watching. I could barely keep my cock erect and do you know how I did it? How I managed to keep it hard? I thought of you."

I picked up my coffee and took a sip as if what he was saying didn't bother me at all. He strode over, took the mug from me and threw it at the wall. The liquid went everywhere, the cream mug breaking into pieces, a chip in the perfect wall where it had hit with force.

He grabbed my chin and thrust my head up.

"I said, are you jealous, Phoebe?"

"Yes," I bit out. "Are you satisfied? I'm jealous. And I was jealous yesterday when you started that shit with my friend. I want you. Is that what you want to hear?" My body was shaking with rage now, and I pushed him away from me and jumped off my stool. I poked my finger in his chest hard. "Despite the fact you have your heart locked in a cage, despite the fact you don't have a penny to your name, despite the fact that sometimes you act like a complete cunt, I was jealous sick because I want you to myself."

I'd backed him up against the wall and it felt so fucking good. My hand dropped to his jeans and I unfastened them, slipping my hand down his boxers and firmly around his cock.

"This is mine. It goes in my mouth and in my pussy and in my arse. Do you understand that's what I need from you, Liam? Fuck the friends-with-benefits, I need you to take a chance. Even though I can't go public with you right now, I need you to be mine."

My eyes fixed on his, the anger and frustration between us was palpable, and if the tension had been visible it would have swirled around the room like an angry storm cloud, gathering itself to wreak havoc.

"You say you're so fucking tough. There's nothing tougher than admitting your vulnerabilities, Liam Lawson."

His hands clutched my shoulders and he quickly switched us around. My hand dropped from his trousers, falling to my side. His hard length pressed into me as he held me to the wall by my shoulder in a firm grip.

"You want my vulnerabilities? I didn't have any, Phoebe, until I met you. None. Not even my mother, not really. Do you know what made me change my plans for how I'd deal with Ivy? When I saw you with Stefan. When I saw him comfort you, trailing his hand down your face. All I could think of was tearing him away from you and screaming that he needed to get the fuck away from you because you belonged to me."

His admission had my heart beating almost out of my chest.

"I thought you were together, Fifi, and it killed me. As I punished Ivy, I closed my eyes and imagined I was punishing you."

"Do it," I told him.

"What?"

"Punish me now. Hate-fuck me right now against this wall."

He pushed his jeans and boxers further down and pulled up my skirt, pushing my panties to the side and thrusting inside me.

"That's for making me think you were with him," he said, slamming into me so hard my back ground against the wall.

I raked my nails down his back knowing I was splitting the skin in places and making him bleed. "That's for letting Ivy put your cock in her mouth."

We weren't kind in our actions, hating each other with every thrust, every scratch. We didn't kiss. Instead, we stared into each other's eyes the whole time. Eyes narrowed and angry, while we told each other with our bodies that we'd passed a line we'd never intended to reach.

A line where friends-with-benefits had become an 'us'.

He spilled out inside my body, his own body juddering with the frenzy and I followed over, going lightheaded because of my racing breath.

"I don't know what happens from here, Fifi." He rested his forehead against mine. "I still don't see how anything good can come from this. Not in the long run."

He pulled out of me and went to grab some kitchen roll from the counter. He returned and began to clean us up. We adjusted our clothing and stood there, facing each other.

"I'm planning to leave Richstone, Liam." It seemed the right time to tell him after all. "I'll explain later. There's a lot you don't know, about me and my family, but right now, I have to get back before my parents ring Lucie and find out I didn't stay at hers after all."

"Just answer me one thing." He ordered. "When? When do you plan on leaving?"

I worried my top lip with my teeth. "As soon as possible. But I need to get my hands on some money so I can start somewhere new. My father has my money out of reach. I need to be able to stay off-grid for a while." I held myself tall. "I'm not saying this because I think we're going to run off into the sunset together, Liam. You just need to know that I don't plan to stay here."

"We'll figure it out," he stated, then his voice dropped lower, softer. "You go now, and I'll see you at the party later. Right now, I need to get my head around the fact that you've sent me into a tailspin and exhausted me with your insatiability."

I laughed and then gathering my belongings, I made my way back to the house.

My father must have been watching and waiting for me, because as the house came into view, he was there, pacing backwards and forwards.

Did I turn back around and run?

No. I would stick up for myself. I would shout and scream this time if he started on me. I would not try to keep this behind closed doors. Not anymore. My mother would find it much harder to deny it, if it played out in front of her eyes or ears.

I closed the space between us, and saw the spittle leave Maxwell Ridley's mouth as he shook with rage, stepped forward and grabbed my jacket. He pulled me up close so that spittle hit my cheek as he raged at me.

"You stupid, fucking little slut. I know what you've been doing." He waved his camera at me. "Do you know what this is, Phoebe? It's a video sent to me by Allen Barratt. He was suspicious of Stefan suddenly announcing he was dating you, and he paid two private investigators to follow the two of you to see what was really going on. With my blessing of course."

"Wh- what?"

"One night. That's all those investigators needed. One. Night. They followed you both home. Stefan brought back an extremely drunk Lucie. You know, the Lucie you were supposedly staying with last night. But you..." he shook the phone again. "You were seen giving oral sex to the rat who is living on our fucking property in my mother's former home. Have you been fucking him there, Phoebe? Sullying the memories of my mother, while you let a piece of shit defile you?"

I pushed my father away, pulling my jacket back down.

"It's none of your fucking business who I sleep with. I'm a human, not your property. I'm not a business deal."

"No, you're a whore."

I slapped him across the face. For a moment we both stared at each other in shock, and then I saw the point the rage snapped his sanity and took over all common sense. His lips pulled back, his teeth bared. His eyes were so wide they showed the whites. With a guttural roar he barrelled into me, grabbing my arm hard and forcing me to the ground. I did my best to fight him off, managing to get to my knees, but I was no match for his rage, so I did all I could do. I screamed and screamed. It wasn't hard as he pulled me across the driveway by my right arm. "You like being on your knees in the gravel, you slut? Here we go then. Enjoy," he shouted as he dragged me through the rough stones on our drive. The pain was excruciating as the skin on my knees tore open, while it felt like my arm would come out of the socket. His grip was so hard I'd be bruised for days. There was no sign of his temper abating and as he let me go, and his leg came up again, I put my hands over my head as this time it was aimed at my face.

But then he wasn't there. After a few seconds of nothing and then the familiar sound of Liam's voice, I moved my hands and turned to where I could hear a commotion. My father was on the ground with Liam punching him straight in the face. Liam laid my father out cold and came rushing over to me.

"What the actual fuck? What the actual fuck?" He said, taking in the state of my bleeding knees.

"It's not the first time," I spat out, in between spasms of pain.

Sounds crunched out across the gravel and my mother came and stood behind us.

"Now do you believe me?" I said, letting my head fall back against Liam. It was all too much. I was on the brink of passing out.

"Get up, Phoebe, before someone sees you," she ordered.

33

Liam

I hadn't been kidding when I'd said Phoebe had sent my head into a spin. I needed some time to think. To reassess what my plans were. I'd only thought about trapping one of the riches or getting out of here at the end of the academic year, following my exams.

Now Phoebe had told me that she planned to escape Richstone. But to go where?

Was this thing happening between us what I said it was, something that couldn't go anywhere? Would I not care if she left? The fact I was concerned about her statement about leaving told me more than I was happy to admit.

Fuck.

I left the kitchen ready to throw myself back on my bed for an hour and then spotted Phoebe's phone on the bedside table. Shit.

As she'd only been gone a couple of minutes, I grabbed it and headed off up the drive after her. If her parents were around, I'd just say I'd found it on the driveway.

When she came into view, I thought I was seeing things.

Phoebe on the ground being dragged across it by her father, who was yanking on her arm.

What the actual fuck?

I took off at speed, and as I got closer, I could hear him yelling at her. He was so gone in his hatred he'd not even heard me approach and he was looking the opposite way when I launched myself at him.

And now? Now I turned to Daphne with an incredulous look on my face.

"That's your fucking response to the fact your husband just dragged your daughter around the ground and was about to put his foot in her face? That she should get up?"

Daphne's cool gaze moved off her daughter and towards me. "If you want to remain in Richstone, I suggest you help get Phoebe and my husband inside, before anyone else sees them. Luckily, it's Sunday and the only staff around are in the kitchens at the other side of the building."

I went to open my mouth again, but Phoebe put her hand over mine and shook her head.

"Let's take th- this inside. I want to see what my d-

346

dear mum has to say about what she now can't deny has been happening."

"This is what you were going to tell me? He's done this before?" I cracked my neck from side to side. I would kill the bastard.

"Liam, please? I need some painkillers and to get my knees cleaned up."

"Okay." I began to help Phoebe to her feet. Daphne stepped forward. "I can take Phoebe, you get Maxwell."

"No," my mouth went tight like I was tasting something bad. I couldn't believe what I was hearing and seeing. In all the shit I'd endured in Sharrow Manor, neither me or my friends had suffered abuse at the hands of our family, no matter their limitations. "He can fucking stay there until I have Phoebe in the house and someone, either you or me, is looking after her injuries."

"Very well. I'll go on ahead and get things out of the medicine cabinet." She walked off leaving her husband, who was now groaning, on the drive. I didn't care if he walked off or dropped dead. I picked up my girl and carried her inside.

My girl. I'd thought of her as my girl.

I swallowed hard. My life was getting more complicated by the second.

I placed Phoebe down on the sofa in the living room and Daphne walked in shortly afterwards carrying a bowl with warm water, cotton wool, and some other medical supplies.

"I'm going to clean your knees, Fifi. It's going to sting. But I have to make sure there's no gravel in there or dirt." I turned to Daphne. "Get us the scotch."

Her lips pursed but she went to the drinks cabinet and passed it to me.

"Your husband's probably come to now, you might want to see if he can stand up and walk himself inside." I told her in a dismissive tone. I didn't need Daphne watching me do the job she should be doing, looking after her daughter and making sure she was okay.

"I'll leave you to tend to her injuries, but I'll be back shortly. We need to talk." With that she walked out of the room. Not for a single second did she lose that haughty headmistress look. Where was the concern for her daughter?

I dipped the cotton wool into the warm water and began to clean up Phoebe's legs. Her knees had taken the worst of it, but some skin was scraped off other parts of her legs too from where she'd been dragged as her skirt had ridden up. She had road rash on her stomach and I cleaned that up too.

Phoebe gritted her teeth throughout, even though at times tears stung her eyes. When everything was clean and dry, I applied antiseptic ointment.

"I'm guessing your first aid skills come from patching yourself and your friends up?" Phoebe tried a smile but gave up and took a swig of the scotch instead.

"You bet. This ain't my first rodeo." I arched a brow. Placing everything down, I sat beside her on the sofa and pulled her in close. "Why, Phoebe? When did this start and what on earth caused it?"

There was silence and for a moment I thought she didn't want to talk about it. Then she took another swig of scotch and started to talk.

"It started a couple of years ago. He'd never laid a finger on me before then. He'd had the occasional mood where I knew to stay out of his way, had yelled at me plenty, but he'd never touched me. Then the dinner parties started in earnest where he began to talk about future husbands. I was sixteen for God's sake so I told him not to be ridiculous. My insolence got me backhanded across the face the first time."

She cuddled further into me. "It's not like it's happened very often, although this last few weeks he's got much worse."

She told me what had happened leading up to her being dragged along the driveway.

"Allen Barratt was suspicious and now he knows what I've been doing with a rat. Stefan's mother will be in her element. She now has power over my mother by the fact that she can delight in my fall from grace."

"Would she accidentally release the footage?"

"No because I'd ruin her," Daphne walked back into the room. She took a seat in the adjacent armchair. "Maxwell is in our bedroom seeing to his injuries and will be staying there."

She picked up the phone from the coffee table.

"Hello, could we have some tea, coffee, and water brought into the living room? Thank you."

"Unbelievable. Why don't you ask a secretary to take notes," I drawled out. "Is there any point where you're going to ask your daughter how she is?"

Hate-filled eyes met mine. "I can see that apart from a few scrapes, she's perfectly fine. He didn't break any of her bones, he just lost his temper because she was caught acting like a slut instead of a Ridley."

It looked like the truth was out, here in the Ridley living room. Phoebe's 'perfect' life was a complete sham.

Daphne said nothing further until the refreshments had been brought into the room and the staff had left.

"So how long has this been going on? I told you to show Phoebe the rough side of life and discourage her from it, not to sleep with her. Did you know that, Phoebe? The man comforting you right now agreed to encourage you to marry a riches and in return I'd pay him a lump sum when he left Richstone."

I felt Phoebe tense up in my arms and so I ran my hand down her arm soothing her while I addressed Daphne. "No. I told you what I wanted you to hear. Anything so that I got my opportunity here. And, yes, before I met Phoebe, I did think of her as a potential opportunity to exploit, but then I did meet her, and I found out she was worth so much more than the shackled life you want to offer her."

Phoebe pushed out of my arms and I thought she was going to push me away, but she just wanted to sit up and face her mother. "You would make financial deals so I married well? You're not much better than Daddy, are you? Parents are supposed to love their children, not use them as bargaining chips."

"Your father's business is sinking fast, Phoebe. So far, we've managed to keep it away from public knowledge but it's only a matter of time. Eddie is working himself to the bone to find investors and sign new publishing deals to breathe life into the company. He is doing his part, getting up early every day and working late into the night. All you have to do is be pleasant and marry someone who has a fortune we can use to back up our own. You're the selfish one. Do you not think you should play your part in the family's upkeep?"

Phoebe huffed, "You tell me I'm acting like a whore? You're my pimp, are you not? Yours is just a more high-class establishment."

Daphne wasn't listening. She carried on with her own speech. "Stefan would have been perfect, but no, instead, you for some reason lie to us saying the two of you are dating. Instead, you're actually hooking up with a rat." Daphne slow clapped. "Now, I have to rethink everything. Because of your stupidity."

"I'm not marrying a riches, Daphne." Her mother's eyes widened as Phoebe called her by her Christian name.

"If you don't do as you're told, I'll release the video myself. I'll let the whole of Richstone see you on your knees giving the rat a blow job. Then I'll disinherit you and let you leave in disgrace and I'll just make Eddie step up and stop his bed hopping."

"You'd do that? To me, your own daughter?"

"What about you see this the other way around? We've brought you up to want for nothing and it's not enough for you. You're all 'more, more, more'. Settling down with a nice guy isn't enough for Phoebe Louisa Ridley, oh no. So with complete disregard for all of us, you embark on whatever this is with a rat from Sharrow Manor. Are you willing to throw your whole family under a bus for him?"

Phoebe tensed up again, her hands clenching.

"She doesn't need to answer that question. What do you want, Daphne? I think we're past listening to your sorry excuses for why you treat your daughter like trash. Yes, yes, she has everything monetary that can be provided, but what about love, Daphne? I might have come from nothing, but my parents loved me. My father loved me unconditionally."

"Not enough for him to stay with you," she smirked.

For a moment I felt like I'd left reality. Winded. Side-swiped. Alternate universe. She'd brought my father's suicide up as a snide comment. I closed my eyes and took deep breaths. I would ruin Daphne Ridley, but she wouldn't press my buttons now. She was goading me, wanting me to reveal my own dark depths. To what? Attack her in return. So she could show Phoebe I was no different to her own father?

I made sure I enunciated each word. Right now, I faced my enemy and they would know by the tone of my voice and the intonation that they were listening to a ticking time bomb that would detonate, but when I said so. "My father's depression took him over and he acted the only way he felt he could. But I'm not going to explain any of this to you further because to you, his death, something that had a monumental effect on me, is nothing more to you than a throwaway insult. You're the trash, Daphne, not Phoebe."

"What do you want, Daphne?" Phoebe repeated my earlier question.

Daphne swept imaginary stray hair from her forehead. "I want this swept under the carpet for now. If you must insist on seeing each other then keep it to the bungalow. Oh, don't look so surprised," she addressed Phoebe. "I know that telling you to stop won't do any good, and I'm confident this will burn itself out in no time. There's no future between a riches and a rat."

Daphne poured herself another coffee and then moved her gaze to me.

"I expect you to put more effort into studying for your exams though, rather than my daughter's anatomy. I have a lot riding on the success of you three students at Richstone Academy. This can lead onto my becoming an expert on the effects of socioeconomics. I've already been drafting a book with the potential to become a huge bestseller, which is also yet another way of lifting the company." She switched her attention back to Phoebe. "Phoebe, you'll be required to attend dinners with the family as usual."

"And what's in this for me?" Phoebe asked.

"If by the time the results come in for your exams, we've managed to turn around our fortunes and no longer need you to secure a partnership, I'll allow you to go to university outside of Richstone. A few years where you can explore this other magical life you believe happens outside of here."

"You've got it all worked out, haven't you, Daph," I said snarkily.

"Liam, you get to stay here in the bungalow, screw my daughter, and if things go to plan, you'll leave with a large lump sum, enough to start afresh somewhere far away from us all. So don't act like you're put out by what I'm proposing. Or am I supposed to believe that if it came to it, you'd choose my daughter over a handout? We're all motivated by money, even those of us who already have it. Perhaps, even more so when you see that life having the potential to slip through your fingers."

Daphne placed her cup down. "All I'm asking for is time. And it will mutually benefit us all. I'll make sure your father never touches you again, Phoebe. I managed to get him to stop before and I will again."

"Wh- what do you mean, before?" Phoebe asked, her bottom lip quivering.

"When he came to see me for therapy. When I first met him. I couldn't exactly say your father consulted me because he'd been abusing his girlfriend, could I? So we told you children it was work-related stress. I fixed him and stole his heart... and his fortune," she smiled as if she deserved a fucking sainthood. There was definitely someone in need of therapy and we were talking to her.

But if we could hold out for the lump sum and for university, then Phoebe and I could leave.

We needed to talk. For her to tell me about her plans

to leave and about whether we could find another way without having to wait for Daphne Ridley's offers which all relied on the company being saved. I'd gamble if the odds were favourable, but this was nothing I knew about. There had to be other options out there.

"What about Stephanie Barratt?" I asked Daphne. "How can you actually stop her from sharing the video. How can you ruin her?"

"Because I know Allen got one of the rat staff pregnant. It cost them a large sum of money to pay for the abortion and the silence," Daphne's upper lip quirked, and she tucked her hair behind her ear. "I'd seen the little looks that passed between them when we'd been at dinner. Being a psychologist has always given me an edge. When she left so suddenly, Stephanie told me that one of her family members was ill, but like I said, I'm a psychologist. I know a lie when I hear one told to me by an idiot. I found the girl and paid her a life changing sum of money to tell me everything, and then I kept this information to myself for a rainy day. Today Allen called and that day came. Stephanie wasn't so smug when I phoned and told her what I had on video myself shortly after Allen's call to your father. She'll say nothing, but obviously there'll be no more talk of you marrying Stefan and we'll adopt a friendly truce for in public."

Those eyes landed on mine again. Probing, assessing, not trusting.

"Don't try anything stupid, Liam. I'll always win. I always do," she said, standing up. "Now if you'll excuse me, I have much to do today, starting with dealing with Maxwell."

She walked out of the room, her speech finished, and I realised that Ivy Sackville wasn't the queen of Richstone Academy. Daphne Ridley was.

But I would knock her off that throne somehow.

Smash her crown and stab her with her own sceptre.

34

Liam

"Come on. I'll take you back to mine and we can digest this morning, get you some pain medication, and see what we do from here."

The effects of the scotch were beginning to take effect, along with the come down from the adrenaline. Phoebe looked exhausted and in total disbelief. She was rubbing at her arms absently.

"Is this really happening?" she eventually said.

Movements sounded outside the door and we both tensed. I didn't know what Phoebe was expecting, but I'd been anticipating her father coming down to confront me. The man had totally taken me in with his welcoming manner, and I was angry at myself for letting him fool me.

But it was Eddie who entered the room. He looked like he'd just finished partying from the night before and maybe he had. Looking from his sister to me, he ran his fingers through his hair and then addressed his sister. "What's going on?"

"You'd better sit down," I told him.

I did most of the talking, Phoebe still sipping slowly at the scotch and becoming increasingly withdrawn. Eddie was largely at a loss for words, not having had a clue what was going on.

He dropped to his knees in front of his sister and grabbed her hands carefully, enclosing them in his own.

"Why didn't you tell me? I would have helped you."

A tear ran down her face as she finally looked at her brother. "I was too scared. I just thought if you were keeping him busy with the business then I would try not to antagonise him until I could get away. I'm going to leave, Eddie. As soon as I can."

Eddie dropped his voice to a low whisper. "Phoebe, I will help you, okay? I'll find out how to access the business accounts. I'll get you some money so you can escape. Just give me some time."

"Your mum said the business is struggling?" I asked him.

He nodded. "It's been better. We are working on it though. My father's been stuck in old ways of working. If he releases the reins a little, I could do more to improve our prospects."

"Then maybe you need to tell your mother that. See if she can give you more control. Let her fight your father on your behalf."

"I'll talk to my mother today and see what I can do.

I'll let them think it's for the family, but this will be for us, Phoebe. I'll take control of the business, and I'll give you control of your own life. I promise."

He placed his arms around her, tenderly and gently.

"Look after her, Liam, while I help sort this shitshow out," he said. We exchanged mobile numbers.

"I love you, sis," were his parting words as he left the room.

"Let's get out of here," I said, and I tried to get Phoebe up off the sofa.

"I'm not feeling so good," she said.

Whether it was the scotch, the shock, or the pain, I held back Phoebe's hair while she puked all over the living room carpet.

I poured her some of the water so she could refresh her mouth when she was finished and told her to spit that onto the carpet too.

"Right, time to take you back to mine," I said.

We took a very slow walk down to the bungalow, but the air was fresh and it sobered her up a little and seemed to bring her around. She didn't say one word the whole time.

After getting inside my place, I opened my bedroom door and pulled back the duvet. I got Phoebe to carefully climb into bed and then I sat next to her.

"I'm going to get you some water and painkillers. You need anything else?"

She shook her head, "I just want to close my eyes and block the world out."

I fetched the painkillers and a glass of water and

helped her sit up and take them. Her eyes were already closing as I left the room.

Phoebe slept for several hours. I kept checking in on her. In the end I'd had to go into the gym and train hard because rage burned through me. Pounding on the treadmill, my thoughts centred around the fact that I felt like a rat in a trap, and all mainly because I'd developed feelings for the woman in my bedroom.

If I didn't give a shit, I'd just threaten to expose Maxwell and the abuse. Yes, I had no concrete proof, but the rumour and Phoebe's injuries would be enough for the gossip to start. It would be enough for Daphne Ridley to pay me to leave.

But it would leave Phoebe and my friends adrift.

It was just a few months, and I wanted the education anyway. It was my insurance if a payoff wasn't forthcoming.

But if I hadn't started to get a fucking conscience... I needed to talk to my friends tonight. They were going to certainly think an alien had taken over my body. Well, until I told them my plans for the party later.

I called Brett and asked for Renee's number. After briefly telling him what was going on, I asked him to ring Daniel and Marlon and get them to mine. Then I called Renee and told her what had been happening with Phoebe and her family.

She couldn't get here fast enough.

"Listen, bring the others if you want. Whatever you

think. I have my friends coming, but we need to talk and deal with a few things, so we'll be going to Ulric's party as planned. It gives you time to speak to Phoebe, see what she wants to do, or just do girly shit, comfort her, paint your nails or something."

"Oh, Liam. We can all see how you've fallen for Phoebe. Your eyes follow her everywhere. I thought it was just lust, I mean she is fit as fuck, but now I'm changing my mind. But I'll pretend you're still a hardass okay? Still leaking testosterone wherever you swagger because you have too much."

"Go screw yourself, Renee Anderson."

"I would, but that need's been taken care of via your friend. See you later, and thank you, Liam. I won't forget this."

As I put the phone down, I realised that this fucking place was changing me.

I was still a rat... but of Richstone.

Everyone had arrived at the house and the girls had rallied around Phoebe once she'd woken up. She'd had some soup and some toast and looked a little less pale, but no less fragile.

"We're going to leave you to it," I told Lucie.

"Thanks. I know you're not being a selfish bastard who still wants to go party, but actually a decent human being who's giving us some private time. It's appreciated."

"Oh I want to go party," I confessed, "but only

because I have a couple of scores to settle and this is the perfect time to do so."

"Be careful, Liam," she warned. "The last thing we need is the rats and the riches at war. Not when so much is now riding on you three staying around and passing your exams."

"Don't worry. Unlike a true rat, I don't leave a trail of piss. Not my own anyway," I winked, and then I called the others ready to leave.

We got in the car and as I started to drive, I began to chat more freely with my friends. "Listen, I'm taking care of Bailey tonight first." Bailey was the red-haired guy who'd said I smelled of shit on my first day.

"What are you planning?" Daniel asked eagerly, ever ready to step up to the plate.

"I don't know yet. Some opportunity will show itself. But it's on. I told him he wouldn't get away with it. But..." I hesitated. "Lucie spoke to me earlier and she was right when she said we can't do anything now that would majorly cause shit for us rats."

Brett met my gaze through the rear-view mirror. "Because of Phoebe? I thought we were finding ways to blackmail the riches? This is a perfect opportunity, so why aren't you taking it? Is there something bigger in the works?"

"I..." I couldn't bring myself to say the words.

"He's fallen for Phoebe."

"You've fucking what?" Marlon, who was riding shotgun knocked into my arm.

"Try not to run us off the road, you twat," I yelled.

"Well, it's hardly surprising. The tin man has a fucking heart? What the actual fuck? Pull this car up right now and explain yourself."

"I'll stop near the bridge, okay?" Marlon was being dropped off back at the bridge given his history with Ulric. It only took a few minutes. A few minutes that gave my friends time to digest my sudden about turn. Marlon was shocked, Daniel ecstatic, and Brett angry.

"I'll leave it for you to argue out with the others," Marlon said, pushing open the car door. "You know where I am with things now. Getting my education in Sharrow still and hoping one of you lot drops me a few quid when you make your millions." Wishing us a good night he headed off back home.

I turned to face the others in the back.

Brett's jaw was taut.

"C'mon then, man. Out with it," I said.

"We're here because of your idea. A better education and/or entrapment. I'm on with things. Have sunk my dick in riches pussy."

"And I'm not asking you to change that, although maybe we should just concentrate on the education side of things and on a pay off from Daphne Ridley at the end? I mean, what if Renee got pregnant, then decided to keep it? What if her family didn't pay you off and you're left with actually paying towards the fucker? We never thought of that, did we? Before I came here, I just saw them as stuck-up rich bitches, but it's not what they've all turned out to be, is it?"

"Now you start this? Now it might have happened already." He thrust the car door open and stepped out. "I'm out of here. I need time to think."

I rolled down my window. "Take all the time you need. I know what I'm saying is a shock. It is to my own ears, so I don't expect anyone else to just roll over and agree. I need time to think too. Maybe I'm talking with these newly discovered emotions and when I wake up tomorrow, I'll have farted them out or something."

That brought a slight smile to Brett's face.

"We'll sort it," he said. "Just go deal with Bailey, and then, yeah, I think you need a good sleep and to pass some wind, because I know what's happened to Phoebe is awful, but bros before hos, remember?"

I nodded.

"And then there were two," Daniel announced from the back of the car.

I sighed. "I am acting weird, I know. I don't know what the fuck's going on with me. That's the truth."

"I can tell you exactly what's going on with you, mate. You met a girl, and for the first time in your life you've realised that your heart isn't encased in stone like you've always said. It was just frozen in ice and Phoebe is thawing it."

I couldn't have this conversation, couldn't face up to that being a possibility, so I quickly changed the subject. "So you and Flora, hey? You think it's the real deal?"

He nodded. "I do, and you know what else? I never

spiked the condoms. As soon as I met her, I knew I wanted her for real. And I know it's not been long, and things could change, but what if they don't? We've agreed to just enjoy the ride."

I smiled. "So, I don't have to ask you to stop because you've not been doing it anyway. Which means, in fact, the only person properly doing what we originally agreed is Brett?"

"Yup. Me and Flora have got caught up in the moment a couple of times, but I'm a firm believer in fate. The dice will lay where they fall and hopefully, Flora and I will live happily ever after whether it's somewhere a bit shitty, or somewhere nice. We'll be in love and we won't care."

I shook my head at my mate. Sometimes I wondered how biology had managed to come up with him.

"You ever think of writing fairy tales, pal?"

"I'm not the one who rescued a girl from the big bad wolf today, Liam. You are."

"Fuck me, you're right." I started up the engine. "Time to party and rediscover where my man parts have gone."

35

Phoebe

"Why did you never say anything? I mean, I never even saw a mark on you. Was I selfish, just not noticing what was in front of my face?" Renee's face was furrowed with concern.

"It didn't happen that often before this last year. I don't know why I didn't tell you. At the time I just felt ashamed and a bit like it couldn't really be happening. But now you all know, it seems stupid to have not told you before and asked for help."

"You can come and stay with me," Flora said. "I'll look after you until you're healed and then you can still stay, so I know you're safe from that bastard. And as for your mother. I always admired her, being a working mum, but now I despise her."

"There's always a room at my house too," Lucie added.

"And you know there is at mine, anytime." Renee squeezed my arm.

"I know. Thanks, all of you. But I'm not making any decisions yet. I can't believe what's happened today. I mean, my dad didn't just punish me for rebelling, he completely lost it. I reckon he could have killed me. Does my mum expect me to go back there? To live with him?"

"Fuck knows. Anyway, shall we get you out of this bed? I've brought you some new pyjamas. We'll redo your dressings and then go sit in the living room. Then it's pizza and girly gossip. Sound good?" Renee said.

I nodded. "Yeah, that sounds really good. As long as you three do most of the talking. I'm just... exhausted."

"Yeah, well, we're not doing *all* the talking, because we want the lowdown on what's been going on with you and Liam. I'm not surprised you're exhausted," Renee winked.

"And we need to discuss the competition because Flora managed her makeover and I've fucked Brett. When's the finishing date, Lucie, because I reckon Fifi can get Liam to sort Ivy now."

"It's already done, so we're all in and done," I told Renee, who stared at me for a second before rolling into action.

"I'll do your dressings. Lucie, get the pizza ordered. Flora, sort everyone a drink and plates. We have lots to talk about, Let's go."

I laughed at my friend. "What would I do without you, Renee?"

"You won't ever have to worry about that." A serious

look came over her face. "Don't ever keep things from me again. You're my best friend. It kills me to know you've been suffering like this and I had no clue."

"I'm sorry."

She shook her head. "No, babes, you have nothing to be sorry about."

"We all need to be there for each other no matter what," Flora announced. "I love you guys. We should say it more often." She turned to me. "I love you, Phoebs."

As she went to turn to Lucie next, we all joined in, laughing at the chorus of 'love you's' echoing around the room.

The other two left the room to carry out their tasks and Renee helped me make my way into the en suite. Opening the mirrored fronted wall cabinet, she exclaimed over the amount of stuff she found inside.

"Is he a pharmacist?" she asked.

"Something like that." I cast my eyes over the different pill bottles, plasters, bandages, creams, and other supplies. The cabinet was crammed. "He's punched at least two people in the last few days. I guess you have to make sure you're covered when you're handy with your fists."

"What are we doing, getting involved with these people, Phoebe?" Renee was rarely serious and the use of my full name, along with her subdued tone, gave me pause.

"Having fun?" I suggested.

"So, that's all this thing with Liam is? Fun? Just until the end of the summer, and then you say your goodbyes?"

I shrugged. "Who says it's even going to last that long? I didn't expect it, so I don't know what's going to happen. My feeling is that I'll go to university and he'll find his next adventure. What about you and Brett?"

"Sex. Pure and simple. In fact, he's so cold towards me when we're not fucking that I'm not sure why he wants me. Though under the sheets it's amazing. I don't think it's anything other than quenching a need for either of us. He sets my panties on fire, but he doesn't warm my heart."

Liam does both, I thought, but I kept my mouth shut.

Once the pizza arrived and I'd eaten a couple of slices while sitting in the soft waffle pjs and new robe my friends had bought me, I felt a million times better than I had when they'd first arrived.

"Thank you," I said, sitting back and resting my head against the back of the sofa.

"Okay, so while we're still eating and you've finished, we want the lowdown on Liam, and on you winning your part of the competition," Lucie ordered.

I saluted her. "Sir, yes, sir." I picked up my water and refreshed my mouth, and then I told them about the times Liam and I had got together and about what he'd done to Ivy. I didn't tell them about how he could be rough with me and how that was what I wanted. That was our private business. But the rest of it, I was happy to share.

"He made her suck his cock? Fucking hell, to be a fly on that wall. I bet she got home and bleached the inside of her mouth."

"You can't mention it to her though, as tempting as it might be. She'll still be giving us shit at school. It just won't have any substance to it."

"Well, that sucks," Lucie giggled, "but not as much as Ivy did. Okay, so how are we deciding the competition winner then? Putting all the names in a hat?"

"I don't want the boat," Flora said, her voice small. "It's where my daddy sees his bitch."

The rest of us looked at each other.

"Let's leave the boats to the Daddy riches, hey?" I said. "I don't need one either."

"Me neither, but thanks, Lucie, for trying to come up with something we don't already own," Renee added.

"Yeah, it was harder than I thought, but... there's still the trophy."

"I don't need a silver rat trap. I have my rat. He's all I need," Flora announced.

We all groaned.

"That narrows it down to us two," Renee said.

"I'd be tempted to hit my father around the head with it and end up in jail, so you have it," I told her.

"Whahhoooo. I won," Renee yelled, getting up off the sofa and doing a little dance. "When do I get my trophy, Luce?"

"It's on order, so sometime next week."

"It will be a reminder when I'm old of the time the rats came to Richstone and I fucked one behind trees and in an old banger of a car I'm unlikely to ever see again. I'll be able to tell my grandchildren about when their granny was a ho."

We all fell about laughing, and even though it made my tummy hurt because of my injuries, it was the best feeling in the world. I might have shit parents, but I had amazing friends. And so maybe, the best thing to do, was to finish my education and go to university because that way I could stay in touch with them all. Not have to cut off all ties. Today had shown me just how much I counted on them.

"Would you go in the bedroom and get me my bag, someone?"

Flora jumped up. "Are you wondering if lover boy has tried to contact you? Awww," she bunched up her shoulders and looked at me like I was a two-year-old who'd drawn a nice picture of her family. Returning a few minutes later, her face was completely changed. "You have a message, but it's not from Liam."

She handed me the phone and I took it from her, swiping across the screen to see the message notification on my front screen.

Mum: We agreed that your father should enter a facility for a time to deal with a new bout of work-related stress. Eddie can take care of the business in his absence. You're safe to return home.

I let out an exhale of disbelief. "Daddy's in therapy. All is well and swept under the carpet. I'm invited back, let me go and grab my things straightaway." My voice was thick with derision.

"Just play the game, Fifi, until you can get out of there for good. The summer will be here before you know it."

I was thinking about my brother. He might soon be in more of a position to help me. But he'd have to be careful. I didn't think for a minute that my mother wouldn't keep a very close eye on things.

Six months. That was the most I'd have to wait before I could get away and go to university. That was the worst-case scenario.

I could manage that. Six months of seeing my friends as much as possible, studying, whatever happened with Liam... and research. I'd start looking at where I could go to university, and where I could go if I wanted to not be found anytime soon.

Renee's phone pinged and we all stared at her. She picked it up and read it and then let out her own sigh.

"I've been dumped. The rat said he doesn't think our hooking up is a good idea. That it's distracting him from his studies, and that he hopes we can still be civil in the group."

"I'm sorry, bestie," I said.

"Ah, don't be. He had the personality of a piece of toast, and I have many, many battery-operated boyfriends to replace him with."

Flora's hands went to her ears. "TMI, Renee."

"So what do I reply?" she asked. "I want to be okay with it and let him know what he's missing at the same time."

"Snapchat him a shot of your pussy with the caption, 'Bye, cunt'?" Lucie suggested.

"Lucie!" Flora said and then started giggling.

"How about you just put, 'No probs,' and then when he's got the horn around you again—because he will, you're gorgeous—you just look at him like he be cray cray and you sashay away swinging those damn fine hips and arse, reminding him of what he turned down," I swept my hand in a flamboyant gesture.

"Yeah, I'll do that." She texted him and put her phone away. "You want me to stay the night or come to mine?" she asked.

"No, thank you. I'm going to stay here," I sighed. "Mum had told me I could move into this place after Liam left, but all my excitement's gone for it now." I thought about how excited I'd been playing designer with Movadi/Andrew, not thinking twice about spending the money because I was so used to it being there. I wondered what Andrew had really thought of me. I might have thought I knew his true identity, but it seemed I'd not even known my own. I'd said I understood why he put on a persona and then I'd acted like a spoiled, little rich girl anyway. I knew now that he'd just humoured me so I didn't reveal his secret, because to do so could have ruined his own life.

"You'll get your own place, away from them," Lucie said.

But would I ever be away from them? Mum had mentioned university. She hadn't mentioned what came after that. And I only got to go to university if the business was back on track.

The girls left after fussing over me and making sure I was back in bed. I looked at the rest of my messages. I had one about a handbag I'd been on the waitlist for which had now come into store. I deleted it. I didn't need another goddamn handbag. And there was a message from Stefan.

Text me when you can talk, and I'll escape and call you. I'm at the party.

I texted him.

I'm free to chat xo

"Hey," he said a few minutes later, and I knew from his voice that he knew stuff. I just didn't know what.

"Whereabouts are you at the party? Can you talk?"

"Yeah, I've walked down the drive, there's no one around. I'm just heading for the park and I'll grab a seat on a bench."

"You'll be freezing."

"I'll be fine. It's you I'm worried about. Liam told me about your dad and about what mine had done. I had no idea he'd had us both followed. I'd thought he was acting weird today. I mentioned us having you round for dinner and he said he'd let me know. Usually, he'd have had my mum sorting the caterers for it within the hour."

"Yeah, I think I was just supposed to dump you from our fake dating."

"You know I'm always here for you, right? Always."

"I know, and likewise. Good luck with whatever heiress they line you up with next," I laughed.

"Yeah, if it's some mean troll, I'm waving my white flag for you to elope with me. They can't make me get married if I already am, right?"

I laughed again. "Thanks for everything, Stefan. Please stay my secret friend, and don't let our parents get in the way."

"Never," he said. "Right, I'd better get back to the party. Shit was getting wild before I left. Ulric's gone all out on the party table. They're all fucking high."

"What about Liam and the others?"

"Liam came with Daniel. No one else. Haven't seen them for a while. Not surprising though. The place is heaving."

"Okay, I'll let you go. Have fun, but stay safe, yeah, and we'll have a sneaky coffee or something when I'm feeling more myself."

We said our goodbyes. I climbed out of bed to brush my teeth and then once more exhaustion overtook me and I fell back to sleep.

36

Liam

Ulric's house was unlike anything I'd ever seen except for in films. I couldn't believe that one family got to live in this vast space. It didn't even look like a house from the outside, with its largely glassed front. More like an art museum. There was security on the doors, as if it were a club. They made sure we all stuck to the rooms we were allowed to go in.

"Fuck me, Liam. This is ridiculous. How can some people be so rich, and then there are people out there homeless?"

"Because life isn't perfect," I said simply.

"I don't need this," Daniel stated, waving his hand around the vast kitchen. It was the size of a basketball court. "I'd like to be comfortable, sure. Not worrying about where the money to pay the bills was coming from, but this isn't me."

"It's not me either, and if it makes you him," I pointed at Ulric, acting like the king he thought he was. "Then I definitely don't want it."

As if he heard me say his name, the man himself looked over and then saying a few words to his band of followers, he moved away from them and began to make his way over to the two of us.

"Didn't think you were coming," he said.

"Been a busy day, but we wouldn't want to miss a party hosted by the King of Richstone Academy. Nice palace by the way."

He smirked, and then took out a walkie-talkie from his jacket pocket. "Security. If Liam Lawson or Daniel..."

"Preston," Daniel added.

"Preston, want to do a tour, show them around. Thanks. Over and out," he finished.

I was torn between wanting to laugh at his pathetic showing off, and resisting the urge to pummel into his features until he could no longer utter commands.

"Well, there's plenty to drink, and plenty to eat, including pussy..." he winked and nodded over to a group of girls whose skirts were definitely higher than their IQ.

"Thanks."

"Although a little bird tells me that Daniel is romancing a riches. You must think you won the lottery, Danny." He tilted his head towards my friend. "But remember, you'll never be able to give her what she really needs. To provide. Enjoy it while it lasts. I've always thought Flora would make the perfect wife. Is she submissive?"

Daniel jumped forward and I put my arms around him holding him back. "He's not worth it, Daniel."

I waited until Daniel calmed down.

"I can give Flora something you can't," Daniel stood tall and imposing and addressed Ulric, who stood around an inch shorter. "Love, respect, and my massive cock. Only a little birdie told me that yours was such a worm it wasn't worth pecking at."

"Your day of reckoning will come, rats," Ulric snarled and then he walked away.

"Remind me why we came here again," Daniel asked me.

"Because they're drunk and stoned and we have scores to settle," I told him. "So let's grab some drinks, settle in, and wait for the opportunities."

I watched and waited, keeping a distance from, but my eye on Bailey Trainor. He chatted to some girls and I watched as he seemed to make his decision of which was tonight's choice of a hook up. Another girl looked hurt. Perfect.

I followed her with my eyes as she walked towards the drinks lined up on the counter. She picked up a glass of champagne and drank the whole thing in one. "I'll be back," I told Daniel. "I'll call you if I need back up."

Standing at the side of the girl, I passed her another glass of champagne and smiled. "You look like you could use this?"

She took it from me and smiled. "Yeah, I really could,

but I'm not sure I should drink any more. I might do something stupid."

"Oh?" I faked sincerity. "You okay? You look a little upset."

"I've been better." She held a hand out. "Casey. You're Liam, right? I'm in the lower sixth, but we've heard all about you."

I shook her hand. "I bet."

She grinned. "Well, my first impression of you is a good one anyway. Thanks for passing me the drink." Her eyes strayed towards Bailey.

"He's not worth it," I told her. "He's one of the King's cocksuckers. You can do better."

That made her laugh. "Yeah, I guess you're right. Looks like I can do better for friends too, seeing as my supposed best friend who knew how much I liked him is the one now by his side."

"His loss," I said, picking up a glass of my own. "Cheers," I told her, and we chinked glasses and drank up.

Soon she was drunk enough she didn't notice me steal her phone. I made my way back to Daniel, explaining my plans and then opened it up.

"Bingo," I said as I found Bailey in her contacts. I opened a new message and typed it.

Please meet me. I'll do anything. Entrance to the maze. Ten minutes?

Ulric's extensive gardens included a summer house and a maze. I didn't expect many to be walking around the maze on a cold night. It wasn't long before I got a reply.

Anything?

Yes, anything.

I want to come in your face.

I said anything.

"Is he looking at her?" I asked Daniel.

"Yep, like all his birthdays have come at once. And of course, because she's lovesick she was looking right back at him."

I waited and then sent another text.

You go first so I know you're definitely coming. I'll follow and see you there.

Oh I'll definitely be COMING.

Bailey broke away from the group, the friend looking pissed off. "Go talk to the friend and distract her while I get rid of the blonde and deal with Bailey," I directed Daniel.

I went back to the girl whose eyes were glazed. "Casey?"

"Yeah?"

"I found your phone on the floor. Look, I think you need to call it a night. You seem pretty wasted. Do you have a driver waiting or anything?"

She looked at me and at her phone. "Can you go in my contacts and phone Simon. That's my driver. Tell him I'm ready and I'll be there in a moment. Then can you help me get to the car? I've drunk too much."

I did exactly that which meant the security guys

thought nothing of me disappearing down the driveway and they weren't covering the gardens, so they didn't see me cut across the grounds and headed towards the maze.

It became clear that the McDowell's had dogs when I spotted a couple of small turds here and there. No doubt they were the handbag type synonymous with most of the riches. I bet they'd never picked up a dog shit in their life. I was looking where I was going trying to avoid stepping in any, while looking forward to delivering a warning punch or two to Bailey's kidneys. Then I suddenly had a better idea.

'Has someone brought shit into class?', 'Found it'.

I took a pair of plastic gloves out of my coat pocket. I never left home without a couple of pairs. They were always so damn useful. I picked up a piece of turd. It was hard and easy to handle, thanks to the cold ground.

And then I picked up pace, heading to the maze and I dipped around the entrance.

"Hello, Bailey," I said, and then while he got his head around the realisation that he wasn't coming in Casey's face, his mouth dropping open either in shock or to plead, I grabbed him by the throat and made him open wide. Stuffing the shit in his mouth it softened, coating his teeth as I kept forcing his jaw closed. It stank, but I was too focused on my task to care.

"You ever sniff me and say you found shit again, and next time it'll be out of my own arse and I'll video it and show it around Richstone," I warned him. "Say a fucking word of what I've done to anybody, and I'll climb through your bedroom window and sit my arse on your fucking face, you hear me?"

He nodded and I let him go. He was retching and making noises I'd never heard before in my life. It was a job well done, both mine and the dog who'd dropped it in the first place. I pulled off the gloves and stuffed them in the hedge and then slipped back past the maze, back into the car park and then returned as if from accompanying Casey. I walked back in like I hadn't just dealt shit out, literally.

"How'd it go?" Daniel asked when I returned after washing my hands thoroughly first.

"Perfect. I'll tell you all about it later. Did anyone notice I was gone?"

"Doubt it, they're all getting even more wasted. Ulric's high as a fucking kite."

"Let's go enjoy the house tour," I jerked my head in the direction of the hall. "While I take a moment to warm up and think about what to do about the king."

The security guy, who introduced himself as Benjy, was friendly and actually looked happy to be doing something other than standing at the foot of the stairs with his colleague. He told us how he'd show us around the downstairs, but the upstairs was off limits. There was no boasting with it being the security guy and he was still clearly in awe of the place even though he worked there.

He showed us into a large room, the frontage of which curved around. It housed a huge pool that followed the curve.

ANGEL DEVLIN

"What I wouldn't do for a dip in the pool," Benjy said. "I mean, have you ever seen anything like it?"

"No," Daniel replied, his eyes looking it all over once more. "I still can't believe people live like this."

"Stupid thing is, it's never even used. Mr McDowall is always too busy for leisure. Mrs McDowall says the chorine would ruin her hair, and Ulric can't swim. It's a complete waste."

"Stupid," I said, a plan forming in my mind.

It was another hour before the tour had finished. The downstairs was just that huge. Home cinema. Several sitting rooms. A gym. A spa room with tables to lie on for a massage. A library. There was even an entire playroom for the dogs. Benjy said the McDowell's owned three Pomeranians, but they were all currently with Mrs McDowell who was visiting her mother for the weekend. I'd been lucky the gardener or housekeeping had been slacking on poop scooping duties.

When the tour came to an end, we both thanked Benjy implicitly, shaking his hand and wishing him well.

"You two dying or something? That sounded a little final." Benjy grinned.

"Ulric only invited us here to show us what he had, and we didn't," I told him. "We'll not be invited here again."

"It doesn't make him happy," Benjy confessed. "You two take good care of yourselves."

"Thanks."

. . .

384

Going back to the party I made my way over to Ulric, who could barely meet my eyes, he was so far gone.

"Have to say, you have a great place, mate. That pool. Would be perfect to go in now. Skinny dipping with all this pussy."

"Nah," Ulric said, but his friends and the other people around him started chanting. "Pool party, pool party." Exhaling loudly, he radioed his security. "I need extra security and lifeguards. We're going to the pool." His face contorted in annoyance. "If I say we're having a pool party, we're having one. Sort it, that's your job." He put his radio away and nodded his head like he was listening to a great R 'n' B track. "Who wants to get wet? Poooool Parrtaaayy."

People began to move, waiting outside the doorway to the pool room. "Keep your phone handy," I told Daniel.

Ulric had clearly quickly been to get changed while everyone waited and he sauntered back in wearing his pool shorts. A couple of his main entourage had clearly borrowed some too.

"Sir, are you sure about this?" Benjy addressed Ulric.

"Not you as well. You don't query my decisions. You're staff. You just do what you're told," Ulric spat out.

As I walked past Benjy, I touched his arm. "I'll keep an eye on the idiot."

"Thanks. The team will too."

People began stripping off and diving in, yelling that it was on the cool side, but heated. I approached Ulric. "You not going in, man?"

"No. I'm gonna relax on a lounger. Probably having

my cock sucked. Isn't it time you went home?" His eyes lit up. "Hey, can rats swim?"

He reached out to push me in the pool. I grabbed him taking him with me. We made an enormous splash, but the room was so loud, no one was paying much attention. Coming up for air, I checked to see if the lifeguards were watching us, but both were too busy dealing with people trying to take glasses into the pool or trying to get in when they were too wasted. It was carnage and I saw security on their radios. I didn't have long.

Ulric was trying to grab hold of me, to get an anchor to come up for air. Not fucking yet he wouldn't. I moved away and then I placed a hand on his shoulder holding him down under the water. Just long enough for him to know what I could do if I wanted. Exploit his weakness. Diving under the water I pulled his shorts off while he struggled for air. Then I grabbed him and hoisted him up, swimming to the edge with him in a grand display of rescue. I shouted for help and Benjy and a lifeguard ran over, helping to pull him onto the side of the pool.

Ulric laid there naked and spluttering, and showing off that small dick Daniel had been told about. My eyes met Daniel's as he snapped pictures, ready to send over the school chat.

Increased security came in and so did Richard McDowell, who I watched apologising profusely on his son's behalf. Security cleared the party faster than a bad fart cleared a room. Richard approached me as I stood with Daniel, getting ready to leave.

"So you're the one who stopped my son from drowning while under the influence," he said.

"Yes, Sir." Daniel and I introduced ourselves.

"Thank you. This won't be forgotten. Luckily, I was only in a restaurant down the road. Thought I could trust him. Never again." He shook his head. "Listen, I know how much stigma has been attached to your arrival. Hopefully, what you did here tonight will improve things. I'd also like to offer you a reward," his voice dropped. "For your silence about what happened here tonight."

Daniel sighed. "Does that mean I can't share the dick pic I took?" he challenged Richard.

Richard only smiled. "Come see me when you've both graduated. Maybe I can make better use of the sharp, raw potential I see here."

He drew a chequebook from his pocket and began scribbling across two cheques.

"Five thousand pounds for your silence, Liam, and five thousand for you to erase the photo, Daniel."

We took the cheques.

"I trust you won't mention this transaction to Ulric," I arched a brow.

"The only information Ulric will be getting is of how to behave under my roof."

We bade farewell and left the house, walking back down the driveway, passing the last few party stragglers who hadn't managed to leave yet. We climbed inside the Porsche. "That was one fucking stonking party," Daniel grinned, waving his cheque. "That's the first part of my savings, for me to start my better future."

"I forget what a badass you can be, Mr. What About the Dick Pic," I chuckled.

"I may end up living somewhere else, but Sharrow lives in my soul," Daniel grinned. "Now can you take me home, because we have school in the morning."

37

Phoebe

I woke to see the bedroom door further ajar. Liam was doing his best to be quiet, but with me being in a strange place and having already slept earlier, I'd disturbed anyway.

"I'm awake," I whispered, the room so quiet apart from his movements.

"Hey." He came over and sat on the bed beside me. "How are you feeling?"

"Like I've been in a fight, but I'll live." I shuffled up the bed. "I think it's time for some more painkillers though." I switched the bedside lamp on, squinting a little as my eyes met the bright light.

"Let me go get the tablets and some fresh water."

When Liam returned, he passed me two capsules and a glass of water and as I took them, he stripped off out of his clothes. My eyes watched him hungrily.

"Not a chance, Fifi. You need to heal." He slipped in beside me, "though a careful snuggle is not out of the question."

I looked up at him. "The man who told me he would ruin me is now asking me if I want a snuggle? Have I taken hallucinogenics?"

His flinty eyes flashed mischief at me. "I made Bailey Trainor eat dog shit tonight, darlin'."

My mouth fell open in shock and Liam bellowed with laughter. It shook the whole bed.

"Oh my god, for a minute I thought you meant it," I said.

His face grew serious.

"Oh, you did mean it. Wow, that's quite an admission."

"He singled me out in class on my first day, sniffed the air, and said he'd found shit. Tonight, I also found some and returned it."

I sighed. "Anything else I should know about?"

"I held Ulric under the water in his swimming pool. Did you know he can't swim? And then I made out like I rescued him, and his father now loves me."

"You were only out a couple of hours. How can you get involved in so much drama?"

"Because I'm a bad." He lowered his mouth and kissed me. "Bad." Kiss. "Boy."

"No, you're not," I shook my head.

He opened his mouth to protest and I put a finger over his lips.

"You're *my* bad, bad, boy."

His lips curved under my finger and he pulled it away and kissed me gently again. "Snuggles," he ordered.

We called in sick for school the next day. It wasn't like my mother was going to come chasing us. She knew I couldn't turn up with my injuries. Liam made coffee, fixed juice, and made cheese toasties and brought them back to bed on a tray.

"I'm going to go back home tonight," I told him.

"Okay."

I tilted my head at him. "You're supposed to fall at my feet and beg me not to leave you."

He winked in return. "I'm making progress, but let's take it one day at a time. You had snuggles. What more do you want from me?"

His question was a joke, but it hung in the air like an icy wind on an otherwise warm and sunny day.

"I've decided I'm going to pass my exams and go to university and then I hope to God I can get a good enough job to get away completely," I told Liam.

"I'm going to pass my exams and go to university, and then I'm going to work damn hard to make sure I have a financially secure future."

"So, we both need to pass our exams," I said. "And that's another six months."

He nodded.

"So, you and me. We take it one day at a time?"

"It's all we've got anyway, Fifi." He leaned over and kissed me. "Your brother could get you enough money for you to leave. Bella Thorne could drop into The Aegean while I just happen to be there and whisk me away. Who knows? We haven't even known each other a month yet."

"So much has happened in that time. I feel like my whole world has tilted on its axis."

His arm came around me, pulling me closer. "I know it's difficult, this stuff with your father, but you have to hope that the only way is up. If I hadn't kept my hope, my determination, I'd be sat sharing a bottle of liquor with my mother."

We ate our breakfast and to anyone looking in from the outside, we'd have looked like a perfectly happy couple and right at that moment it's exactly what we were. And I'd take as many moments like that as I could.

My wounds healed and I returned to school. Ulric and Ivy still continued with their barbs, but on the whole, things were settled. Liam had appeared to save the 'King', and as time passed and Richstone didn't suffer any adverse effects of having a rat live there and three attend school, other scandals took over the riches' conversations.

Weeks passed and I got used to living with my mother. Being ships that rarely passed in the night. Dad stayed wherever she'd sent him. Eddie was working but had told me there would be no quick escape fund, the business just didn't have the funds right now.

So I studied hard. Liam helped me with the maths that was my weakest subject and I helped him trust that he could try to be in a relationship.

One day at a time.

It was the Easter holidays and Flora had requested everyone meet in a new and upcoming bistro, situated just behind Richstone Main Street. It was her eighteenth birthday. Her parents were insisting on a glitzy celebration where they would pretend to be happily married at the weekend, and so Flora demanded we all come and celebrate her actual birthday as she wanted to. With her best friends and her boyfriend. She'd asked that cards and presents be left for the official event and asked that we just come with a large appetite and be ready to enjoy ourselves.

Liam pulled up just outside the restaurant in the Porsche. Climbing out, I went to stand at the side of him. "Put the keys in your bag, Fifi," he asked.

It was pathetic, but I smiled because it seemed like a couple thing to do. He caught my look and shook his head, "Women." I punched him in the arm, and he grabbed me and kissed me.

Lucie made a puking noise as she approached. "Purlease. I want to be able to eat."

Soon everyone was gathered around. Drinks were ordered, starters and main courses also noted down by the staff. The birthday girl had pride of place in the middle of the table with Daniel at her side. They were still as loved up as ever. It was lovely and nauseating at the same time.

The waitresses poured a glass of champagne for everyone and then left us to it. All drinks were held aloft and Daniel stood ready to say a toast.

"To the birthday girl," he said, and held up his glass.

"To the birthday girl," we replied and held up our own. We clinked glasses and then took a sip. But Flora didn't. Her eyes twinkling, she passed her glass back to Daniel.

"We have extra news to celebrate," she said. "We're having a baby, and Daniel has proposed."

As six pairs of eyes looked at the two of them in shock, Renee was the first to recover herself. "That's fantastic, babes. Many congratulations. Can I see the ring?"

"Well, I don't have one yet. We've a lot to sort out. You're the first people we've told. As you can imagine, it's not going to be the easiest of times," Flora shrugged her shoulders. "I mean you're our best friends and look how you just took the news."

I stood up and tapped my champagne glass with the end of a fork.

"My dear Flora," I said. "You are one of the most genuine, lovely people I know. Your heart is large, and you will be the most amazing mummy. You and Daniel might not have been together long, but your love for each other shines out like the brightest stars. Yes, we're shocked. It was only two months ago that the two of you met, but you totally have our support and a band of auntie and uncles waiting to meet Baby Flor-Dan."

Flora's eyes were glassy, her mouth pinched tight with emotion. Daniel squeezed her hand and they shared an intimate smile.

"To Flora and Daniel and the baby," I said, and everyone chinked glasses and cheered the happy couple, even though I knew that inwardly, no doubt everyone shared the same thought.

What the fuck?

Flora's father would unleash hell.

The couple would have a lot to battle in their pursuit of happiness.

But looking at how they stared at each other, I knew they'd come through it.

Liam squeezed my knee under the table and I turned to him.

"They'll be fine," he said.

"One day at a time," I replied, and he nodded.

The rest of the meal was amazing, the food incredible. Daniel excused himself to go to the loo and the other three guys got up to go with him, making us all laugh.

"I thought it was girls who visited the bathrooms together?" Lucie folded her arms across her chest.

They left. "They're giving Daniel a grilling and leaving us with the opportunity to do the same with Flora," I said.

"I really could use a pee though," Flora whined. "I'm

surprised I've managed this long; my bladder has been pathetic in holding my wee lately. Come with?" she asked me.

I nodded and followed her to the bathroom.

When we walked inside, she turned around to me.

"I've done something a bit stupid," she said.

Given she'd already got pregnant to and engaged to a rat, I had to wonder what was coming.

She waved her phone at me while turning it on. "I've got a spy cam... on Daniel."

"Flora!"

"I know, I know! But I wanted to know his true feelings when he talked to his friends. I knew he would at some point during the meal. I bought a small recording device. It's hidden in his tie. He thinks I bought him a new tie and put it on him, but I did it to spy and what if he finds out? He'll think I don't trust him," she panicked.

"Flora." I grabbed her hand. "You bought a spy cam because you're feeling insecure, that's all. Now you can either forget all about it and remove his tie as part of some seductive striptease, or you can watch now and put your mind at ease." I hugged her. "Don't forget your hormones will be all over the place right now. You're allowed to act a little crazy."

She let out a slow breath through her pinched mouth.

"Practicing for when it comes?" I laughed.

Her fingers flew across her screen. "I'm going to listen."

Crackly voices came on, but they were distinguishable.

"...fucking mental," was the first thing we heard, from Brett. Flora looked up at me.

"At least one of them was bound to say that. We're all eighteen and they were supposed to come here to better their prospects, not get one of their classmates up the duff."

"Why am I mental?" Daniel protested. "Was that not the whole point of us coming here? To get a riches pregnant or blackmailable? That was what you said wasn't it, Liam? That was your big plan for us. And you fucked Renee with spiked condoms, Brett. This could have been you. But it doesn't matter anyway because..."

Flora's face paled, while I stood there for a moment in complete and utter shock.

"I have to get out of here." Flora ran from the bathroom, pushing past me. I tried to block her in the doorway, but she yelled. "Phoebe, let me out of here."

I opened the door, and she ran.

"Flora, wait," I shouted as she ran straight out of the front door of the restaurant.

"What's happening? I heard Flora shouting." Daniel was behind me.

"She knows. She knows it was part of a grand plan."

His face went as white as hers had. "No. No, she's wrong. Yes, it started that way, but then it was love. And she was as careless with the contraception as I was."

"She's not thinking straight. She's upset." I took the Porsche keys and threw them at Daniel. "The car's outside. You drive, and I'll look for her. She can't have got far. Then let me speak to her first, okay?"

"Okay."

We got inside. Daniel started the car and began to drive down the street. He was frantic. "I fucking adore her, Phoebe. Love her. What a mess. How did she...?"

"There's a camera in your tie. She wanted to hear you tell your friends the news," I lied. I'd tell Flora the cover story for her doubt when I caught her up. They'd be okay.

"Today is supposed to be a celebration and it's all gone to shit. I need to find her. She has to know how much she means to me. I'd die for that girl," he said, his voice breaking.

Daniel and Flora were the real deal. No matter whether a rat or a riches, they were in love. I didn't let myself think of what I'd heard in the bathrooms; right now I just needed to find my friend. I'd think about Liam afterwards.

"She's there. Pull in," I yelled, while I wound my window down. "Flora," I shouted at her. "It's fine, it's all fine. Stop panicking."

My friend turned around and stopped. Her eyes were puffy and red, but she looked at me out of breath, with such hope, and walked towards the car.

Beeep. Beeeeep.

"Move out of the way, rat boy." Ulric's annoying tone, coming loudly from behind us, spoiled what I was antici-pating would be a Hollywood style romantic ending. Trust him. His car was behind ours and he repeatedly beeped his horn for us to move.

"Give me a minute, Daniel. I'll sort everything."

I got out of the car and holding my index finger up at Flora, I mouthed, "One minute," then I walked down to Ulric's passenger door. I tapped on the window and he wound it down. "Give them a minute, Ulric," I said.

His nose turned up in a sneer. "Give them a minute for what?"

"They had an argument and they're about to sort it. That's all they need, one minute."

"I'm done giving these rats another fucking second, bitch," he announced and set off.

It all happened in slow motion.

Flora walked down the street to the side of the Porsche and stalled, clearly wondering whether to get in and listen to Daniel, or whether to walk down to me. She looked from one of us to the other.

Ulric revved the engine and as he drove past, he veered his car in towards Daniel as if he was going to clip it. Daniel swerved to the side, but then must have accidentally hit the accelerator as the car lurched forward.

And straight into and over Flora.

I saw it all.

I heard it all.

My mind couldn't process the horror.

Daniel jumped out of the car, his screams and my screams joining together to form a sound that nails down a blackboard couldn't have held a candle to.

People dashed out of nearby shops and restaurants.

I heard shouts for ambulances and 'don't look' and

people retching. Maybe one of them was me as I swayed on my knees, trying to stay conscious, just in case my friend lived.

You saw her, she's dead.

Dead.

Dead.

Dead.

There was not the slightest chance my friend and her baby were still on this earth. I'd seen a horror my mind could not accept.

Tears coursed down my cheeks as I entered a hell I could never have imagined.

Sirens sounded in the distance.

Arms came around me. I heard Liam's voice.

I couldn't speak. But I knew one thing.

My friend was dead because of Liam. And Liam would pay. I would cause him as much pain as whatever was happening to me now. It was like my body was being pulled apart in strings as wide as a hair, each as painful as the stab of a knife.

They would all pay: Liam, my parents, Ulric. Daniel, if I found he tricked her.

I threw up on the pavement, the sirens growing closer.

Flora was dead. My beautiful friend with her huge heart of gold.

I'd died alongside her.

If I came back, I wouldn't be the same.

Liam had said he'd ruin me and he had.

That was the last thought I had before everything went black.

TO BE CONCLUDED IN BAD BAD GIRL

Read the book description after the playlist that follows.

PLAYLIST

Spotify
open.spotify.com/playlist/
1T7pahAPN2SYdfnYmuos4b?si=JJ9tdlOjRx-
a16rs1o1KcA

Taylor Swift
Getaway Car
Miss Americana & The Heartbreak Prince
Cardigan
My Tears Ricochet
Dancing With Our Hands Tied

Harry Stiles, Falling
Shawn Mendes, Wonder

BAD BAD GIRL

Tragedy has rocked Richstone and the 'rats' and 'the riches' may never be the same again.

Reeling from recent events, Phoebe Ridley finds herself numb. While she tries to come to terms with her grief, one thing keeps her focused.

Revenge.

With a list of people she vows to ruin, this good girl is going bad. Very, very bad.

And Liam Lawson? The guy who started the rats' pact to ensnare one of the riches? She's saving him for last. Using him for his body and letting him believe they have each other despite their differences, she'll bring him to his knees before she escapes Richstone for good.

There are still games to be played.
Secrets to be revealed.
And all hell to break loose.

Liam and Phoebe will face each other for a final
showdown... a last shot at love... literally.

geni.us/BadBadGirl

ABOUT ANGEL

Angel Devlin lives in Sheffield, UK, with her long-suffering partner and son, and her beautiful Whippet furbaby.

When she's not thinking up dark and dirty book scenarios, she spends her time looking at the house thinking 'oh my god, what happened' and hoping it's a tornado and not the fact her head was too busy in her work. Then she takes the dog for a very long walk.

She also writes paranormal romance and dark suspense as Andie M. Long.

For more of her crazy, follow links are below

Instagram: @andieandangelbooks.
Reader group: www.facebook.com/
groups/1462270007406687

Facebook: www.facebook.com/angeldevlinbooks

OTHER ANGEL BOOKS

Other Angel books with delicious bad guys/downright
dirty billionaires

B.A.D. Inc Series

Torment
Ride
Bait
Provoke
Break

Double Delight Series
Sold
Submit
Share

The Billionaires Series

The Billionaire and the Virgin
The Billionaire and the Bartender
The Billionaire and the Assistant